COMHAIRLE CHONTAE ÁTHA CLIATH THEAS
SOUTH DUBLIN COUNTY LIBRARIES

MOBILE LIBRARIES
TO RENEW ANY ITEM TEL: 459 79~ ~
OR ONLINE ^~

D0364478

Praise for *Dead Ends*:

'Life-affirming, sad, hopeful ... I was up reading it until 3 a.m. I loved this book because of its sensitivity and its promises. Billy D stole my heart as I'm sure he'll steal yours.'

Jenny, *Wondrous Reads*

'Beautiful, bold and utterly fearless. A story that will stick with the reader long after they close the book. We need more YA books like this – I loved it!'

Carly, *Fiction Fascination*

'Heart-breaking for all the right reasons.'

Laura, *Sister Spooky*

'I loved this touching story of friendship, self-discovery and belonging.'

Beth, *Thoughts from the Hearthfire*

'An excellent read ... I'm going to be pressing my copy into the hands of other readers. I want everyone to spend time with Dane and Billy D.'

Jenni, *Juniper's Jungle*

'A real coming of age book ... A great read.'

Sarah, *Sarah's Book Reviews*

'There are not enough stars to rate this book. It read like a screenplay for the visual mind and I loved every word.'
Michelle, *Teacher Moloney King*

'One of those books that completely draws you in making you not want to put it down for even the briefest moment. I thoroughly enjoyed every page.'
Kirsty, *The Overflowing Library*

'*Dead Ends* had me racing through my emotions . . . Sometimes I could be laughing and hurting at the same time, but that just goes to show how incredible it is!'
Raimy, *Readaraptor*

'A truly heart-warming tale of friendship, redemption and self-discovery.'
Sahina, *Reading Between The Lines*

Praise for *Butter*:

'Powerful and courageous.' *Booktrust*

'Incredible, poignant and affecting.'
Jake Hope, children's librarian and Blue Peter Judge

'Dark and humorous.' *Telegraph*

DEAD ENDS

Erin Lange

ff

FABER & FABER

First published by Bloomsbury USA in 2013
First published in the UK in 2014
by Faber & Faber Limited
Bloomsbury House
74–77 Great Russell Street
London WC1B 3DA

Typeset by Faber & Faber Ltd
Printed and bound by CPI Group (UK) Ltd, Croydon, CR0 4YY

All rights reserved
© Erin Lange, 2013

The right of Erin Lange to be identified as author of this work has been asserted in
accordance with Section 77 of the Copyright, Designs and Patents Act 1988

A CIP record for this book is available from the British Library

ISBN 978–0–571–30882–8

FSC
www.fsc.org
MIX
Paper from
responsible sources
FSC® C101712

2 4 6 8 10 9 7 5 3 1

For Matt, who somehow keeps me grounded
and lets me soar all at once

1

I had a foot on some guy's throat and a hand in my pocket the first time I saw Billy D. He was standing across the street, staring – not even trying to be sly about it – just staring without a word, without even blinking.

'What are you lookin' at?' I called.

His mouth fell open in a silent little O, but he didn't respond. He didn't leave either, just kept on staring.

Something gurgled inside the throat under my foot, and I glanced down. The guy looked like he might be struggling to breathe, but his face wasn't red yet, so I turned my attention back to the other boy.

'Get out of here! Or you're next!'

That was kind of an empty threat. Even from across the street, I could tell by his vacant expression, that slack jaw, and the strange way he hunched his shoulders that he was different – probably in special ed. And I didn't beat on those guys.

Standards, y'know?

'Hey, you deaf or something? I said *get lost!*'

He hesitated, shuffling first to the left, then to the right. He looked once more at me and at the boy under my boot, then moved his gaze to the pavement and stomped away.

Freak.

The hand in my pocket closed over a piece of gum. I popped the stick in my mouth and refocused on the task at hand. Below me, surrounded by pavement grit and gravel, that face was definitely turning a little pink. I lifted my foot and kicked a loose bit of rock so it pinged off the guy's shoulder. It must have stung because he winced between gasps for breath.

'You think that hurt? That's nothing compared to what I'll do to your *car* if you mess with me again.'

He hadn't found his voice yet, which was lucky for him because he was probably just dumb enough to say something to piss me off even more. He pulled himself up to a sitting position and crawled along the pavement towards the street, where the door to his bright red Mustang still hung open. It was restored vintage, from back when Mustangs were still cool. He was halfway across the road when I called out. 'And you better find another way to school. If I see your car on this street again, you'll have a broken windshield and a broken face.'

The guy finally pulled himself up into the driver's seat and turned just long enough to glare at me before slamming the door shut. I responded with a raised fist, and even though I was still on the pavement and couldn't possibly touch him, I heard the door locks click. I had to laugh.

What a pussy.

The Mustang roared around the corner and disappeared. I scratched my palms out of habit, but it wasn't necessary. The itching had evaporated with the car.

It always started like that – with the itch. I would feel it in the centre of my palms, a buzzing sensation I couldn't ignore. If I did try to ignore it, the itch would spread like a spiderweb, radiating out to the edges of my hand, tingling down to my fingertips. Closing those fingers into a fist and giving that fist a landing pad was the only way to scratch the itch.

I never knew what would trigger it. It could be as subtle as a guy rolling his eyes when I spoke up in class or as obvious as some asshole in a bright red Mustang rolling down a window and asking why I couldn't afford a car. Not much I could do about the former – I was this close to getting kicked out of school as it was. If it wasn't for my good grades, they'd have shoved me out the door already. But the latter would get a guy dragged out of his car for a lesson in pavement humility. I would have done more to the Mustang moron, but the freak across the street had

3

distracted me. Something about his eyes – kind of slanted and round at the same time – unnerved me. I felt like I was being judged – a feeling that normally made my palms itch. But in the case of the slack-faced kid, it made me want to scratch my head instead of my hands.

The turd in the red Mustang was right about one thing. What kind of self-respecting sixteen-year-old didn't have a car?

I kicked rocks aside as I shuffled down the pavement. I wasn't the only junior at Mark Twain High without a car, but I was one of the few. Columbia, Missouri, wasn't exactly the home of the rich and famous, but most families could at least scrape together a few bucks for a clunker.

I turned the corner in the opposite direction the Mustang had gone. Haves to the right. Have-nots to the left. I pulled myself up a little straighter, as if the guy in the Mustang could still see me. Who needed four wheels when I had two fists?

The further I walked, the more overgrown the yards became, the deeper the peels of paint on the houses. My street was the last one before those houses and yards became trailers and gravel driveways. I rounded the corner and spotted the now familiar removals van parked directly across the street from my own house. That thing had been there for almost a week, blocking my view of just about everything else from my bedroom window.

How long does it take to unpack a U-Haul?

I cocked an eye at the house next to the van, wondering what kind of lazy neighbours were moving in to drag the 'hood down even more, and pulled up short. On the front steps of the house, another set of eyes met mine – eyes so distinct in shape I recognised them instantly. Just like before, the kid watched me without blinking. Maybe it was because he was a safe distance from me, or maybe it was because he was too dumb to sense the danger, but he didn't look away when I caught his gaze.

'It's rude to stare,' I challenged him.

He adjusted his backpack in response, shifting it higher on those strangely curved shoulders. He was short and a little bulky, so the move, combined with his awkward, stooped posture, made him look top-heavy. Actually, everything about him fell sort of heavy, from his eyelids to his arms. I waited a moment to see if he'd tip over, so I could have a good laugh, but he held his balance.

'It's *stupid* to stare,' I tried again.

He blinked.

What was that? Fear? Mocking?

I waited for the itch, but it didn't come. It was tough to get mad at someone when I had no idea what he was thinking. Finally, I pointed a warning finger in his direction.

'You're lucky I don't beat up retards.'

A shadow passed over his face – a glimmer of emotion.

'I'm not a retard.' He said it with some force, like he actually believed it.

Even his voice made it clear he wasn't like other kids. It was a little high – *still waiting for puberty, this one* – and it sounded like his teeth were getting in the way of his tongue.

'I'm not a retard,' he repeated, louder. He stamped his foot for emphasis.

'Fine, fine.' I turned my pointed finger into a hand held up in surrender. I wasn't looking for a fight with some challenged kid. I just wanted him to stop eyeballing me. 'But enough of the ogling, got it?'

I turned towards my own house and was halfway there when his voice rang out again.

'Your clothes don't match!'

What?

I spun around. He had his arms folded across his chest in a smug gesture. *This*, he must have thought, was the final word in insults. Inexplicably self-conscious, I glanced down at what I was wearing. How could jeans and a hoodie not match? I looked back up to ask him – genuinely ask him – what the hell he was talking about, but the steps where he'd been standing were empty. I got only a quick glimpse of a backpack disappearing into the house.

2

I slammed the front door closed to announce my homecoming and tossed my backpack in a corner. The next stop was usually the remote control, but today I reached for the curtains covering the front window instead. From this angle, the U-Haul blocked most of my view, but I could see half of the first- and second-floor windows of the house across the street. I squinted, trying to see inside those windows, but they were dark.

'What are we looking at?' Mom perched on the arm of the couch and pressed her face right next to mine, peering out the window.

'The new neighbours.'

She was so close that when she smiled, I felt her cheek lift up to touch mine. 'Oh, goody, where? I've been trying to spot them all week.'

'They're inside now.'

'You met them?' She pulled away from the window and flopped backwards on to the couch.

'Well, one . . . kind of.'

'Who is it?'

'Some hunchback with a staring problem.'

I finally wrenched my face away from the window and let the curtains fall back into place. Mom was frowning now.

'That's not nice, Dane.'

'Good thing no one ever accused me of being nice,' I said, taking over the sofa cushion next to Mom.

'That's what you always say.'

'That's because it's always true.'

Mom laughed. 'Okay, Mr Mean, go shave your face, and I'll make dinner.'

'Nice try.'

'Come on, please? For Mommy?'

We were both laughing now.

'No way,' I said, fingering my chin. 'Stubble makes me look tough.'

'It makes you look like a hoodlum.'

'Who says "hoodlum"?'

'Grown-ups, that's who,' she said.

'Oh, you're a grown-up now?'

It was just a tease, but Mom's face tensed up, and I immediately wished I could take it back.

I used to think it was cool that my mom was younger and better-looking than other moms, until guys my age started staring at her in a way that made me sick. But as embarrassing as that was for me, it was worse for Mom.

Once, when my facial hair first started coming on, we were out at a restaurant, and the waiter asked us how long we'd been together – as in, *together*. I don't know who was more grossed out, me or Mom, but on the way home, she stopped at a pharmacy to buy me a razor and a can of shaving cream. She told me what she could about how to do it, but shaving your legs is a lot different from shaving your face. I got thirteen cuts that night. I'd thought they made me look tough, but Mom had cried. It was months before she started nagging me about the stubble again.

'Well, *you* don't look as "grown up" as you think,' she said. She reached out to flatten the chunk of my hair that always stuck up in back. 'Not with this little baby cowlick you've got going.'

I shook her hand away and reached for the lock of hair myself, smoothing it down out of habit.

'My own Dennis the Menace.' She smiled. 'You get in any trouble at school today?'

'Not today.'

'Good.' She patted my leg and stood up.

I followed her into the kitchen. 'Mom, I wanted to talk to you about – Hey, why are you cooking dinner, anyway? Don't you have a class tonight?'

She pulled a bag of stir-fry out of the freezer and tossed a frying pan on the hob, deliberately ignoring my question.

'Mom?'

She kept her back to me, but I could hear guilt in her voice. 'They cancelled my Wednesday classes. Not enough people were showing up.'

Mom taught yoga and Pilates at a local gym and got paid by the class. No students meant no cash.

'Shit,' I said.

She lifted her shoulders like it was no big deal, but I could tell by the heavy way they fell back down that she was worried – worried about making rent this month, worried about feeding me, worried about putting petrol in the car. *Her* car.

She fired up the hob and emptied the frozen bag into the frying pan. 'Anyway, what did you want to talk to me about?'

'Well, maybe it's not a good time, but . . .' I hesitated. 'I wanted to ask you about getting a car.'

Her laugh revealed more irritation than humour. 'You're right, Dane. It's not a good time.'

She flipped the stir-fry with more force than was necessary.

'I could get a job,' I said.

'You could get a better job if you went to college.'
She turned to face me finally. 'Which you won't be able
to do without a full ride. Your grades are key to getting
a scholarship. I promise you will regret it if you let a job
interfere with your schoolwork.'

'My grades are awesome,' I said.

'And they're going to stay awesome, because you're not
getting a job.'

'Or a car,' I grumbled.

'That's right,' she said, ripping dishes out of the cabinet
and slamming them down on our tiny kitchen table.
'Because I'm a terrible mother.'

'I didn't say that. And I didn't mean to piss you off. It's
just that—'

'Just what?' She stopped setting the table and looked at
me with one hand on her hip.

'It's just that when you were my age, you had a car.'

And then the conversation ended the way it always did.

'Dane, when I was your age, I had a *kid*.'

*

The bullshit of it was, she *could* afford to get me a car. The
proof was staring me in the face as we ate dinner in silence.
Across the kitchen table, on the wall above Mom's head,

hung dozens of tiny little frames. And there wasn't a single picture in any of them. These frames were for tickets. Lottery tickets. Each one a winner.

Mom played the lottery whenever she could afford it, which wasn't that often compared with the other lotto junkies out there. But unlike those losers, Mom won – not just a lot, but always. She had an unnatural lucky streak when it came to those little scratch-off tickets. We would probably have been rich if she'd just take that luck to Vegas for a weekend. But Mom was convinced the luck would run out as soon as she tried to cash in on it, and she said she was saving up that luck for something big.

I glanced around at the linoleum floor peeling up at the corners and the mismatched kitchen chairs. So far, it looked like her lucky streak was confined to those tickets, sealed inside frames and hung up on the wall to torture me. Most of them weren't worth much – a dollar here, five bucks there – plus a couple of hundred-dollar winners that it had hurt me to watch her lock away. If they had all been small like that, I wouldn't have minded so much.

But there was one ticket – right in the centre with a slightly larger frame than the rest – that I had begged Mom to redeem. One shining ticket . . . worth five thousand dollars. I'd been sure that ticket would break her bizarre habit. Obviously, this was the stroke of luck she'd been saving up for. I exploded when she told me it was going on the wall with the rest.

'Half a year's rent!' I screamed. 'A car! College!'

I tried everything, but my protests were ignored. Mom said the big win was just proof her luck was building. That was when I realised her little game of karma was more than a quirky habit. It was a sickness.

Now that ticket had been hanging on the wall for three months, and according to the Missouri Lottery website, it was due to expire in another three. Every time I saw it, I felt more furious, more concerned about Mom's sanity. That single ticket stuck out, taunting me with its possibilities.

That one ticket made my palms itch.

I wrenched my gaze away from the frames. Pretending they weren't there was the only way to not go mad living so close to something I couldn't have. I let my eyes fall on Mom instead.

She looked so *normal* – and truth be told, she was pretty damn cool as far as moms go – but clearly she was completely bat-shit crazy.

3

The walk to school was pretty straightforward – three turns and a cut across the baseball diamonds – so it wasn't hard to spot him tailing me. I had just veered off our street when he popped up on the opposite pavement, stomping along with that weird hunch and his face aimed down at the ground. He was so focused on where he was putting his own feet that I wouldn't have even guessed he was following me if I hadn't taken my shortcut through the gardens.

Sometimes, when I was running late in the mornings, I would cut through a cluster of houses that surrounded a grid of flower gardens. The houses all had back doors that opened up to a courtyard with brick walking paths, which zigzagged through square brick pens, each containing a different type of flower. The flowers didn't do much for me, but it was nice to know the gardens were there – that something that pristine still existed in our neighbourhood. It was the kind of place I might take a girl who deserved flowers. Too bad most of the girls I knew were the kind who had already been *de*flowered.

I took the path that angled to the right and spotted him out of the corner of my eye taking the one to the left. He still wasn't looking at me, but when I slowed down near a patch of yellow flowers, he slowed, too, over by some pink ones. And when I bent down and pretended to tie my shoe, he literally stopped to smell the roses.

I couldn't imagine what kind of trouble this kid was looking for, but I was going to find out. I stayed in a crouch and pushed one foot back into a runner's stance. Then I launched off the ground and sped out of the gardens as fast as my feet would go. The crooked paths slowed me down, so I hurtled into the air and cleared the last brick flower box with a single flying leap. I didn't look back to see if he could keep up; there was no way the little stomper was coordinated enough to catch me.

Certain I'd left him in the dust, I leaped behind the first house I saw as soon as I was clear of the gardens and waited, chest heaving, back pressed up against the siding. I heard his heavy shuffling footsteps coming through the grass a few seconds later and pounced.

I burst out from behind the wall. 'Why are you following me?'

But I might as well have shouted *'Boo!'* because I gave the kid such a scare he only stammered and started to wheeze. His bent posture went ramrod straight, and his hands balled into fists near his face. I supposed this was the desired effect, but instead of feeling gratified, I was freaked out. The last thing I needed was to get blamed for some retard's hysterical fit.

'Hey,' I said, gripping his shoulder. 'Relax.'

He obeyed, slowly unclenching his fists and controlling his breathing.

'Yeah, like that,' I said. I let go of his shoulder and crossed my arms. 'Now, why are you following me?'

He gulped some air and said as quickly as he could, 'Because of the guys who said they would get me and because you know the way to school and because of the boy you beat up—'

'Which boy?'

His eyes widened a little, and when he spoke, I heard awe. 'You beat up a lot of boys?'

'Not your business.'

'The one in the car.'

'You know him?' I asked.

He shrugged. 'No.'

'Then why do you care?'

'You ask a lot of questions,' he said.

'You better start answering them. I like being followed about as much as I like being stared at. Or having my clothes insulted.'

His eyes moved down my outfit, but if he found any fault, he was smart enough not to say so. Instead, he lifted his face back to mine. 'I'm afraid of some boys at school. But they're afraid of you. If I walk to school with you, I don't feel scared.' He held up his hands in a 'what are ya gonna do?' move, but his facial features never changed.

I wondered who those guys might be. I couldn't think of anyone at school worth being afraid of, but then again, I wasn't short like this kid. He was built like a little boulder, but if he had to reach up to fight back, he could be in trouble.

'You go to Twain?' I asked.

'Yeah.'

'Freshman?'

'Yeah.'

'Down's syndrome?'

'*Obviously*,' he said, like he was talking to the dumbest person on earth. He rolled his eyes and shifted his backpack upwards. I noticed his tongue poked out a tiny bit; it rested on his lower lip and pulled back only when he spoke.

'So you think following me around without my permission is going to *keep* you from getting your ass kicked?'

'Well, not now,' he said.

'Good.' I turned in the grass and moved towards the street.

'Now I'll tell them how you're scared of me.'

I tripped over my own feet trying to spin around and stumbled backwards on to the pavement. 'Excuse me?'

'You ran away from me.' He joined me on the concrete and stamped the dew out of his shoes.

'Dude, I didn't run away from you.'

'Uh, yes, you did. You went *over* the flowers and everything like this.' He flattened his hand and made a sailing motion with his arm. He swung it high, right in front of my face, and added a *shwooo* sound effect. I resisted the urge to push his arm away.

'I was running to get ahead of you,' I said. 'So I could . . . so you would . . .' Then I shut up. The running thing seemed pretty stupid now.

'So you could scare me,' he said.

'I guess.'

'That's why I followed you. Because you scare people.'

'Well, congratulations. You're scary, too. Following me is creepy.'

'It's only creepy if we don't walk *together*.'

I pressed my fingers to my temples. I did not have time to argue with someone who had an answer for everything. We were late to school as it was, and I couldn't afford another detention. So I did the only thing I could think of and started moving down the pavement. It was a moment before I realised he wasn't moving with me. I sighed, and without looking back, I flicked my wrist, motioning for him to join me.

'Walk,' I commanded.

He hurried up next to me. 'Thanks, I—'

'No talking,' I interrupted, still staring straight ahead as we walked. 'No crying, no staring, no comments on my clothes. But mostly no talking. And if we see anyone from school, you scram to the other side of the street.'

I glanced over to see if he was paying attention. He nodded eagerly.

'If you break any of these rules, you get knocked on the head, got it?'

'Got it,' he said, then immediately broke the rules by talking. 'My name's Billy Drum. But everybody calls me Billy D.'

'Don't care.'

'Who are you?'

I smirked. 'I'm your worst nightmare.'

'You're not my worst nightmare. My worst nightmare is about a snake and a—'

'I *don't care*.'

'My next-door neighbour Mark calls you *"that dick"* but

that's not your name. I know what a dick is, and it's not a name. In my life skills class, they call it a penis. But I know it's also called a dick, and it's definitely not a na—'

'*Dude!* I don't want to talk about dicks with you.'

'What do you want to talk about?'

'I want to—' I threw up my hands, then paced a few steps backwards down the pavement and forwards again. 'I don't want to talk about anything! Go away!'

Billy was unfazed by my outburst. I picked up my pace, and he adjusted his stride to match mine. 'Okay, but if you tell me your name, I'll tell Mark, and he won't call you *"that dick"* any more.'

'That little punk knows my name, and I'm gonna kick his ass later for calling me a dick.'

'Okay, then will you tell *me* your name so I don't call you a dick and get *my* ass kicked?'

I sighed and covered my face with my hands. 'Dane, okay? My name is Dane Washington.'

'Washington like the president?'

'Yeah. Like the president.'

'That's awesome.'

'If you say so.'

His steps became lighter, almost a skip. 'Now I'll call you Dane, and you won't kick my ass.'

'I might kick your ass anyway if you don't shut up.'

'You said you don't beat up retards.'

'You said you weren't a retard.'

'I'm not.'

'Okay, then.'

'Okay, then.'

He fell quiet for a few blissful seconds, then: 'Does that mean you can still kick my ass?'

I dropped my chin to my chest and closed my eyes. This was going to be the longest walk to school ever.

4

The trek across the baseball diamonds was treacherous. I half sped, half slid across the damp grass, intent on getting to first period on time. Billy D. struggled to keep up, and the panting from exertion kept him quiet. I moved faster, but he managed to stay at my side. I was secretly impressed by his speed, given his short legs. I allowed myself a quick sideways glance to see how he was moving so quickly, and just as I looked, his whole body lurched forwards, and I heard the squeak of his sneakers slipping on wet grass.

My arm shot out instinctively, my fingers finding his elbow.

'Ow!' he complained as I pulled his arm backwards to stop the fall.

We both skidded to a clumsy stop at the edge of the school car park. He pulled his arm away and squirrelled up his eyebrows. I tried to figure out whether it was anger or confusion on his face, but I just couldn't read it.

'You were about to fall,' I said. It came out sounding like

an apology, so I added a snort to my next words. 'You're welcome.'

'Oh.' Billy's brow smoothed out, and he rubbed his elbow. 'Thanks.'

'Whatever.'

His face broke into a smile that showed off more of that oversize tongue and revealed tiny gaps between all his teeth. 'Meet here after school? To walk home?'

'Listen, Special Ed, I'm not meeting you anywh—'

'I'm Billy D. And I'm not in special ed.'

He stomped off before I could reply, and I was left once again wondering how the kid managed to get the last word while I stood around looking like the idiot.

*

I slipped into my first class just before the bell. Raindrops smacked the window, cutting through the drone of Mr Johnson's lecture. I scowled at the clouds gathering outside. The drops were going to turn into a downpour, and the walk home would be even more slippery than this morning's.

I glared around at the rest of my classmates, wondering how many of them had four wheels and a roof to carry them home warm and dry after school. Getting through winter without a car was rough enough, but at least you could bundle up. Spring brought the cold rains that soaked through everything, no matter how many layers you put on. And even though the calendar had barely flipped from February to March, spring storms had already arrived.

My eyes fell on a waterfall of wavy dark hair. Nina Sinclair was good scenery, so lucky for me we had almost all the same classes. She also didn't treat me like a thug, which meant she was one of the few people at school I actually bothered with. Unfortunately, bothering with her bothered her boyfriend. I slid my gaze to the right, and sure enough, there he was, next to her, giving me the evil eye.

Calm down, asshole. I'm just looking.

I made sure he was still watching me and deliberately aimed an air kiss at the back of Nina's head. The kid – Timmy or Tommy or some other jockstrap name – clenched a fist on top of his desk. I smiled and made a fist of my own, with my longest finger popping out of it.

If there was a ruder gesture than that, he didn't have time to make it, because Mr Johnson caught him turning around and put him on the spot with a question.

I figured that would be the end of it, but Tim-Tom didn't like me having the last word – or the last finger – so he pulled a move that too many guys before him had pulled.

As soon as class was over, he slung an arm around Nina and turned to mouth at me over her shoulder: *You wish*.

That was a mistake.

'Hey, Nina,' I said.

She turned, spinning right out of the boyfriend's arm. 'Hi, Dane, what's up?'

'Just sayin' hey.' I smiled and saw Nina blush a little as she returned the grin.

I was always surprised to get that reaction from girls, but it had been happening a lot lately. Maybe it was the stubble.

'Well, see you in algebra,' she said.

She moved to take Tim-Tom's hand, but it was balled into a fist.

'I'll catch up,' he told her.

He waited for both Nina and Mr Johnson to leave the room, then turned to me, face beet red.

'What's the deal?'

'What do you mean?' I scooped my textbook and notepad off my desk and moved to brush past him, but his hand caught my chest, ever so slightly pushing me backwards. The itch started circling my palms. It wasn't so much the touch that bothered me – more the fact that he wasn't afraid to do it. Most guys knew better.

'I'd move that,' I said, nodding down to his hand.

He gritted his teeth and added more pressure to my chest. 'Nina's my girlfriend.'

This was going to end badly for me no matter what. A fight would land me in the disciplinary office, but if I backed down, word would be all over school by the end of the day. I had a millisecond to weigh my options, but all I could focus on was the itch.

'Really, you want to move your hand now.'

'She's not into you, got it?'

'Last chance.'

'She doesn't do trailer-trash losers who—'

And that was all he said before my fist hit his left eye.

'I don't live in a trailer,' I said calmly, shaking out my hand.

But I don't think he heard me through his own girlie squeal.

He pressed both hands over his eye and stumbled back, knocking a few desks out of place.

'What is this?' Mr Johnson's voice boomed from the doorway.

Guess I wouldn't be seeing Nina in algebra after all.

Within seconds, we were on our way to the warden's office.

Tim-Tom had cried something about me hitting him, which I didn't bother to deny. But I told Mr Johnson he'd touched me first to make sure I wasn't the only one bound for detention.

My palms were still tingling when we took our seats outside the office.

'Hi, Mrs Pruitt.' I winked at the secretary.

'Dane.' She gave me a thin-lipped smile. 'Shame to see you under these circumstances again.'

I shrugged.

Mr Johnson and Mrs Pruitt ducked their heads in a whispered conversation, as if it was a secret from us why we were there. Then Johnson left and Pruitt rapped on the warden's door. Just above her fist, a little plaque gleamed gold with black carved words: THEODORE BELL, DISCIPLINARY OFFICER. Pruitt pushed the door open without waiting for an answer.

'Ted? Dane Washington and another boy here to see you.'

As always – Dane Washington and 'another boy'. With an introduction like that, who could disagree that the odds were against me? I spent the most time there, so naturally I was the one who most likely deserved to be there. 'Another boy' would be sent back to class without punishment.

Mrs Pruitt waved us into the office and closed the door. I knew the routine and sat silently, but Tim-Tom launched right into his side of the story. He blathered on for almost a whole minute before he noticed the warden's hand in the air, a quiet command to shut up. The warden studied us for a moment, paying particular attention to the swollen tomato that used to be Tim-Tom's eye socket. Then he swivelled his chair ever so slightly towards me.

'What happened?'

'*You're* asking *him*?' Tim-Tom pointed at his busted eye. 'I'm the one who got hurt.'

The warden kept his gaze on me, waiting.

'He put a hand on me; I asked him to move it; he kept it there and called me a name; so I hit him.' I knew the warden liked it short and sweet.

'I didn't touch him!' Tim-Tom burst out.

The warden flicked his eyes towards the noise. 'What is your name?'

'Toby Smith.'

Huh. Toby. Close enough.

The warden finally gave him a chance to tell his side of the story – an elaborate lie about how I'd tripped, and he'd put out a hand to try to catch me, but instead of thanking him for the help, I'd punched him for no reason at all.

I chuckled and raised a hand. The warden nodded.

'I would like to revise my statement. I didn't hit anyone. His face actually fell into my fist.'

The warden's mouth twitched, then he launched

into the usual speech about words being just words and violence being something else entirely. I glared at Toby. I knew what was coming next. The warden went on to say that an unkind word is not enough to provoke a punch. He told Toby we should all be careful about putting hands on people, in case the touch is misunderstood, but that, in this case, it didn't sound like a violation of school rules.

I watched Toby's face through the entire speech.

Was that a smirk?

I didn't mind so much getting called down to the disciplinary office. The chairs were comfortable enough, and Mrs Pruitt's candy dish was always full of jelly beans. She'd let you have as many as you wanted, no matter how much trouble you were in.

I didn't even mind when the warden lectured me about self-control and respect. But there was one word he always stuck in that speech that got my palms itching.

'Unprovoked.'

That was what he called it when I threw a stick into the spokes of Jimmy Miller's bike and sent him face-planting into the gravel next to the bike rack. But Jimmy had stolen my English report, changed the big red A to an F, and taped it on my locker for everyone to see – for everyone to think I was some kind of failure.

And when I smashed up Brian Chung's art project

because I'd overheard him telling someone I was a dirtball who needed a shower – the warden called that unprovoked, too. The word pissed me off every time. It was like saying people had permission to go around treating everyone like shit, but nobody had a right to shut them up.

Was he blind? Couldn't he see Toby sitting there right now, provoking me with that smirk?

Apparently not, because a second later, 'another boy' was dismissed.

Once the door was closed again, the warden slid a sheet of paper across the desk to me without a word. I knew the drill, and he knew I knew it. Take the paper home to Mom, have her sign off, showing she knows I'm a bad boy, then drop the slip in the warden's pigeonhole on my way to detention tomorrow.

Really, they would've saved a lot of paper if they'd just given me something reusable, like one of those little coffee cards with boxes for stamping. Ten detentions earn you one free suspension! In fact, my card would be almost full. At Twain, it took only seven detentions to get suspended, and this one made six for me. It would've been a hell of a lot more, but Mom convinced the principal to wipe my slate clean at the start of second semester. Principal Davis cared a lot more about straight As than a straight attitude. He wasn't about to lose one of his top performers.

Now I was back on the brink – one detention away from suspension. A single toe out of line after that, and I'd be expelled. Mom couldn't afford private school tuition, so for me, that would mean enrolment at the alternative high school – the place for thugs, dumb asses, and people with no hope of going to college. In other words, just about all my old friends.

Almost everyone I ran around with in junior high had disappeared from Twain by the end of freshman year. The ones who'd stayed in touch dropped me one by one when they turned sixteen and started getting cars. Maybe they didn't want to haul me around. Or maybe those cars drove them into the kind of trouble only alternative-school kids could understand. I didn't care to find out. I wanted to stay at Twain as much as Mom and Principal Davis wanted me to, but dicks like Toby made it impossible.

I snatched the paper and stuffed it into my backpack.

Mom was just going to love this.

5

Rain was dumping so hard outside school I didn't even bother to lift the hood of my jacket or try to use my backpack as a shield. I just dived straight into the downpour. The quicker the assault, the faster the misery would be over. All around me, the pounding of the rain mixed with slamming car doors and shrieking girls hurrying across the car park. One noise pierced through the rest.

'Dane! Dane, wait up!'

I ducked my head, pretending not to hear him, but in an instant he was at my side, splashing across the muddy baseball diamonds.

'It's raining,' he said, a little breathless.

'I didn't notice.'

Every step through the field was another spray of mud on my jeans from Billy's stomping. I snapped my head in his direction, intending to tell him to tread a little lighter when I noticed the splashing wasn't just an accident of his heavy footfall. His eyes were fixed on the ground, deliberately seeking out the biggest pools of water. He hopped from foot to foot, puddle to puddle, intentionally making a mess with every step. His face was split open in a wide grin, and his eyes crinkled at the corners.

Something in his expression caused me to swallow my words. I didn't speak again until we hit the street.

'You go that way.' I pointed down towards the road where I'd first spotted him. 'I'm going through the gardens.'

'Then are you going to beat up Mark?'

'What?'

'Mark. You said you were going to kick his ass later.'

Billy ignored my instructions and followed me up the grassy lawns, retracing the path we'd made that morning. The rain was letting up now, turning into a mist.

'Oh.' I shrugged. 'Maybe.'

Billy squinted and pushed back a chunk of wet hair. 'All bark and no bite.'

'What?'

'That's what my dad would have said. When people say they're going to do something but don't do—'

'I know what it means,' I said.

'And sometimes it's "all talk and no ac—".'

'I *know*,' I repeated.

'So are you gonna?'

The clouds above us turned a lighter shade of grey as we reached the gardens' crooked brick pathways.

I had a good enough reason to confront Mark, but I wasn't looking for a fight at the moment.

I wondered sometimes if Mark and I should have been friends, growing up on the same street and all. But there were a lot of kids on our block, and I'd never made much effort to get to know any of them. I didn't get chummy with the kids at school, either. I was always too embarrassed to invite any of them over to see our ugly house and meet my crazy mom. I was waiting – until we moved to a house with a kitchen floor that didn't peel, until Mom stopped framing lottery tickets – but nothing ever changed, and by the time I realised it wasn't going to change, I'd already made more enemies than friends.

'I'll give that tool a pass for now,' I said to Billy. 'I already got a detention for fighting today.'

We stepped out of the gardens and into the first streaks of sun breaking through the clouds. It was that strange sunlight that shows up only after a hard rain and washes everything in gold, so even our shit neighbourhood shone.

'You got a detention?' Billy's eyes widened until they were nearly popping out of his head.

'It's no big deal.'

'I almost got a detention once, at my last school. It was a really big deal. Mom got in a big fight with the teacher because he said I deserved it—'

34

'Let me guess. For talking too much?'

'No, for going berserk.'

'What?' I stopped and looked at him.

'I have a really bad temper,' Billy said in a cheerful voice. 'I used to have fits – that's what my doctor called them. Mom calls them tantrums, but I don't really think—'

'Get to the point.'

'The point is – I used to go all crazy when I got upset, and I got upset at the teacher.'

'About what?'

Billy thought for a moment. 'Don't remember. But I didn't get detention. Mom still calls me her little berserker, even though I don't go berserk any more.'

As we walked down the pavement in silence, I thought about the first time *I* went 'berserk' on somebody.

I couldn't remember the kid's name now, but he used to ride bikes down our street with Mark. I remembered how he shoved the kickstand of his crappy bike down into the icy pavement in front of my house. I was building a snow fort, and he started bragging about how his dad taught him to make an entire igloo out of snow. I ignored him at first, like I ignored all the loser kids on my block, but he kept talking. He went on and on about how his dad taught him to change the chain on his bike and was going to show him how to fix up a car when he got older.

I felt the itch for the first time there, kneeling in the snow. It was like the icy clumps I was piling on to my fort were stabbing me right through my gloves. I kept making fists with my hands, trying to scratch my palms with my fingertips. Open. Close. Open. Close. The itch didn't go away.

And I still didn't say anything, which seemed to irritate the kid. He went right on with his one-sided conversation, shuffling through the snow to lean over my fort and make sure I heard every word. He told me all about how his dad took him camping and mini-golfing and swimming, and how I wouldn't know anything about any of it, because I didn't have a dad.

I should have pummelled him right then, but all I could think to do was lie. I told him my dad was an astronaut and that he was never home because he was in outer space studying aliens. It was one of many stories I kept in my back pocket as a kid to pull out whenever anybody asked me about my dad. But this boy wasn't buying it. I would never forget his response.

'My mom says your mom doesn't even know who your dad is!'

It happened so fast I wasn't even aware that I had caused it, but all of a sudden the snow fort was flattened, and that punk was splayed out in the middle of it, with blood

36

flowing from his nose. It spilled into the rubble of white below him, making it look like a giant cherry snow cone. The itch in my palms was gone.

It wasn't what he said about my dad that provoked the punch. It was more that – even as a kid – I had a good idea of what he was saying about my *mom*.

I remembered running inside and crying in my room after that first fight. I was sure the kid would tell and that I'd be in big trouble. But the trouble never came. In fact, the kid never said a cruel word to me again. After that, I used my fists on a few other big mouths. Success, every time.

I cocked my head at Billy as we turned down our street. 'What did you mean – "would have said"?'

'What?'

'You said your dad *would* have said "all bark and no bite". Is your dad . . . is he, like, dead or something?'

'No.' There was a flicker of an expression on Billy's face, but I couldn't make it out.

'So where is he?'

'He's—' He shifted that heavy backpack higher on his shoulders, causing him to hunch forward further than normal. 'Not here,' he finished.

He glued his eyes to the tarmac and walked faster, right down the middle of the road. I didn't press him any further. I knew as well as anyone how annoying it was to

37

be asked questions you couldn't answer – especially about an absent parent.

Instead, I reached up to unzip Billy's backpack.

'What's in here that's so heavy, anyway?'

'Hey!' Billy spun on instinct, causing something big and flat to tumble out of his pack and on to the wet street. I snatched it up faster than he could and brushed off the muddy gravel clinging to the front.

'What's this?'

'Duh. Can't you read?' He pointed to a huge word on the book's glossy cover and sounded it out. 'At-las.'

'Nobody says "duh",' I told him, flipping the atlas open. 'You have a geography class or something?'

The pages settled on a map of West Virginia. Just below and to the left of Charleston, in squiggly handwriting, were the words 'Big Ugly'. They were circled with red marker. I leaned in to take a closer look, but Billy snatched the book out of my hands.

'I don't need a geography class,' he said. His voice sounded calmer than his movements. He was fumbling with the zip on his backpack, trying to stuff the atlas back inside.

'Okay,' I said.

'I'm awesome at geography.' He tugged the zip hard over the corner of the book.

'Fine.'

'I could *teach* geography.'

'All right. Relax.'

He slung the now zipped pack on to his shoulder and looked me dead in the eye. He spoke in a deliberately reassuring voice. 'Don't worry, Dane. I'm not going to go berserk on you.'

'Um. Thanks . . . I guess.'

We continued the trek down the centre of the street until our houses rose up on either side and we silently moved to opposite kerbs.

I stopped on my pavement and looked back.

'Hey, Billy D.'

'What?' He turned.

'My dad . . . he's not here either.'

Billy watched me for a few seconds, expression unreadable. Then, in a flash, his face lit up with a smile.

'Okay, then.'

'Okay, then.'

6

It's the calm *after* the storm, and it's typical of Mom and me. We'd had a tornado of a fight, when I'd handed her the detention slip and offered my excuse. Now it was the silent breakfast that always followed one of those storms. And by breakfast, I mean coffee for Mom and a soda for me. I took advantage of the silent treatment to finish up an algebra assignment at the kitchen table. Mom sat across from me, pressing a lotto ticket into a new frame.

I put the final bracket on my last equation and slammed my textbook shut.

'How much?' I asked.

Mom cleared her throat. 'Dane.'

'How much?'

She closed the clasps over the backing and turned the frame over to check that it was centred. 'Five dollars.'

'Five dollars that could have bought me lunch today.'

'Stop that.'

'Stop what?'

'Stop acting like we don't have enough money to buy you lunch.'

'Do we have enough money to pay the rent this month?'

'Of course we do. Now that's enough. I don't want to start again this morning.' She stood and moved to the junk drawer, sifting around for a nail to fix the frame to the wall.

I swept my arm across the embarrassing display. 'We probably have enough for an entire year's worth of rent. Too bad we're using cash as wallpaper.'

Mom slammed the drawer shut and flew towards the table with such speed, I actually jumped out of my seat.

'You're right, Dane! Maybe I should start framing *these* instead!' She snatched my detention slip off the table so fast it made a snapping sound in the air. 'God knows we have enough of them.' She flung the paper away, and I caught it as it fluttered downwards.

'I said I was sorry.' I sounded like a little kid.

Mom only pressed her lips together and went about hanging her new treasure.

I watched her for a minute, taking in her blonde hair and her pale skin stretched over lean muscles, shaped by years of yoga and Pilates and whatever else she taught over at the gym. She looked strong, like me, but otherwise we were night and day. My brown hair and tan skin reflected all the dark inside, but Mom's look was a disguise, because underneath she was just as stormy as me sometimes – and just as tough. I didn't know who I matched on the outside, but inside, I was all Mom.

I had a sudden urge to hug her or make her laugh, but I knew she wasn't ready to make nice, so I packed up my bag and silently left for school.

*

I stuck to the pavements, taking the usual route. Halfway to school, I heard Billy D. huffing and puffing behind me. His feet caught up with mine at almost the exact spot where I'd put the kid with the Mustang in his place.

'Why didn't you wait for me?' he asked.

'Wait for you for what?' I picked up my pace.

'To walk to school.'

'When did I say we could walk together?'

'You didn't, but . . . but I thought—'

'You thought wrong.'

Billy paused, thinking, then burst out laughing. '*You* thought wrong.'

I rolled my eyes. 'Oh yeah?'

'Yeah. I thought we were walking together; you thought we weren't. And look, we are! So *you* thought wrong.'

I opened my mouth but couldn't think of a retort. How

could something that made absolutely no sense be so hard to argue with?

*

Billy followed me all the way to the warden's office.

'Don't you have somewhere to be?' I asked him, pulling open the office door and nodding at Mrs Pruitt.

We crossed to her desk at the same time, me reaching in my backpack for my signed detention slip and Billy reaching for Mrs Pruitt's candy dish.

'Good morning, Billy D.' She smiled and patted a chair next to her desk.

'Morning.' Billy climbed into the chair and started shoving jelly beans into his mouth. The sight of him looking so at home in the disciplinary office pulled me up short. I froze with the detention slip half extended to Mrs Pruitt.

'What are you doing?' I asked him.

'Billy delivers messages for me before school,' Mrs Pruitt purred. 'And during his lunch hour.'

I wished she wouldn't answer for him.

'You don't eat lunch?' I asked.

'He eats in here sometimes,' Mrs Pruitt said.

'He can speak for himself. He's not retarded.'

43

Mrs Pruitt held her breath in shock. When she finally let it out, a string of disconnected words rode the exhale. 'Didn't say – horrible word – detention would be good for – of course not retar – disable – challenged—'

'Mrs Pruitt,' Billy interrupted, either ignoring or totally unaware of her internal struggle. 'Dane can't have detention today. He has to walk me home. He keeps the bad kids away.'

'Our own resident bodyguard, eh?' The warden leaned in the doorway to his office. 'What's this about a walk home?'

'Dane walks with me so other kids won't pick on me,' Billy said.

'That true?' The warden raised an eyebrow at me.

No, I thought. *Well, not entirely, anyway.*

Three walks sure didn't make me a bodyguard, and I'd tried to dodge every one. But it wasn't a total lie, either.

I looked from Billy to the warden. 'Kind of.'

'Well, *kind of* won't get you out of detention.'

That perked my ears up. I crossed my arms, the detention slip still in my hand.

The warden looked back and forth between me and Billy. 'I think Principal Davis would like this,' he said.

'Like what?'

'You helping a new student. Billy here could use a – a—'

44

He snapped his fingers. 'An ambassador, of sorts – someone to show him around.'

'So?'

'So volunteering to be that ambassador could go a long way towards cleaning up your record.' The warden nodded at the paper clutched in my fist. 'Maybe it could even get one or two of those black marks expunged.'

'So . . . what? You'll erase my detentions if I carry his books or something?' I gestured at Billy, who was on the edge of his seat, listening.

The warden lifted his chin. He knew he had me. 'I'll have to run it by the principal, but for now let's just say . . . Billy is in here every day. If he says you're being a good ambassador, perhaps your next detention won't be an automatic suspension.'

'Perhaps I won't *get* another detention.' I mocked his condescending tone.

The warden laughed. It was three months to the end of the school year, and we both knew the chances of me going that long without a detention were nil.

'Fine, I'll show the shortstop around.'

Billy huffed. 'I'm not a shortstop. I'm Billy D.'

'Well, *Billy D.*' I spread my arms to indicate the room. 'This is the disciplinary office.' I jerked a thumb behind me. 'Out there's the hallway. All those little doors? Those are classrooms.' I cocked my head at the warden. 'I can show him the bathrooms, too, but I'm not going to hold his—'

The warden was in my face in a flash. 'This is serious,' he hissed. 'You are. One. Mistake. Away.' He jabbed my detention slip with his finger on every word. 'From getting suspended. After that – expulsion.'

'I know.' I was ashamed to hear a tiny squeak in my voice.

'I am offering you a chance. Principal Davis thinks you're smart – so smart that keeping you in school keeps him off my ass.'

I heard Mrs Pruitt clear her throat.

'So prove it. Prove you are smart enough to take a deal you don't deserve.'

'Okay,' I said, shifting uncomfortably under his towering stance. 'How does this deal work?'

The warden backed off a step and looked over his shoulder at Billy, whose eyes were bulging now at the scene. 'Billy D., you said Dane helped you out with some kids who were picking on you?'

'No,' I said. 'I never even met—'

'I'm asking Billy,' the warden interrupted me.

'He walked me to school, and no one bothered me,' Billy answered honestly.

The warden pulled the detention slip from between my fingers, crumpled it into a ball, and tossed it expertly into a bin by the door. 'That's a good start,' he said.

I gaped at him. 'No detention?'

'It's still on your record.' He pointed at the crushed paper in the bin. 'Still number six. But you don't have to serve it here at school. You walk Billy home tonight instead.'

I'd rather be in detention.

'Like getting out of prison for good behaviour,' I said.

'More like parole.' The warden smiled. 'Step out of line, and you go right back in.'

I narrowed my eyes. 'What else do I have to do?'

'Anything Billy needs.'

'Like wha—?'

'*Anything* he needs. But you can start by showing him a little more respect. In fact, show some respect for *all* of our special education students.'

So he is in special ed.

Billy twisted his lips and looked like he might protest, but the warden pushed on.

'Billy may have Down's syndrome, but he's extremely high-functioning.' He paused and made his next words sharp. 'He certainly doesn't need your help to *go to the bathroom.*'

He backed into his office, pointing at me as he went. 'Just show me you give a shit for once, okay?' Then he slammed the door.

Mrs Pruitt cleared her throat again and waved her hands as if to shoo away the whole nasty business.

'Well!' she said, pulling a file from one of her desk drawers. 'I'll just mark that detention served, then.' She winked at me and patted Billy on the shoulder. 'Looks like you owe your friend Billy here a favour.'

I frowned. 'I don't do favours.'

But between the crumpled-up detention slip in the bin and the big grin on Billy's face, all the evidence seemed to suggest this was one favour I couldn't avoid.

7

It wasn't even a day before Billy came to collect.

I was leaning against Nina Sinclair's car after school, blocking her door just enough to keep her from getting in but not enough to be obvious, and pretending to chat her up about algebra, while I was really calculating which was hotter – her long hair or her long legs.

I'd just got a laugh out of her when Billy came stomping up.

'I thought of my favour,' he announced.

My eyes threw fireballs in his direction, but the watery look in Nina's eyes doused the flames.

'Oh, sweetie, what was that?' She spoke in a sickening baby voice and bent over with her hands on her thighs, as if Billy D. were a small boy and not, in fact, her exact same height.

'I was talking to him.' He poked a finger at me.

'Oh, sorry.' Nina looked taken aback for a second, but she was mushy-eyed again when she tilted her head up to me. 'You look after him?'

49

'Well, it's not really *looking after*—'

'Does he have Down's syndrome?'

'He can hear you, y'know—'

'That's really sweet.' She leaned in close and fluttered her eyes down towards the ground. 'And really hot.'

I felt a warmth spread from my face all the way down below my belt.

'Yeah, you know.' I slung an arm around Billy's neck and pulled him towards the baseball fields. 'Gotta look out for the little guys.'

Nina smiled, and I kept Billy in the headlock until she was in her car and pulling away.

When I finally loosened my grip, he pushed away hard. 'I'm not little.'

'You're a little bit stupid, though.'

'I'm not stu—'

'I don't mean it like that. I mean it's stupid to interrupt a guy when he's trying to hit on a chick.'

Billy frowned. 'You were trying to hit her?'

'No, hit *on* her. It's just an expression, like—' I shook my head. 'Forget it.'

We reached the street and walked in silence until we came to the slope that led up to the gardens. We paused, deciding which way to go, then without a word, we both passed the hill and continued down the pavement.

'You said you thought of your favour,' I said.

'Oh, yeah. I need you to help—'

'No.'

'What?'

'Whatever it is, *no*. I'm walking you home. That's my detention.'

'But Mr Bell said you're the amb – the umb—'

'Ambassador,' I said. 'And don't call me that. And don't expect me to hold your hand or wipe your butt, either. I'll show you around school, but I'm not doing any bullshit favour you can come up with like . . . like helping you clean your room or something.'

'I don't need you to help clean my room. I need you to help find my dad.'

I stumbled on the pavement and had to search Billy's face to see if he was joking. He wasn't. I backed up a step with my hands in the air. 'Whoa. That is . . . that's just . . . way heavy.'

And way too close to home.

Billy didn't look surprised. With his eyes narrowed and his jaw set, he looked – *what was it?* – calculating.

'Mr Bell likes me,' he said.

'So?'

'So he won't give you detentions if you help me.'

I didn't like where this conversation was going.

51

'No deal,' I said, and kept walking.

Billy scurried to keep up. 'If you help me find my dad, I'll help you find yours.'

Again, I was stopped in my tracks. 'Dude, who said I wanted to find my dad? That's . . . that's . . . none of your business, that's what that is.' I paced the pavement, feeling my palms begin to itch. 'And who says I don't know where my dad is?'

'Mark.'

'What?'

'Mark says you don't know *who* your dad is.'

Mark had really given Billy an earful in his first week in town. I pounded a fist into one of my itchy palms. 'Okay, this time I *am* going to kick his ass.'

'Do you?' Billy asked.

'Do I what?'

'Do you know who your dad is?'

'I told you it's none of your business!' I pointed a finger in his face. 'And you shouldn't listen to mental defects like Mark.'

'And you shouldn't say "mental defects".'

I dropped my hand. 'I didn't mean it like . . . I didn't mean, y'know . . .'

Billy stared.

'Anyway.' I shook off his stare. 'If you're such good

friends with Mark, ask him to help you find your dad.'

'We're not friends. He just walked me to school once.'

I was sure Billy meant he *followed* Mark to school.

'I bet he wouldn't help me,' Billy said. 'But you will.'

'Why is that?'

'Because if you don't, I'll tell Mr Bell.'

'Tell him what? That I won't solve your family crisis? Yeah, go ahead. I'm sure he'll throw me right out of school.'

Billy shook his head. 'No. I'll tell him you won't help me at school. That you're not a good ampassator.'

'Ambassador,' I said, and stared hard down at Billy. 'You're joking, right? You wouldn't lie to the warden and get me a detention and maybe kicked out of school just because I won't do you some impossible favour.'

Billy didn't answer, but he met my gaze without blinking, and the look in his eyes said it.

Yes, yes he would.

'That's . . . You can't . . .' I chased him as he started moving down the street again, waving my arms and desperately trying to find the words. 'That's *extortion*!' I finally cried.

Billy gave me a blank look.

'Blackmail,' I said.

Billy shrugged. 'I don't know what that means. But I'm supposed to tell Mr Bell if you don't help me. And if you don't help me, you get in trouble. So you have to help.'

I was beginning to wonder if there wasn't an evil genius brain under that innocent expression. I wanted to be pissed, but – *damn it* – I was secretly impressed.

'Okay, kid. I guess you got a deal.'

'I'm not a kid. My name is—'

'I know, I know. Your name is Billy D. Fine, *Billy D.*, I'll help you find your dad, all right?'

I had no idea what kind of a mess I might be getting myself into, but it didn't look like I had much choice. Something told me the warden just wouldn't buy it if I told him the friendly new kid with Down's syndrome was blackmailing me.

'Awesome,' Billy said. 'And I'll help you find yours.'

'That's okay, I don't want—'

But Billy was already pounding down the pavement, babbling on about when we should get started and how long it might take.

Two turns later, at the end of our street, he finally became aware of me again.

'I need another favour.'

The kid had nerve.

'You have to teach me to fight.' Billy pulled himself up straight and pounded a fist into a palm the way he'd seen me do earlier.

54

I started to laugh, but the intense look in his eyes cut me off. 'Oh, you're serious.'

'*Dead* serious.'

I half smiled. That line sounded like something Billy had heard a tough guy say on TV. 'Yeah, I'm pretty sure teaching you to fight is the *opposite* of what Mr Bell wants,' I said.

'So you won't do it?' Billy narrowed his eyes at me.

My half-smile opened all the way, imagining what the warden would think if he knew he'd just traded in my detentions for fighting lessons.

I gave Billy's shoulder a soft slug. 'That's exactly why I *will* do it.'

8

Billy may have been a berserker – whatever that meant – but he'd obviously never thrown a real punch. Only a few days after promising the kid I'd teach him to fight, I already regretted it. It would have been easier to take my chances with the warden than hang my Twain High career on Billy's demands.

I thought we'd cleared the toughest hurdle just convincing Billy's mom to let him leave our street. I had waited on the pavement while Billy promised her we were just going to 'hang out' and that we wouldn't go far. But Mrs Drum hadn't appeared to be listening. She was a frazzled-looking woman with suspicious eyes, and she'd stood in the doorway, staring right past Billy down to me. It was obvious she thought 'hang out' meant do drugs and that anywhere beyond our street was too far. But Billy had begged, and she'd finally relented, making him promise to be home by dark.

I pressed my fingers over my eyelids and leaned back against the splintering wooden post of a swing set. 'I don't know what to tell you, dude. It's not that hard to hold a fist.'

'It is for me.'

I opened my eyes and saw Billy sitting on the end of a faded yellow plastic slide. The park with the beat-up old playground covered in gang symbols and rust was the best place we'd found to get a little privacy. It was too much of a crap heap to draw any kids during the day, and the thugs who used it as a meeting place for drug deals or a canvas for spray paint never showed up until after dark.

Billy looked at his hands, splaying the fingers and forcing them to stay straight. When he rested his hands, those fingers curved in slightly. He could make a thick fist, but he had a hard time holding on to it. Every time he landed a punch, his fingers went slack, and so far he'd hurt his own hands more than he'd hurt me.

I pushed off the pole and stood up straight, shaking off my frustration.

'Okay, one more. This time hit me here.' I pointed at my stomach. 'It's soft. It won't hurt.'

Billy shook his head. 'You're not teaching me right.'

'I'm not – what?' I flinched. 'Screw you, Billy D.! I'm doing you a favour. And I don't do—'

'I know,' Billy interrupted. 'You don't do favours.'

I snapped my jaw closed.

'You should show me how to hit harder or—'

'It's not just about strength. It's about form.' I tried to sound like I knew what I was talking about. No one ever taught me to fight. I always just followed the itch.

I sank down on the ground next to where he sat pouting on the slide. 'This isn't going to work.'

His face fell. 'But you said—'

'I know, but what can I say? I can't teach you.'

'Why not?'

I threw up my hands in frustration. 'Because I'm no Mr Miyagi, and you are *definitely* not the Karate Kid.'

'The what?'

'Don't tell me you haven't seen that movie.'

'What's it about?'

'It's this oldie from, like, the eighties. It's all about a shrimp dude who becomes the greatest fighter who ever lived, basically.'

'Like me.' Billy grinned.

'No, man, *not* like you. That's the point.'

'It's only the first day,' Billy protested. 'Don't worry. You'll get better at teaching me.'

I gaped at him, speechless. Yes, obviously, I was the one sucking it up here and not the kid who couldn't hit a target if his life depended on it.

While I sat there stunned and half admiring the kid's

confidence, he dragged his backpack over to the sandbox and pulled out his atlas. He sat on one of the cracked wooden railway sleepers framing the sand with his legs crossed, the heavy book open in his lap.

I tried to sit back and enjoy the temporary silence, but the longer Billy searched the pages, the more I wanted to know what the hell was so interesting about a bunch of maps. I moved to sit next to him on the railway sleeper. 'What're you looking for in there?'

Billy didn't look up. 'My dad.'

I shot him a sideways glance.

'Strange place to be looking for a dad,' I said. 'Unless he's a paper doll, I don't think you're gonna find—'

Billy stabbed one of the pages with a stubby finger. 'Truth or Consequences!'

I pulled back at the volume in his voice. 'Dude, don't get all heavy on me. I was just making conversation.'

'No, look. Truth or Consequences.'

He moved his fingers, and I saw the words printed there in the dent he'd made on the map of New Mexico.

'That's the name of a town?' I asked.

'Yep. That's an easy one, because it's on the map.' He thumbed through the soft, worn pages of the atlas. 'But there's lots of towns with funny names that aren't on the maps.'

'Yeah, but what's that got to do with—'

'See.' He let the pages fall open. 'In Oregon, where I used to live, there's a place called Boring. But it's not in the atlas, so I had to write it down.'

'But, Billy—'

'And there used to be a town called Idiotville.' He laughed as his fingers traced a line from the handwritten Boring to a dark scribble where he'd crossed out *Idiotville*. 'But it's not there any more. And there's lots of Borings. There's one in Maryland and Tennessee and—'

'Billy D.!' I had to shout it to get his attention.

He lifted his eyes from the atlas like he was coming out of a daze, and I made the universal symbol for 'time-out' with my arms.

'That's all cool, man, but you said you were looking for your dad.'

'I am.'

'Yeah, I'm not getting it.'

Billy spread a chubby hand across the map, smoothing out the page.

'My dad told me all the names of the towns. He made lists, and I'd find which state they were in and where to put them on the map.'

'And?'

'And he's in one of them. I just don't know which one.'

I studied Billy's face, but his expression was far away, lost in Hooker, Oklahoma, or some other place.

'When's the last time you saw him?'

'At home,' Billy said. 'A couple months ago. Or . . .' He screwed up his face, thinking. 'Maybe a lot of months ago.'

'Didn't you just move here?' I asked.

Billy went back to flipping the pages of his atlas. 'We went some other places first.'

'So your dad's not back in – where did you say? Oregon?'

Billy shook his head. 'No. I called our old house. I memorised the number. But it's someone else's number now.'

'Cell phone?'

A faint shade of pink filled Billy's cheeks. 'I don't have it any more.'

'Why not?'

'Mom deleted it from my phone.'

'Oh! Nasty divorce or something?'

I'd had a buddy go through that in junior high. His dad wouldn't pay child support, so his mom stopped letting him see his dad on the weekends. He was the first of my friends to get booted from Twain over to the alternative school after the warden busted him with drugs.

Billy picked at the corner of the atlas, ignoring me.

I crossed my arms and tilted my face up to the sky. 'Man, I know you want me to help you with this dad-hunt-whatever, but you have to at least give me a place to start.'

Billy held up the atlas and finally met my eye. 'Start here.'

'Makes more sense to start in Oregon,' I said.

'He's not there.'

'You're so sure—'

'Even Mom says he's not there. She says he moved. And I know he would only move to one of *our* towns. But it wouldn't be Boring, because Dad said he'd *never* live somewhere called *Boring*—'

'What's your dad's name?' I asked.

'Paul Drum.' He twisted his head to look at me, his eyes squinted. 'Why?'

'Because we can look him up on the Internet – find out where he is.'

Billy rolled his eyes. 'Duh. I tried that.'

'Dude, I told you to stop saying "duh".'

'There are, like, a billion people named Paul Drum,' he said. 'And they're all in Detroit or San Diego or places you've *heard* of. My dad would never live anywhere you've heard of.'

'So you haven't even tried to call—'

'No. He's not in those places.' Billy snapped the atlas

shut and hugged it to his chest. 'He's in one of these places.'

He rocked back and forth, hunched over the book.

Instinctively, I reached out to pat his back. It was an awkward gesture, and my hand wasn't used to it, so I hit him a little too hard, and he had to kick out a foot to keep from going headlong into the sandbox. I gripped the back of his shirt to pull him upright.

'Okay, Billy D. If you say he's in one of those funny-name places, that's where he is.'

When Billy looked up at me with a small smile, I didn't regret lying to him. If it made the kid feel better, then let him think his dad was hiding in that atlas.

It had been a long time since I'd scoured old photo albums looking for shots of me as a baby in some guy's – *any* guy's – arms and even longer since I'd entertained silly dreams of a dad showing up to claim me, but I still remembered what it felt like. And I couldn't deny – back then, if I'd had an atlas, or any sort of treasure map that might help me find my dad, I would've clung to it, too.

*

The walk home felt longer after the fighting lesson, so about halfway between the playground and our street, we parked our butts on a bus-stop bench, agreeing to let wheels carry us the rest of the way. A smelly drunk was slumped in the corner of the bus stop shelter, snoring loudly. I stared at him – like I stared at a lot of strangers – searching for something familiar. I always looked harder at the bums and thugs, afraid one of them might be the man I was supposed to call Dad.

The bus squealed to a stop in front of us, and we climbed on. It was crowded with nine-to-fivers on their way home from work, and there was nowhere to sit. I grabbed on to a metal bar, but Billy didn't have to. A woman in a cheap-looking suit got up from her seat and motioned for Billy to take it. She gave him a patronising smile as he took the seat, and he smiled back. There were a few other smiles of pity around us – more people who would have given their seat to Billy as if he couldn't stand up like anyone else, like his unusual face somehow meant his legs didn't work.

The woman who gave up her seat smiled at me, too – a silent 'atta boy' for being such a Good Samaritan, hanging out with the Down's syndrome kid. I returned her smile with a scowl.

We got off the bus at the end of our street, and my feet were barely on the pavement before I told Billy, 'That's not cool, man.'

'What's not cool?'

'You shouldn't have taken that chick's seat.'

'Why not?'

'Because of why she gave it to you.'

Billy's expression flickered confusion.

I sucked in a breath and tried to figure out how to explain delicately.

'She gave it to you because she thinks you're retarded.'

Delicacy was apparently not my thing.

Billy frowned. 'No, she's just nice.'

'Billy D., do you ever notice people being nice to only you and not anyone else?' I asked as we walked.

Billy thought for a moment. 'Maybe.'

'Doesn't that bother you?'

'Why would it bother me?'

'Because . . . because they're only being nice to you because they feel sorry for you.'

Billy looked up at me in surprise. 'Why do they feel sorry for me?'

I caught his eye. 'Really?'

'Really.'

'Dude, because you look different. Obviously.'

'Oh.' Billy looked down at his feet.

I rushed to explain. 'I mean, at least they're nice, y'know? Better to be nice to someone different instead of mean or something. But still . . . they're judging you. They're making a decision about you based on how you look . . . like—' I snapped my fingers. 'Like people think I'm a jerk just because I don't go around grinning at everyone all the time.'

'Yeah.' Billy's eyes lit up with understanding. 'And like that piece of hair that sticks up on the back of your head.'

My hand flew to my head automatically. 'What?'

'People probably think you don't brush your hair, but I bet you do, because I've seen you try to push that hair down, and it won't stay, no matter how much you brush your hair, I bet. But people don't know that.'

Slowly, deliberately, I pulled my hand from the clump of hair in question and felt my scalp tingle as the hairs stood back up, one by one.

'Yeah, that's not – I didn't mean . . . the point *is*, Billy . . .' I took a breath. 'People shouldn't treat you different just because you look retar—' I choked on the word. 'Because you're – whatever – challenged or something.'

Billy stopped. We'd reached our houses. 'You treated me different,' he said.

'What? No, I didn't.'

'Yeah, you said you wouldn't beat me up – because of how I look, right?'

He stared at me, his expression empty. He wasn't judging me – just stating the obvious.

'Shit,' I said. 'I guess I did. I'm sor—'

'Who else won't you beat up?'

We were standing in the middle of the street between our houses, and it was getting dark fast. I backed up towards my kerb, to get out of the road. 'Girls,' I said as I walked backwards. 'I don't hit girls.'

'Why not?'

'Dude, because it's just not cool to hit girls.'

Billy thought about that for a minute, then nodded. 'Who else?'

'I don't know, Billy. I'm tired, okay?'

'Okay.' He stomped away to his own kerb but turned back before he reached the front step. 'Hey, Dane.'

'Yeah?' I could barely make out Billy's silhouette under his dim porch light.

'Your mom's the blonde lady, right?'

'Right. Why?'

'You don't look like her.'

'I know.' I hesitated. 'I don't know who I look like.'

'I bet your mom knows,' Billy offered.

'What?'

Billy shrugged. 'You don't look like her. But she probably knows who you *do* look like.'

Of course I'd thought before that I must look like my dad, but how had it never occurred to me that that would mean my mom knew who he was? I smiled in the dark.

Whatever people thought about my mom . . . whatever *I* had secretly thought about her . . . I was sure now that she was not those things – that she knew who my dad was and probably always had.

Billy's shadow moved towards his front door.

'Billy D.!'

'Yeah?'

'Walk to school tomorrow?'

I could almost see his face spreading into a smile. 'Okay, then.'

'Okay, then.'

9

'And how is Dane treating you?' I asked Billy, doing my best impression of the warden.

'Fine,' Billy said in a bored voice.

'Is he showing you around school?'

'No.'

I grabbed Billy's arm, turning him around. We stood toe-to-toe on the pavement halfway to school.

'No, Billy, you say *yes*.'

'But I don't need you to show me around school.'

I threw my hands up. 'Not the point.'

I'd been coaching him on what to say to the warden ever since we'd stepped off our street. So far, I was sure a suspension was right around the corner.

'Whatever,' I said, walking again. 'Just tell him I'm helping you, okay?'

'I will.'

'Good.'

'When you start helping me.'

I wheeled on him. 'What do you mean? I'm teaching

69

you to fight, aren't I?'

His sour expression told me that wasn't the favour he was referring to.

'Dude, I'll do what I can to help you track down your old man, but that's going to take time. You need to make sure the warden thinks I'm helping you now. Besides,' I said, lowering my voice, 'if you don't keep me out of trouble at school, you won't be holding up your end of the bargain, and I won't have to help you find your dad at all.'

Two could play at this game.

'That's—' Billy huffed and turned a little red in the ears. 'That's—'

'Blackmail?' I said. 'Yeah. Tell me about it.'

I should have won that round, but the way Billy's eyes and mouth turned down at the corners sent an uncomfortable little wave of guilt through me.

'Fine, let's try this again. You're sure your dad's not back in Oregon?'

'I'm sure,' Billy said.

We moved down the pavement.

'And he didn't tell you where he was going?'

'Nope.'

'He just moved and didn't call you?'

Billy's smile faltered. 'He doesn't have our number.'

'Why not?'

'Because Mom keeps changing it.'

Wow, that woman had really been burned.

'Hey, what's she doing?' Billy pointed ahead to the corner of the next street.

I followed his finger to a car parked right in the middle of the intersection. A woman in a tight skirt was kicking her tyres and shouting swear words at no one in particular.

'What's wrong with her?' Billy asked.

'Who cares?'

A few steps later, almost to the corner, the woman spotted us. She threw her arms up in a hallelujah gesture.

'Oh, thank goodness! Can you help me?'

'Help you what?' I asked.

She flung an arm backwards towards her car. 'This piece of sh— this piece of junk broke down. It just *stopped*. I'm driving, and it sputters and chugs and then just *stops*!' She planted her hands on her hips, waiting for us to look as shocked by this news as she was.

'And?' I said.

'And – well, could you look at it maybe? See what's wrong?'

I sighed. This happened to me a lot. Maybe it was the stubble or the fact that I lived in work boots and jeans, but for some reason, people – especially female people – always assumed I knew something about cars.

One of Mom's boyfriends tried to teach me about cranks and gear shafts and whatnot once, but I shut him down same as I did every guy who pretended to be my dad. I wouldn't have minded learning from an uncle or a grandpa or something, but I didn't have any of those, and Mom assured me if I knew them, I wouldn't want them anyway.

Normally I would have told the cougar with the car I couldn't help her, but Billy was standing right there, watching me like he expected me to fix it – like he expected me to be able to do anything. So I tried to look confident as I stepped over and opened the bonnet.

I peeked in and immediately backed up, coughing. Something in the mess of engine parts was smoking slightly.

'Oh yeah.' I hacked. 'You've got a problem.'

'Oh no! What is it?' The woman leaned away from the car as though it might explode at any second.

'It's – um—' I moved back to the engine and reached for a part, stalling for time. The bit of metal I touched seared my fingers. 'Shit!'

I stuffed my hand in my pocket, wincing. I didn't want Billy or the woman to see I'd burned myself.

'Oh, God. It's really bad, isn't it?' The woman moaned.

I nodded. 'Yeah, yeah, I can't fix this without . . . y'know, without my tools. You should call a tow truck.'

'What a crock of shit!' a husky voice chimed in.

I whipped around at the sound of wood skidding against concrete. A skinny boy with shocking white hair hopped off a skateboard behind me. *No wait – not a boy – a girl.*

Her flat chest, deep voice, and supershort crop of bleached hair had thrown me off, but as she grabbed her board and joined me at the front of the car, I could see everything about her face screamed girl. It was all soft skin, long eyelashes, and bright red lips.

I felt my hand fly up to flatten my cowlick. 'Excuse me?'

She leaned over the engine, ignoring the smoke. 'Looks like you just overheated,' she said to the woman in the tight skirt. 'When's the last time you changed your oil?'

The woman waved a hand. 'Oh geez, who knows?'

The white-haired girl rolled her eyes. 'Well, the smoke is clearing out. When this cools off, it should start up again, but I'd drive it straight to a mechanic.' She pointed down the road, past the baseball diamonds. 'You know where Ray's Auto Repair is? On Oakland? Just down there to the right.'

The woman nodded. She seemed encouraged by the confidence in the girl's voice.

'You might need to flush your coolant system.' The girl lowered the bonnet and dropped her skateboard to the street. 'Ray'll give you a good deal. Tell him Seely said to hook you up.'

The woman thanked the girl over and over while I stood to the side feeling like a jackass.

With one foot on her board, the girl waved goodbye to the woman and turned to us. 'A tow truck?' She sneered.

'What makes you think her car will restart?' I snapped back.

The sound of the engine coming alive and the car peeling away answered my question.

The girl laughed. It was a low sexy laugh, and I wanted to hear more of it, but I scowled at her anyway.

'It's okay.' She gave my arm a light punch. 'I'm sure you would have fixed that engine right up. Y'know . . . with your tools.'

'Guess we'll never know,' I mumbled.

'Can I ride your skateboard?' Billy suddenly spoke up.

She eyed him, looking unsure of whether it was rude of him to ask or rude of her to say no to a kid with Down's syndrome. 'Well . . . I don't usually let strangers borrow my board.'

'I'm Billy Drum. But everyone calls me Billy D.'

'I'm Seely. Everyone calls me Seely.'

Billy laughed.

Seely looked at me, waiting.

'Oh. I'm Dane.'

'Yeah, I know. I've seen you at school.'

She had? Why hadn't I seen her? It seemed like I would remember that crazy Wite-Out-coloured hair, but she was probably one of those posers who changed their hair colour every week, trying to prove how 'different' they were.

'You go to our school?' Billy asked.

'Yep.'

'What grade are you in?'

'I'm a sophomore.'

'How do you know about cars?'

'My dad owns a bike shop. He works on motorcycles.'

'Is your dad Ray?'

I almost laughed. This girl had no idea how long an interrogation from Billy could go on.

'Who?' she asked. 'Oh, from Ray's Auto. No, Ray is a friend of my dad's. Wow, you ask a lot of questions.'

'Get used to it,' I muttered.

'I'm getting to know you, so we won't be strangers, so I can ride your skateboard,' Billy said.

You had to admire the honesty.

'Tell you what,' Seely said. 'If we see each other again, we won't be strangers next time, and then maybe I'll let you ride. Deal?' She talked to Billy so easily, like she'd been negotiating with guys like him all her life.

'Deal.' Billy clasped his hands together. 'I hope we see each other soon, then.'

Seely smiled. 'Me, too.'

And when she said it, her eyes shifted ever so slightly to me. Then she had both feet on her board and was sliding off towards school.

'I like her,' Billy announced as we headed across the ball fields. 'Do you like her?'

Let's see. She humiliated me in front of the hot old lady; she made me feel like a jerk for not recognising her when she recognised me; and she made it painfully obvious that having a dad will give even a girl a bigger man card than I had.

'What's not to like?'

10

It was almost a week before Billy brought up his dad again. We'd spent so much time sparring in the park next to the playground and so much effort convincing Billy's mom that it was safe to come home after dark as long as I was with him that we hadn't had time for anything else.

And I definitely owed him this favour. I didn't know what he was saying to the warden and Mrs Pruitt, but in a matter of days they'd gone from keeping a reproachful eye on me to going out of their way to wave and smile when they saw me in the halls. Billy was keeping up his end of the bargain. At least in the eyes of the jail keepers, I was becoming less hoodlum, more hero.

Billy was sprawled on his stomach in the grass after one of our sessions at the park, his face inches from the atlas open in front of him.

'Why are you always staring at that thing?' I asked him. 'It's not like you're going to find anything new in there.'

'I find new stuff all the time,' Billy said without looking up.

I dropped into the grass next to him and peeked over his shoulder. It looked like the same boring maps to me. 'How's that?' I asked.

'I follow the clues.'

Billy pointed to the bottom of the page, at a single line of neat handwriting – too neat to be Billy's own.

'What is that?'

'My dad wrote it. There are lots of them.' Billy flipped through the pages, and here and there, one of the maps would have its own footnote, inked in that same uniform print. There were at least a dozen of them. 'They're clues,' Billy said.

'Clues to what?'

'New towns. See?' He held up the atlas so I could read the line written under the map of California.

It's better than two in the bush.

I stared at it for a second, then shook my head. 'I don't get it.'

'Mom always says "A bird in the hand is better than two in the bush".'

'Yeah, I've heard that,' I said, still confused.

Billy flipped fast through the pages as he talked. 'I looked it up on the Internet. My dad showed me how. There's a place called Bird-in-Hand here.' He let the atlas fall open to a map of Pennsylvania and pressed his finger to a spot where he'd written *Bird-in-Hand*.

I raised my eyebrows. 'That's really smart, Billy D.'

He beamed at me, but a second later, a shadow passed over his face, and he went back to staring at the book. 'But I don't understand all of them.'

I watched Billy for a moment and felt things clicking into place. 'So . . . you think if you can figure out all those clues, one of them will tell you where your dad is?'

Billy sat up, his eyes wide. 'You think so, too?'

No, not really.

But I knew my job: keep the kid happy, keep my ass in the warden's good graces.

'Can't hurt to figure out the clues, right?' I pulled the atlas into my lap. 'Do you know this one?'

The page was still open to Pennsylvania, and at the bottom, the handwritten line read: *Here, Mom and I both met and married. Different, but the same.*

Billy read the clue out loud, using his finger to follow the words and sound them out. He stumbled in the middle over 'married' and 'different', and I finished for him.

'That's easy enough,' I said. 'Where'd your parents meet and get married?'

Billy shrugged, his face blank.

'You don't know? Just ask your mom.'

'Mom gets mad when I ask questions like that.'

79

I nodded, wondering what had happened between Billy's parents to make them split up. It obviously hadn't been pretty, but it also wasn't fair of Billy's mom to not even let him talk about his dad. I felt a surge of empathy for Billy. Whatever beef my own mom had with my dad, she got even by never telling his son who he was. What was it with these moms and their misdirected punishments?

'Well, it's still easy,' I said, getting to my feet. I held out a hand to drag Billy up, too. 'You and me – we're going on a scavenger hunt.'

*

There wasn't much to scavenge. Billy's house was pretty bare – just a couch and a coffee table with a small TV in the living room, a foldout table and chairs in the kitchen, and mattresses flat on the floor in the bedrooms. Everywhere else was a sea of boxes still waiting to be unpacked.

'What are we looking for?' Billy asked, dragging one of the boxes into his room on my orders.

'Photo albums,' I said. 'Pictures from your mom and dad's wedding.'

Billy scrunched up his face. 'Mom would be mad.'

'Good thing she's not here, then,' I said, cracking open the box.

It was a Saturday, and Billy had promised that his mom was gone all day working weekends. He didn't know what she did, which I thought was weird, but I didn't press. I wasn't all that interested, and I could tell by the sparse furnishings it wasn't anything too impressive anyway.

Billy helped me dig through the first few boxes, but he quickly lost focus. Every box contained some new distraction.

This is the Megatron Transformer Dad got me for Christmas.

This is the picture I drew in kindergarten that Dad put up on the fridge.

This is the ticket from when Dad took me to the zoo, and we spent a whole hour at the monkey cage watching them pick bugs off each other – Dane, did you know the monkeys pick bugs off each other? And then they eat them. They eat the bugs!

Billy's stories made me want to smile and scream in equal parts. It was nice hearing about having a dad from someone who wasn't throwing it in my face to hurt me.

But I would never have stories like that.

And with every memory from Billy, I felt a little more pissed at his mom for taking him away – for keeping him from making more memories. I hoped my mom hadn't done the same. I even hoped for one small second that she *didn't* know who my dad was, because at least that would be a pretty damn good reason for not telling me.

I was about to give up on the boxes when my hand closed over the edge of something thick and flat.

'Billy D., I think I found one.'

'A photo album?' He dropped his Megatron toy and crawled over to me.

'Yeah.'

I pulled the album from the box and blew the dust off its cover. A picture on the front showed two hands with fingers interlaced, wedding rings in sharp focus.

Jackpot.

'You found it!' Billy clapped and bounced around on the floor.

I cracked open the cover, almost as eager as Billy to see if I was on the right track. The binding creaked as I opened it – too loudly. I stopped moving, but the creak continued. It wasn't the photo album making the noise, I realised. It was the front door. Billy and I locked eyes, and I saw my own panic reflected in his when we heard his mom's voice call, 'Billy? You home?'

We jerked forward simultaneously, both aiming to leap to our feet and smacking foreheads instead.

'Ow.'

'Shit.'

'Billy?' Mrs Drum's voice was closer, moving down the hall. I dropped the album back into the box, and Billy tossed the biggest pieces from his toy collection on top of it. The split-second teamwork covered the evidence just as Mrs Drum's face appeared in the doorway.

'What are you doing?' she asked. The question started with a smile, but her eyes slid from Billy to me as she spoke, and by the time she reached the question mark, she was scowling.

'I said no visitors when I'm not home.'

I returned the stare and tried to make mine even fiercer. She had no right to be giving me that look. What had I done to her, besides keep her kid entertained while she worked long hours and kept secrets? *You're welcome*, I thought.

'I'm showing Dane my toys,' Billy said.

It was a decent cover. Half-truths are really the most believable lies. But I felt a twitch in my stomach as Mrs Drum's eyes slipped down to the box. She let out a tired sigh. 'Fine. I don't have time to argue. I have to go back to work. I just came to pick up – I mean, we're out of—' She rubbed her eyes. 'Oh, it doesn't matter. Just please stay home for the rest of the day. And no visitors after dark,' she said pointedly.

Billy agreed, and we followed his mom into the kitchen, where she grabbed an industrial-size bottle of bleach and a handful of old rags. I took in her clothes, a uniform of papery grey pants and a matching top, like dreary doctor scrubs.

'Where do you work, Mrs Drum?' I asked, using the voice I used with girls at school.

Apparently it *only* worked on girls at school, because Mrs Drum snapped her head around and fixed me with a look like I'd just let out a string of curse words.

'Why?' she asked.

I stepped back in surprise. 'Just making conversation,' I said.

She watched me for a second longer, then turned to Billy. 'No visitors after dark,' she repeated, and disappeared out the door.

Billy and I were back in his room, unearthing the photo album, the instant the door closed. We didn't even have to study the pictures. Billy's mom had made it easy for us with a label right inside the cover: *Our wedding, Cancún, Mexico.*

I read it out loud to Billy, and he wrinkled his nose. 'That's not in my atlas.' He pulled the book out of his backpack and showed me the front cover. 'United States of America.'

I frowned, thinking. 'What does the clue say?'

Billy flipped to Pennsylvania and recited the line printed under the map. I noticed he read it much faster this time, almost like he had already memorised it. I wondered how many of the clues he knew by heart.

'Both met and married,' I repeated, mumbling to myself. 'Different but the same.'

'What does that mean?'

Different but the same. 'Did they meet in Cancún?' I asked.

Billy huffed and crossed his arms. 'I told you I don't know that stuff.'

'Well, where are your parents from?' I pressed. 'Where did they grow up? Oregon?'

Billy shook his head. 'No. Here.'

'What?' I started in surprise. 'Here in Columbia?'

'Here in Missouri.'

I jumped to my feet and started pacing like I expected the movement to shake my brain loose or something. 'Where in Missouri?'

Billy waved his arms, frustrated. 'I don't know, Dane. But Mom said, "Missouri is home. We're going home."' He pouted. 'You're asking a lot of questions.'

'Annoying, isn't it?' I raised my eyebrows.

Billy just scowled.

'Different but the same.' I paced some more. 'Mexico and Oregon. Mexico and Missouri.' I stopped in my tracks and flashed a smile at Billy. 'Mexico, Missouri!'

'Huh?'

'It's a town! It's a town with a stupid name right here in Missouri.' I dropped to the floor and flipped eagerly to the map of Missouri. 'Look, you don't even have to write it in. It's already there.'

I pointed out Mexico to Billy – less than an inch away from Columbia on the map. 'I bet that's where they met. And see? There's a clue at the bottom of this page, too.' I was talking fast. 'I think that's why some pages have clues and some don't. There's a pattern, like an order to it, and you have to find the right order until you get to the end . . .'

I'd said too much. I could see it in the way Billy's face lit up.

'I'm not sure . . .' I stumbled. 'I didn't mean . . .'

But I couldn't backpedal as fast as Billy could run full-steam ahead.

'Can we go there?' he asked.

'Go where?'

'To Mexico.' He uncapped a pen and drew a careful circle around Mexico, Missouri.

'Dude, I doubt your dad's in—'

'Just to see,' he said, perfectly calm.

I still didn't think the clues led anywhere except to more maps, but it couldn't hurt to check out one little town. Anything that kept Billy happy kept me out of trouble at school. And on top of that, I admitted only to myself, I sort of wanted to help the kid find his dad. A dad like that, who bought you Christmas presents and took you to the zoo and let you spend an hour at the monkey cage, now *that* was a dad worth finding.

'Yeah, we can go there sometime,' I said. 'On a weekend when I can borrow my mom's car.'

'You can drive?' Billy asked.

'Of course I can drive. I'm sixteen.'

'But you always walk,' Billy said.

I pulled my eyes down to the floor, suddenly very interested in a dark stain on the worn-out carpet. 'That's just because I don't have a car,' I muttered.

'You should get a red car like that boy.'

'What boy?'

'The one you beat up.'

I looked up. 'Oh, that douche in the Mustang? I would never drive the same car as that loser. He thinks he's a big shot just because he's got wheels.'

'Is that why you beat him up?' Billy asked. 'Because he has a car and you don't?'

'No, that's not why I . . .'

I hesitated. It wasn't just that the jerk had a car and I didn't. It was that he had the freedom that comes with a car – and I didn't.

87

'Yeah,' I said to Billy, shocking even myself with the confession. 'Yeah, maybe that was part of it.'

Billy nodded. 'You hit people who have stuff you don't.'

'Nah,' I said. 'I just hit people who have it coming.'

'Have what coming?'

'You know – people who are asking for it.'

Billy's eyes bulged. 'People *ask* you to hit them?'

'No, it's not—' I half laughed, half sighed. 'I just mean people who deserve it.'

Billy nodded again, but he didn't look like he understood so much as he was bored of the line of questioning.

'You want to see something cool?' He jumped up and pressed his nose against the bedroom window. 'Look. My room is right next to Mark's room. You can see inside it.'

'Who would want to?' I said. 'The only action in Mark's bedroom involves Mark and his own—'

'Well, you can't see any more,' Billy said. 'He talked to me through the window when we moved in. But then you walked me to school, and he closed the curtains, and now we can't see.'

'Who cares? Sure, if it were Nina Sinclair's bedroom . . .' I leaned back against Billy's mattress, fantasising.

'She's boring,' Billy said. 'Seely is cooler.'

'Who?'

'Seely, with the skateboard.'

88

'Oh, Wite-Out?' I cocked a sideways grin at Billy. 'You got a thing for her, huh?'

Billy's wide cheeks turned pink, and he looked away. 'I just like her skateboard.'

I pictured the red lips popping out from under that white hair and imagined the husky voice coming from that tiny body. She was annoying, but I wouldn't mind seeing her bent over under an open bonnet. There was something kind of hot about a girl who knew her way around an engine – especially since *I didn't*.

'Yeah,' I said, closing my eyes and letting a new fantasy take over. 'I kind of like her skateboard, too.'

11

'And then, in Worms, Nebraska – that's not really a town, just a bunch of houses in the same place – we went to a carnival.'

'Uh-huh.' Mom nodded.

'And my mom let me ride this one ride that spins around really fast all by myself.'

'Uh-huh.'

'And I didn't even get sick.'

'Good for you!' Mom grinned at Billy.

He'd taken her on a stop-by-stop tour of his trip here from Oregon – everywhere from Snowville, Utah, to Frankenstein, Missouri, which apparently had a lot of cemeteries and not much else. I'd lived in Missouri my whole life and never heard of it. And I could have lived the whole rest of my life and happily never heard about it again.

It had been more than an hour of this, and Mom still seemed riveted.

She kept piling cookies and crisps in front of Billy, and between those and his big atlas he'd spread across our kitchen table, I'd been pushed over to a corner, where I was trying to catch up on algebra and block out their conversation. But it was kind of hard to ignore when your mom went all Betty Crocker with the new kid. The only reason I'd let him in after school was because he was all excited to show me something he'd checked out of the school library, but ever since we'd walked in the door, it was like he'd forgotten all about it.

'I would love to take a road trip like that,' Mom gushed.

'*My* mom didn't want to go. I had to say "pretty please with sugar on top".'

'Why didn't she want to go?'

Billy dropped his eyes to the table and twisted a cookie in his hands. 'She doesn't care about those places.'

'Well, she obviously cares about you, if she took you to them. You are a lucky guy, Billy.'

'Not as lucky as you!' Billy exclaimed. He threw an arm up towards the wall of unclaimed tickets. 'I wish I could do that. It's like magic!'

Trust Billy to not only not judge our crazy house, but also embrace it like it was the coolest place he'd seen since Ketchum, Idaho.

Billy turned his chair to marvel up at the lottery tickets, and Mom caught my eye behind his back.

I love him, she mouthed.

I ducked my head into my algebra textbook, pretending to ignore them both.

'Really, Billy, you don't think my tickets are weird?' Mom pushed.

'No way.' Billy knelt to face my mom over the back of the chair. 'I saw a show on TV about people who won the lottery and spent all the money. They couldn't help it; the lottery made them loony tunes. And they ended up *poorer than before they won.*' Billy punctuated the sentence by throwing his arms up in the air. 'Isn't that nuts?'

'That *is* nuts,' Mom emphatically agreed. 'Greed is dangerous.'

'This way,' Billy said, gesturing at the wall, 'you're a winner forever.'

Mom leaned over the table, reaching a hand out to Billy. She was practically slobbering on him.

'Oh, Billy, you simply *have* to come over more often.'

'I'm done!' I snapped my book shut a little too loudly. 'Um . . . with my homework, I mean. Billy D., you want to show me that thing, or . . . ?'

Billy looked surprised that I was still in the room. 'Oh, yeah.' He slid a sidelong glance at my mom, which I took to mean the 'thing' wasn't for her eyes.

'Let's go to my room,' I said.

'Okay, but . . .' Billy looked down at the cookies.

Mom took the cue and pressed a pile of imitation Oreos into his hands. 'Take them with you. Come back if you want more.'

'We'll be fine, Mom,' I said, pushing Billy and his backpack out of the kitchen and down the hall.

I locked my bedroom door behind me. 'Okay, this better be good.'

'It's awesome,' Billy said. He sat on the dirty carpet and pulled a tall, flat book from his backpack.

'What is it?' I dropped down to the floor next to Billy and leaned in.

'It's a *yearbook*,' he breathed.

His breath was the sound effect to match my own deflating anticipation.

'A yearbook? Seriously? I've been waiting an hour to see some lame yearbook?' I grabbed it from Billy's hands. 'It's not even a new yearbook. It's some old mouldy year.' I checked the date on the front. The year I was born. 'I don't get—'

Oh.

There was only one person I knew who went to Mark Twain High sixteen years ago.

'Is this my mom's yearbook?'

I opened the pages without waiting for a response. Billy knelt beside me, peeking around my shoulder.

'You said she was fifteen when you were born,' Billy explained. 'And I'm really good at maths' – I happened to know Billy was, in fact, in remedial maths, but I didn't interrupt – 'so I figured out which yearbook she was in.'

'Okay. So?'

'I bet your dad's in there, too.'

I snapped the yearbook shut and held it away from me like it was contaminated. 'Whoa. Who asked you to look up my dad?'

'Nobody asked me. I did it because I'm nice.' He looked very pleased with himself, which only pissed me off more.

'I told you,' I said, seething. 'I don't want to find my dad. I don't want to talk about my dad. I don't give a *shit* about my dad.'

Billy leaned away from me, but he didn't look scared. 'You didn't tell me all that.'

'I told you enough,' I said, flinging the yearbook back into his bag. 'What did you expect to find in there, anyway? I don't even know my dad's name.'

'Duh. Somebody who looks like you.'

I froze for a second, almost tempted by the idea, but then shook my head.

'No way. Sorry, but he could look like anybody. I could look like anybody. What are we going to do, look up every guy with dark skin and dark hair, track them down, and ask them if they slept with my mom? Not cool, Billy D.'

Billy's shoulders slumped, and I could see he hadn't thought that far ahead. Just like with his atlas, he'd decided the answers were in a book – like books were magical yellow-brick roads with dads at the end of every one. My palms began to itch. Billy had made me think – even for a second – like him, like there was a secret inside one of those books. He'd made me feel dumb and childish, and I wondered why the hell I was hanging out with someone so retar— *damn*, I couldn't even *think* the word any more. *Someone so . . . not like me.*

I stood up and growled down at Billy. 'My dad is not in some yearbook. I don't need that or an atlas or anything else. If I wanted to find him, I could. I wouldn't need your help. I don't *want* to find him, okay?'

Billy zipped up his backpack and stood, unfazed. 'Okay. We can look at it later.'

'I don't want to look—'

'Anyway, I have to go home. My tummy hurts from the cookies.' Billy's eyes widened, and he pointed a finger at me. 'Don't tell your mom!'

'Trust me,' I said, 'I'm not telling my mom about this. I've asked her about my dad before, and she totally freaks out—'

'No,' Billy interrupted, one hundred per cent serious. 'Don't tell her what I said about the cookies.'

*

After Billy left, I sat at the kitchen table pretending to write a paper for English. I stared at the notepad under my hands, but I didn't see the words written there. My senses were all focused on Mom instead – the sound of her opening and closing the fridge, the smell of her shampoo, and the feel of her eyes on me.

'How's the homework going?'

'Fine.'

'English?' she asked, sitting across from me.

I didn't look up. 'Uh-huh.'

I was afraid to say anything more than a few syllables. Billy had opened up something inside me when he opened that yearbook, and even though I knew it would lead to nowhere good, all my thoughts were now focused on asking Mom a question – a question I hadn't asked in a very long time. Of course, I had asked variations of it over and over as a kid, and she had given me answers that ranged from half-truths to what I suspected were out-and-out lies. Finally, after a few heated conversations that had ended with her crying behind her closed bedroom door,

I'd dropped it. I never meant to drop it *forever*, but the more time that passed, the harder it became to bring it up again. But Billy had set something simmering, and now it was at a full boil.

'Mom, do you know who my dad is?' I blurted.

Her mouth fell open. '*Excuse me?*'

'Do you – well . . .' I didn't know how else to word it.

'What exactly are you implying, Dane?'

I stumbled over 'I didn't mean—' and 'uh, uh, uh' and just *ick*. The weight of what I was really asking her fell all over me, and I wanted to sink into the floor.

Did I really just ask my mom if she was a slut? It was the very accusation I'd defended her against the first time I ever threw a punch. I blamed Billy for planting crazy ideas in my head. This kind of thing was exactly why I didn't want to go looking for my dad. Too messy.

And now Mom was right across from me, barely keeping a lid on that temper I understood so well and waiting for me to say just the wrong thing.

I wanted to drop the whole disgusting conversation, but the pressure of her staring at me was too much. Plus, I had to know. As gross as it was, I had to know if she at least knew who he was. I mean, there had to be a reason she hadn't told me, and if it wasn't that she didn't know . . .

Oh shit. Oh God. No.

It was too sick to think about. It was worse than talking to Mom about sex – way worse. I tasted bile in my mouth.

'Oh my God, Mom, were you – did someone *do* something to you?'

'What?' She kept her eyes narrowed at me, trying to figure out whether I was insulting her again. Then her eyes opened up, and all signs of anger melted off her face.

'Oh geez! No! I wasn't raped, if that's what you're asking. Honestly, is that what you think?'

I recoiled at the word 'rape' and wished even harder that I hadn't started this whole awful conversation.

'No, I'm sorry. Shit.'

Mom and I were mirror images with our heads in our hands, looking anywhere but at each other.

'I'm sorry I asked,' I said to the table. 'It was stupid.'

'Dane, I need you to understand something.' Mom pressed her fingertips together in front of her mouth and forced herself to look into my eyes. 'The reason I never talk to you about your . . . your father . . . is not to protect myself. I wasn't rap—'

I winced.

'I wasn't attacked,' she went on. 'And I wasn't sleeping around.'

I sighed. I had known that, deep down, but it was good to hear Mom say it.

'The reason I don't talk to you about him is to protect *you*.'

I raised an eyebrow. That sounded like a line, but I wasn't going to protest when she was so close to spilling the beans, so I kept my mouth shut.

'The truth . . . or the thing is . . . damn.' Mom whispered the last word and looked away, towards the wall of lottery tickets, towards all the things we should have had but refused to claim. When she turned back, her eyes were liquid. One tear escaped down her cheek as she said quietly, 'He didn't want you.'

It was soft, the way she said it, but it punched me hard in the gut. I wanted to puke again but in a whole new way – like I could upchuck my whole heart.

Mom rushed to fill the silence.

'But *I* really *did*, honey. I wanted you *so* much. It's his loss. It's always been his loss, because you are so great—'

'It's okay, Mom.'

'No, it's not. I'm sorry. But do you see now why it doesn't matter who he is?'

No. It matters more than ever.

'Yeah, I see.'

I realised right then that I *did* want to know who he was. I didn't want to go find him for some lame father-son reunion. I didn't really want to find him at all. I just wanted

99

a name. I wanted to know who was making my palms itch right then – whose face belonged at the end of my fist. But I wasn't angry for myself. I was angry for Mom. I was pissed that she had to apologise for that bastard, that she had to shed tears for him – or for me, because of him.

I reached forward to take Mom's hands. It made me feel like the adult.

'Mom.'

'Yeah?' Her tough voice was back, but I could still hear a little sniffle behind it.

'If he doesn't want me, I don't want him, either.'

She met my eyes and squeezed my hands as if afraid I would pull away. 'Are you sure?'

I held her gaze. 'I'm sure.'

As Mom wrapped her arms around my neck, I added to myself: *Sure if I ever do find him, I will beat him until even he doesn't know his name.*

12

After a couple of weeks of Billy tagging along to and from school, I'd forgotten to be embarrassed being seen with him – forgotten to notice other people noticing us. The only times I remembered we might look strange walking side by side were once when I heard a rumour that Billy must be my little brother and whenever Nina Sinclair gave me that weepy 'aren't-you-sweet' smile. I pretty much stopped talking to her after a few of those.

Our walks were mostly a tug-of-war between Billy trying to get me to decipher codes from the atlas and me trying to give Billy bonus fighting lessons. I knew I let Billy down whenever I couldn't figure out his dad's cryptic messages, so I tried to make up for it with the extra-credit fight-club stuff. I'd been teaching him to stand a little taller and firmer, to get a good stance for leg swipes. He'd managed to knock me off my feet a few times, and I noticed he wasn't hunching so much now when he walked.

We were practising those leg swipes on one of our walks home when a flash of white ahead of us caught my eye.

'Hey, Billy D., isn't that your girlfriend?'

Billy followed my line of sight, then ran ahead, arm straight out in front of him, waving like a maniac. 'Seely! Seely!'

Seely skidded to a stop and used the back wheels of her skateboard to do a 180-degree spin. 'Hey! Billy D., right?'

'Right!' Billy made a fist and did a little elbow tuck like he was celebrating a victory. 'You remember me.'

'Sure I remember you, little dude.'

'I'm not little,' Billy corrected. 'I'm – I'm big enough to ride your skateboard.'

Seely tapped the end of the board with her toe to make it pop into the air. She caught it one-handed without taking her eyes off Billy. 'That's right. I said you could ride it if we met again.'

'Yeah, 'cause we're friends now.'

I caught up with the two of them and shrugged over Billy's shoulder at Seely. She *had* promised.

She hesitated only a second before plastering on a big smile and passing the board to Billy. 'Okay, friend, let's see if you can stand up on it first.'

'Yes!' Billy dropped his heavy pack right there in the street and stepped on to the board. Seely steadied him with two hands, then one, then let him fly around on his own. I noticed he was using his fighting stance to keep balanced.

Seely and I both sat on the kerb to watch Billy, impressed and – speaking for myself – a little proud.

'He's pretty good,' Seely said.

I snorted. 'Not like riding a skateboard is very hard.'

'It is for some people,' she said.

I glared sideways at Seely. 'If you mean people like Billy D., you're wrong. He can stand on a piece of wood as good as anybody.'

'I didn't mean *people like Billy D.* I just meant *people*. It's not as easy as you think.'

My arms relaxed at my sides, and I looked away so Seely wouldn't see the little smile of relief that slipped on to my lips before I could stop it.

'Why do you ride a board, anyway?' I scoffed. 'Didn't you say your dad owns a motorcycle shop or something? Why don't you have wheels?'

Seely pointed to the street, under Billy's feet. 'I've got four of 'em.'

She winked as Billy slid by and laughed at her comment.

'Anyway,' she went on, 'I have to *earn* the big wheels. I'm logging hours at the shop for my dad. He had to lay a bunch of people off when the shop started losing money. So I'm helping him out to earn cash.'

'You gotta pay for your own car? With a mechanic for a dad?'

'Fifty-fifty. Every dollar I earn at the shop, he matches. When we have enough money combined, we'll buy something classic but busted from Ray's, then fix it up together.'

'How much is enough?' I asked.

Seely shook her head, and her short, spiky white hair moved with it. 'I don't know. Every time I go to Ray's, I see something I like better – and by better I mean more expensive.'

I began to wonder just how much money she'd saved up already – if it was even half of what Mom had hung up on the wall.

A clatter in the street spun both of our heads. The skateboard was on the ground, wheels up, and Billy was facedown. Seely and I moved at once, sprinting towards Billy. I got there first.

'Billy D., you all right?'

He groaned, his face still on the road. I nudged his shoulder with my boot.

'Real gentle.' Seely elbowed me aside and crouched down next to Billy. She swatted my boot out of the way and replaced it with a soft hand on Billy's shoulder. 'Hey, friend, are you hurt?'

The groaning gave way to a giggle, and Billy finally rolled over to face us.

Bits of gravel stuck to his cheeks, and he had road rash on his chin, but he was smiling. 'That was awesome.'

We all laughed, and I stuck a hand down to help Billy to his feet. 'Now *that* is how you take a hit.'

'Pretty tough,' Seely agreed.

She kept a smile on her face while she inspected her board. It was two whole minutes before she declared the board intact and let that fake smile melt into a real one. She dropped the board to the ground and put one foot on it.

'Guess I'll see you guys around.'

'You live in this 'hood?' I asked.

'Close enough.' Seely pointed over a row of houses. 'I live about ten blocks that way. You know where the park is, by the strip mall?'

'We know,' Billy said. 'We go to the playground there.'

I hung my head, swinging it slowly from side to side.

'Oh yeah?' Seely kept her voice polite, but I could hear the laughter in it. 'The playground?'

'Yeah, with the yellow slide and all the drawings.'

'He means the graffiti,' I said, looking up. 'And we don't *play* there. We just hang out there sometimes.'

'Whatever,' Seely said. She put the other foot on her board. 'Maybe I'll see you over there sometime.'

'Cool,' Billy said, his eyes on the skateboard.

Seely pushed off down the street and waved. 'See ya, Billy!' She nodded at me. 'Dane.'

I nodded back but didn't say anything. I didn't realise I had my hand on my head, flattening my hair, until after she had disappeared around a corner.

13

I found myself scanning the cafeteria the next day for a shock of short white hair, but apparently Seely had a different lunch hour. *Too bad*, I thought as I weaved my way out of the cafeteria to the patio outside. I could have used the company.

I dropped my tray on to one of the patio's concrete picnic tables. I used to have a spot inside, freshman year. But as my friends got kicked out of Twain one at a time, it got harder to hold on to the table, until finally I was the only one left, and I just gave up on the cafeteria altogether.

The patio was usually pretty empty, but today a familiar face threw himself on to the bench across from me – Jake something-or-other. He used to sit with my crowd sometimes last year, when we made room. He reminded me of one of those little yappy dogs that think they're bigger than they are and try to take on Rottweilers. Actually, Jake tried to take on everyone. As often as he picked fights, it was kind of a miracle he hadn't been kicked out yet himself.

Marjorie Benson sat next to him and gave me a short

nod. I used to look forward to seeing Marjorie around school, but most of my old crew had seen enough *of* her to spoil the mystery. Still, she was hot enough that I couldn't figure out why she'd be sitting with Jake, until I realised most of her friends probably went to the alternative school now, too.

'What's up, Dane?' Jake asked, forking a bite of something brown and vaguely meat-like into his mouth. A few drops of gravy landed on his shirt, and he kind of smeared them in with his fingers.

This was the company I'd been left with when my friends evaporated.

'Nothing,' I muttered. 'You?'

'Ah, you know. Usual. Putting freshmen in their place.' He gave me a conspiratorial grin, but I felt something stick in my throat.

'Which freshmen?' I asked. I narrowed my eyes at Jake, trying to decide if he was the type to pick on a kid like Billy – if Jake was the one who had scared him.

'Any freshmen. All freshmen. How should I know?'

'Any named Billy Drum?' My tone made Jake lean back a bit.

'I don't think so. Who's that?'

'Is that the special-ed kid you've been running around with?' Marjorie asked in a bored voice.

'What do you know about it?' I snapped.

She waved a hand like it was old news. 'Nina Sinclair was talking about it in gym. She says you walk him to school – like you're volunteering for some charity programme or something.' Marjorie laughed. 'She obviously doesn't know you very well. Stuck-up twit. You didn't go out with her, did you?'

Jake cut in before I could answer. 'What's that about, Dane? You some kinda hero now?'

'Not a hero,' I grunted, embarrassed. 'But if I find out you've messed with him—'

'No way. I wouldn't hit a retard. And I sure as shit wouldn't hit a friend of yours, man. Swear.'

'He's not a retard. And he's not my friend.' I lowered my eyes to my tray on that last bit, knowing it was a lie. It felt strange to defend Billy in one sentence and insult him in the next. But I didn't like hearing what our hanging out was doing to my reputation. It was fine if a girl like Nina thought I was some kind of guardian angel, but I didn't want a bunch of guys getting wind of it.

I took a bite of my sandwich. 'We have a kind of deal going.'

'A deal? Like you're doing him a favour or something?'

I looked sharply at Jake. 'I don't do favours.'

Jake laughed. 'Well, I wish you'd do me a favour and

create some action around here. Been getting pretty boring.'

'Yeah, Dane.' Marjorie winked. 'When *is* the last time you got any action?' She bumped my leg under the table with her foot, and I slid away out of her reach. I appreciated tough girls – girls who'd grown up in the trailers next door to my own street and who knew how to handle everything from whisky bottles to white-trash insults. Both would get knocked back in a single slug. I appreciated them, but I also knew to stay away from them.

'Not the action I meant.' Jake rolled his eyes. 'I want to see you take someone out like when you made Jimmy Miller flip his bike. That was epic!'

'Any more epic moves like that, and I'm at the alternative school.'

'Better there than here,' Jake said. 'Bet it's not boring, anyway.'

'If you say so.'

'Stare much?' Marjorie said to someone over my shoulder. I turned to see who she was talking to and saw Mark shuffling by. I sneered at his khaki pants and knock-off polo shirt – obviously something his mommy had put together from a second-hand shop. Who did he think he was, wearing some rich kid's cast-offs and trying to look like he lived anywhere but on my street?

'Oh, look, it's the big mouth,' I jeered.

Mark caught my eye for only a split second before looking away and pretending he didn't hear.

'Stop,' I ordered.

He did stop, and when he turned, I saw him puff up his chest a little bit. 'Yeah?' he said, trying to sound tough.

I swung my legs to the other side of the bench to face him square. 'I heard you've been telling my whole life story to your new next-door neighbour. You got a reason for that? You got a crush on me or something?'

Marjorie and Jake howled behind me, and their laughter made me feel stronger, meaner. 'Well?' I pushed.

Mark seemed to summon all his courage. His skinny little arms tensed as his hands curled into fists. 'Maybe Billy D.'s the one who has a crush on you,' he said. 'He's the one who likes guys.'

'What's that supposed to mean?' My own hands were fists now, and they were wrapped in the itch.

'I caught that pervert looking in my bedroom window,' Mark spat.

I was on my feet and in Mark's face in an instant. I heard Jake scrambling over the concrete table behind me. 'Say that again,' I dared Mark, the heat of my breath on his cheeks.

Mark's eyes darted back and forth between mine, his

brain probably boiling over with the fight-or-flight instinct. He should have run for it, but it wasn't like any kid from our neighbourhood to back down – even a shrimp like Mark. 'I said your friend Billy D. is a pervert,' he repeated. 'And you probably are, too.'

My hand grabbed the front of his fake designer polo, and the force behind it pushed him backwards into the patio's brick wall. I twisted the fistful of cloth until it was squeezed tight against his neck. His head made a gritty sound as it moved back and forth against the bricks.

'You really don't know when to shut your mouth,' I growled.

Jake leaned casually against the wall next to Mark and whispered in his ear. 'Nice move, dumb ass. My friend Dane is about to erase you from the planet.'

Something about Jake in that gravy-stained shirt with his creepy whisper and dangerous look in his eye – something about a guy like that calling me *friend* caused me to loosen my grip on Mark's collar.

Jake saw the slack and flipped his eyes from Mark to me. 'What?'

I gave Mark's shirt one more rough shake before letting go and spitting at his feet. 'Not worth it,' I said. I tried to sound like I'd made some calculated decision to let the kid go, but the truth was, looking at Jake had suddenly felt like looking in a mirror, and I didn't like my reflection. Mark probably deserved to get knocked around, but maybe – just maybe – I had started it this time.

Mark inched away from the wall, straightening his shirt. He looked at me with a question in his face, as if asking permission to run away now.

I nodded once. 'Go.'

Mark scrammed, and Jake threw his hands in the air. 'Lame! There's not even a lunch monitor around. You totally could have taken him down and gotten away with it.'

I shrugged, hoping I looked bored instead of weak. 'He would've told. Anyway, he lives across the street from me. I can handle him later.' I moved back to the picnic table, where Marjorie was still picking at her lunch, looking utterly uninterested in the almost-bloodbath in front of her. I shoved the last of my sandwich into my mouth and scooped up my tray.

'Later, Marjorie.'

'Later.' She waved.

When I raised my hand to wave back, I realised the itch had faded but not gone. I was glad I'd managed to keep myself out of the warden's office, but some part of me still wanted to give Mark what he deserved.

14

Seely showed up at our next fight session on two feet. I spotted her gliding across the park as smooth as if she were on her skateboard. The graceful movement didn't match her tough, punky exterior.

'Where's your board?' I called out.

She yanked a thumb over her shoulder. 'I just live across the street.' In her other hand, she was swinging a plastic bag full of something colourful. As she got closer, I saw it was candy, wrapped in shades of pink and purple.

'Easter swag,' she said, holding up the bag. If we didn't get a day off from school, I would have forgotten all about Easter. Outside of Christmas and birthdays, Mom and I didn't celebrate much. She tried hiding eggs for me when I was a kid, but I always found them too easily. One year, she was so determined to hide them well that even she couldn't remember where she'd stashed a few of the hard-boiled ones. Months later, when a rotten smell led her to discover the nasty old eggs inside an unused flowerpot, we called off the egg hunts forever.

'What are you guys doing?' Seely asked.

'Fighting,' I said, at the same time Billy said, 'Looking for our dads.'

Seely's eyes flipped back and forth between us.

'I'm teaching the kid to defend himself,' I said, hoping Billy wouldn't speak up again.

'Yeah, we fight. Then we talk about our dads,' Billy said. So much for hoping.

'Your dads, huh?' Seely sat down next to Billy in the grass, where he was already pulling out the atlas. Before he zipped the backpack, I noticed the yearbook was still inside.

Seely unwrapped a piece of chocolate and passed one to Billy.

'No candy. Mom says.' He opened the atlas, ignoring Seely's outstretched hand.

Seely offered it to me instead. I took it. It was the good stuff, with nuts and caramel – not the cheap junk from the Buy & Bag.

'See,' Billy began. 'We figured out *my* dad is in one of the towns on my maps.'

I didn't correct Billy's 'we'.

'What are these riddles on some of the pages?' Seely asked. She read one out loud. '*Everyone thinks he lives in the North Pole, but he really lives here*. Santa?'

'Santa *Claus*,' Billy corrected. 'That's in Indiana.'

Seely munched on piece after piece of candy while Billy walked her through the atlas, showing her the clues. He struggled reading a few, and Seely helped him without being a mush about it. But most of them he rattled off without even looking at the page – not so much reading as reciting from memory. He babbled on about which ones he needed help solving and which ones he'd figured out all by himself. By the time he was done, Seely had a pile of wrappers at her feet.

'What about your dad?' she asked me when Billy finally took a breath.

I waved a hand. 'I'm just helping Billy D.'

My dad was none of her business.

Seely shrugged off my answer and went back to inhaling candy.

'These names are great,' she said with her mouth full. She pointed at the atlas in Billy's lap. 'Crapo, Maryland? That's hysterical.'

I sat on Billy's other side, and he flipped through the pages, pointing out his favourite funny names. Some of them were in his dad's neat handwriting and others were in Billy's big, childish scrawl. We all smiled at Toad Suck, Arkansas, and Bummerville, California.

I stopped him at Dickshooter, Idaho. 'That's where Mark should live.'

Seely burst out laughing, and Billy joined in, even though he probably didn't quite get it.

Seely grabbed the atlas from Billy. 'Sandwich, Massachusetts,' she said, her mouth half full of candy. 'And Cheddar, South Carolina. This book is making me hungry!'

We were already cracking up when she turned the page and shrieked, 'Chocolate Bayou, Texas!'

Billy and I just lost it, leaning into each other we were laughing so hard. The sugar high from the candy made all the names funnier, and by the time we got to Mosquitoville, Vermont, Seely was rolling on the ground, and I was clutching my side. Billy's belly laugh came out in a stilted 'HA HA HA' that only made us crack up harder.

'Dude, that sounds like –' I gasped for air between my own wheezy laughs – 'like a dog barking.'

Seely snorted and spat a little chunk of chocolate-covered peanut out her nose. Billy and I roared.

'Ow, that huuuurt,' Seely cried, but even in pain, she couldn't stop laughing.

When we finally ran out of breath, we were spread all over the lawn. I stared at the sky, trying to remember the last time I'd laughed that hard. The only person I ever made laugh at all was Mom, and it was never quite that fun. The clouds above us were turning a threatening shade of grey and moving towards each other from the east and west. A warm breeze spun white dandelion debris into the air.

'I think it's going to storm,' I said.

When no one answered, I looked over and saw Seely sitting up with the atlas balanced on her knees. After a moment, she said, 'You could try an online directory, you know – just look him up.'

I sat up. 'Yeah, I thought of that already.' Now I understood why Billy had said 'duh' when I'd suggested it. 'But there are too many Paul Drums. Hundreds of them, all over the country. It would be crazy to try to call them all.'

Billy rolled over in the grass. 'I wish Dad had a cool name like one of the towns. Then he'd be easy to find.'

'Doesn't your mom know how to find him?' Seely asked.

Billy went back to picking at the grass.

Seely looked at me with a question in her eyes, and I gave a tiny shake of my head.

'Well, anyway, I didn't mean looking him up by just his name.' Seely closed the atlas and ran her thumb along the spine. 'I meant start by looking up the town – every clue leads to another town, right?'

Billy pulled himself upright and stared at Seely. 'Yeah.'

'So . . . solve a clue, look up the town, and see if your dad is listed. One town at a time.'

Why didn't we think of that?

'You could start with the clues you've already solved,' Seely went on. 'Look for Paul Drum in all of those first.'

'Yes!' Billy got to his knees, leaning in towards Seely and the atlas. 'Let's do it. Let's do it right now. Do you have the Internet on your phone?'

'I don't have the Internet,' Seely said, holding up a beat-up, old flip phone.

'Me, neither.' Billy frowned.

They both looked at me.

'Yeah, right,' I laughed, producing my own cheapo cell. 'This thing barely makes phone calls.'

'Well, we'll just use a computer,' Seely said. 'That's faster, anyway.'

'I don't have a computer,' Billy said. 'I have to use the ones in the library at school.'

I pictured the folding table and chairs that substituted for a dining-room set at Billy's house and felt a tug in my gut. I knew Mom and I weren't the poorest people in Columbia, but now I realised we weren't even the poorest people on our street.

'I don't have a computer, either,' I said.

'I do.' Seely looked back and forth at us and grew shy all of a sudden. 'I mean, if you don't mind my help. I don't want to butt in—'

'That's great,' Billy said.

'Yeah, cool!' I said. I swallowed hard and glanced away from Seely. 'I mean fine, whatever.'

'And you live right across the street.' Billy got to his feet. 'Let's go right now.'

I stood, too, and pointed out the dark clouds that had finally come together above us. They were swirling, and the electricity in the air was making our arm hairs stand up on end.

'If we don't get home now, we're going to be walking back in a tornado.'

Billy stamped a foot. 'But it's not even dark yet!'

'Well, I'm not your mom, dude. Do whatever you want. But I'm going to try to catch the bus, so I don't get soaked.'

Seely put a hand on Billy's arm. 'Yeah, it's gonna get nasty. You better go. We'll do it tomorrow.'

Billy scowled up at the sky. 'Tomorrow is Saturday?' he asked.

'All day,' Seely said.

'Fine.' Billy pouted. He shouldered his pack and started to pound his way across the park.

The first drops of rain fell as Seely and I joined him. At the edge of the park, she pointed out her house and made us promise not to show up too early.

'Okay,' Billy said. 'But if it rains again, we're still coming over.' He narrowed his eyes at me. '*I'm* not afraid of storms.'

15

Seely's house was like one giant garage. The kitchen counters were covered in tools, drill bits and metal parts I didn't recognise. There was a diagram of some kind of engine taped up to the mirror in the bathroom and a table with a big, round saw set up in the living room, right in front of the TV.

The homiest room in the whole place was the actual garage, where at least there were some dusty couches and a stereo. The computer was in the garage, too, so that's where we were hanging out, drinking sodas, and finishing off Seely's Easter candy.

'This is awesome,' I said for the fifth time, gawking at the garage.

'It's okay,' Seely said.

'Okay?' I swept an arm to indicate the vast space, big enough for two motorcycles, a truck, a living room setup, and an industrial-size workbench. 'It's bigger than my whole house – than *your* whole house.'

'Yeah, we expanded it when we moved in. I helped build

it, but only because I thought that meant we'd keep the house, y'know, a *house*.'

'But this is perfect,' I argued. 'Any guy would want to live here.'

'Exactly. Any *guy*. But I'm not a guy, in case you didn't notice.' She glared at me.

I had noticed, but it was easy to forget. I'd never met a girl who could rip a belch like Seely or who knew so much about cars. Talking to her was like talking to a dude, but *looking* at her was definitely like looking at a girl, even with her short hair.

'I like it 'cause it's warm,' Billy said.

We'd both forgotten our bus fare and had had to walk the whole way to Seely's in a downpour. Seely had fired up a pair of heaters and aimed them at the sofas in the garage, but we were still pretty soaked.

I tilted my head towards the computer on the workbench. 'Does that dinosaur even work?'

It was old-fashioned and boxy, like the TV in Mom's bedroom.

'Of course it works. My dad built it.' Seely propped herself up on a stool in front of the computer and turned it on.

'I thought your dad fixed motorcycles,' I said.

'He does. One builds bikes. One builds computers.'

Billy and I looked at Seely, then at each other, then back at Seely.

Seely spun her stool towards us while the computer fired up.

'It's funny. You guys have no dads, and I have two. I guess we all have our own issues.'

'Two dads?' I asked.

Seely licked a smudge of chocolate off her thumb. 'Well, three, if you count bio-dad, but I don't.'

'What's a bio-dad?' Billy asked.

'Biological, like, I have his DNA, but I don't know him or anything.'

'What about your mom?' I asked.

'*Bio*-mom,' Seely corrected. 'Don't think much about her, either. They're not my parents, really – more like participants in a science experiment.'

My face must have looked as flat and clueless as Billy's, because Seely just laughed at both of us.

'My dads wanted a kid, but gay couples aren't exactly at the front of the adoption line, y'know? So they got some sperm and a good friend with a vagina to—'

'Whoa, whoa!' I held up my hands. 'Too much information.'

Seely laughed again and reached for another piece of candy. 'The point is, some kids get the-birds-and-the-

bees talk. I got the one about test tubes and surrogates.'
She ducked her head next to Billy's, crossed her eyes, and
let her tongue loll out the side of her mouth. In a voice
even lower and more gravelly than her normal husk, she
growled, 'I was created in ze laboratory like ze monster of
Dr Frankenstein.'

Billy rolled to one side on the couch, giggling.

I raised an eyebrow. 'But your dad – or, *one* of your dads
– is a mechanic.'

'So?'

'So that's like a . . . a *dude* job.'

Seely rolled her eyes and dropped her empty candy
wrapper on to the workbench next to the computer. 'You're
an idiot.'

Maybe I *was* an idiot, but if I needed schooling, surely
Billy D. did, too. I looked at him and adopted that voice
Mom used when she was trying to talk about so-called
grown-up things.

'See, Billy, the reason Seely has two dads is because—'

'Because you're so lucky,' Billy breathed. He was
looking at Seely, but his expression was far away, staring at
something no one else could see.

'Yeah, I am,' Seely said. She gave me a pointed look and
turned back to the computer. I wished I hadn't insulted
her dads.

125

I pulled a second stool up next to Seely's.

'Hey, I'm, uh—' I stammered quietly. 'I'm, uh . . . um . . .'

'Sorry?' Seely offered.

'Yeah.'

'You're not very good at it.'

'What?'

'Apologising.' She didn't meet my eye. 'It's fine, whatever. I'm used to it. So, Billy D.' She looked past me to Billy, who had the atlas out already. 'What's first?'

Billy consulted his maps. 'I don't know which one's first.'

'We don't even know if one clue leads to another,' I said. 'That was just an idea I had.'

'Makes sense,' Seely said. 'But we don't have to go in order. Just pick a town you figured out already.'

'Burnt Corn, Alabama.' Billy was all business now. 'B-U-R-N-T.'

Seely had pulled up three different websites, each with little boxes to search people by name and city. She typed 'Paul Drum' and 'Burnt Corn' in all the appropriate boxes and set the search engines spinning.

'No results,' she said after a few seconds. 'Next.'

There were no Paul Drums in Bird-in-Hand, Pennsylvania, or Spunky Puddle, Ohio, either.

Billy's list of towns was short, and we were burning

through them fast. With every 'next' and 'nope' from Seely, the room grew quieter. We were letting Billy down.

After Santa Claus, Indiana, turned up another dead end, Seely suggested we take a break, but Billy insisted we keep going. It wasn't until Mexico, Missouri, came up empty that Billy finally slammed the atlas shut and crossed his arms. I think he was just a little too hopeful about that one. He'd been wanting to go to Mexico, and I could see now how much he really hoped his dad was that close.

I wanted to tell him it's not that easy to find dads – even when they probably live in the same *town* as you.

Instead, I opened the atlas again to Missouri and nudged Billy. 'So we solve this clue, then.' I pointed to the riddle written under the map. 'We solve all of them – get a longer list.'

Seely sat on Billy's other side and read from the bottom of the page. '*This is what happens when you don't give up.*' She chewed a fingernail. 'Try, try again?'

'No,' I said. 'The clue would have to be, "If at first you don't succeed".' The last word caught in my throat, and I sat up straight on the couch. 'Hey, what about that? If you don't give up, you succeed, right?'

Billy's eyes widened a little, and some of the shadows that had clouded his expression began to clear away. His head spun from me to Seely and back again. 'Can we . . . ?'

'I'll look it up,' Seely said, hopping back over to the computer.

I held my breath along with Billy as the keyboard *click-clacked* under Seely's fingers.

'I can't find any place called Succeed,' she finally said.

Billy and I exhaled in matching sounds of disappointment. I wanted to be right about the clue, if only to give Billy something to hold him over for a while – to make him feel like we were getting somewhere.

'But wait,' Seely said.

We crowded behind her, drawn to the excitement in her voice. A website flickered on the computer screen, loading a large map image. When it finished, a name appeared in the centre of the map, at the junction of two state highways: Success, Arkansas.

'Success!' Seely said. 'What happens when you don't give up.'

She spun on the stool and gave us a big grin. Billy and I grinned, too – at her, at each other. Then, in unison, we both dived for the atlas on the couch. I got there first, but I tossed the book in Billy's lap. 'Go for it.'

Seely and I crowded in next to Billy, looking over his shoulders as he quickly passed Alabama, Alaska, and Arizona. I was holding my breath again when he turned the page to Arkansas. I don't remember letting the air out of my lungs, but I definitely felt my ego deflate. All we saw under the map of Arkansas was a blank space.

Right. Of course there was no clue in Arkansas. Hadn't I looked at those maps a hundred times? But if I'd looked a hundred, Billy had looked a thousand, and even he had been caught up in the moment enough to forget that Arkansas was not part of the chain.

'Well, that's okay,' Seely said, her voice a measure too cheerful. 'We'll figure it out.'

Billy sank into the couch cushions and pulled the atlas close to his face.

'Maybe we should just look for Paul Drum in all the towns you have marked,' Seely continued. 'Your dad showed you a lot of these places, right? Not just the few with clues. Maybe the one he's in is already—'

'Or maybe he's not in any of those towns,' I said.

Seely shot me a pointed look.

'What?' I said. 'I'm not saying give up. I'm just saying maybe we're barking up the wrong tree.'

'It's the right tree,' Billy said, his voice muffled behind the huge book.

I could sense Billy losing confidence in the search – in me. If he didn't think I was holding up my end of the bargain, he wouldn't hold up his, and Billy was the only thing keeping the warden off my back.

'What if we just find more town names on our own?' I said, moving to the stool in front of the computer. 'Come on, Billy D., Burnt Corn is the only one in Alabama? That can't be right.'

'What are you doing?' Billy stood behind me and peered at the computer as I flew through search-engine results. Seely watched over my other shoulder.

'I'm looking for stupid city names in Alabama.'

'They're not stupid,' Billy said.

'Bam!' I punched the screen with my finger. 'Check it out. *Intercourse*, Alabama.'

'No way.' Seely leaned in, and I could smell her citrusy shampoo. 'Is that for real?'

I clicked on the map that popped up in my search and zoomed out until we could see state borders. 'Billy, do you know what "interc"—'

'I know what "intercourse" means,' Billy snapped. 'We learned about it in my life skills class. It's when a man and a woman—'

'That's okay,' I stopped him. 'I know what it means, too.'

That discovery triggered a new kind of search that probably wasn't very helpful. We spent the next hour looking up the filthiest names we could find. There was another Intercourse, in Pennsylvania, where we also discovered Virginville. By the time we got to Sugar Tit, South Carolina, and Spread Eagle, Wisconsin, we were all cracking up.

'Oh no. Oh, gross,' Seely said. 'That can't be a real place.' She was looking at the screen, where I'd just pulled up a map of Beaverlick, Kentucky.

'I don't get it,' Billy confessed.

I turned to Seely for help, but she backed away laughing with her hands up. 'Don't look at me.'

I shut down the computer and slung an arm across Billy's shoulders. 'Come on, Billy D., I'll explain it on the way home.'

16

'Billy, you have to pay attention!'

He was supposed to be spinning away from my punches, but I'd just landed the third one in a row.

'I am paying attention.' He massaged his cheek with his fingers.

Mostly, I threw soft punches – swinging fast but pulling up just before contact, so he could feel where I was aiming. But I put a little force behind the last one to wake him up.

'You're not,' I said. 'You're not even trying.'

Billy dropped his hand, and I could see a tiny bruise turning his cheek from pink to blue.

'I'm tired,' he said.

'We've only just started.'

'I'm *bored*.' He crossed his arms and pouted.

'Look,' I said, 'I don't care if you learn this shit or not. If you don't feel like fighting today, we can just go home—'

'No!' Billy stamped a foot.

'Well, I have better things to do than hang around this crappy park with some idiot who can't even focus for two min—'

The blow to my gut came so fast, it knocked me clear off my feet. I landed hard on my ass in the sandbox.

Billy towered over me. 'I'm not an idiot.'

I groaned and clutched my stomach.

Billy clasped his neck in pain. He'd head-butted me – so hard it had nearly taken the wind out of me. I had to laugh.

'Good move, Billy D.'

Billy just scowled.

I struggled to sit up and pointed to his neck. 'If you're going to ram people like that, you need to bend all the way over and hunch your shoulders behind your ears. Like this.' I stood to demonstrate. 'Then push off with your legs and throw your whole body into it.'

Billy was still frowning, but he imitated my position.

'Good,' I said. Billy was a natural shoulder-huncher. 'Now let's try this. I'm going to go to punch you, and you do the spinout like I showed you, but at the end of the spin, come around my side and do your head-butt.'

Focused now, he took a position in front of me, ready to do the manoeuvre.

I raised my arm in a fist but paused. 'Hey, Billy D., I'm sorry I called you an idiot.'

He nodded. 'I know.'

Then I swung. And in one lightning-fast move, my arm was flailing in the air, and the force of Billy's head was in my side, pushing me to the ground.

When I caught my breath, I got to one knee and gave Billy a thumbs-up. 'Damn, you *are* the Karate Kid. You're like . . . the Karate Kid in part three, when he's already a rock star!'

Billy gave me a blank stare.

'Okay,' I said, standing. 'We need to rent that movie. It's a crime that you don't know what I'm talking about.'

'It's a crime?' Billy's eyes widened.

'No, it's just an expres— Never mind.'

'Again?' Billy asked, stepping in front of me, ready for another swing.

'Nah, I think you've got that move, man.' I took a deep breath and felt a sharp pain slide along one of my ribs. 'I might need a minute.'

Billy plopped down on the edge of the sandbox and opened his backpack. *Good*, I thought. *Just read your atlas so I can heal*. But it wasn't the atlas he pulled from the bag.

'I want to show you something,' Billy said. The yearbook was in his hands.

I stared at the yearbook, trying to decide whether I was pissed or just exasperated. Of course he hadn't taken it back to the library. Why would he? Because I said so? I was fast learning, Billy did whatever damn thing he wanted, regardless of instructions from me or anyone else.

Billy opened the yearbook, and I noticed some of the pages were marked with tiny blue Post-its.

'Your mom was a sophomore, but none of the sophomores look like you.' Billy turned to the first Post-it. 'But some of the juniors and seniors kind of—'

'I told you I'm not interested in some lame yearbook,' I interrupted. 'We can't tell if someone's my dad just because he has the same colour hair.'

'What if his hair sticks up like that?' Billy pointed to a picture on the page. The face under his finger was lighter than mine, and the eyes were too close together, but the chunk of hair standing up at the back of his head was hard to ignore. My hand went to my own hair automatically.

'And this one.' Billy flipped to a new page. 'His chin is all big and pointy like yours.'

I had to admit, our faces were shockingly similar.

'But Billy—'

'And this one—'

'Billy!'

'What?'

'Yeah, they look like me. But don't you get it? If you look hard enough, they *all* look like me.'

135

This I knew from experience, from years of studying faces – in the grocery store, the launderette, the car wash. That guy's eyes – wide like mine. That guy's mouth – wearing my same scowl. Yes, I'd had years of practice seeing exactly what I wanted in the faces of strangers. But they couldn't all be my dad, and I'd figured out a long time ago that probably meant none of them were.

'That one doesn't look like you.' Billy pointed to a skinny face with acne and glasses.

I laughed. 'Yeah, and for all we know, he's my dad. See how pointless this is?'

'It's not pointless,' Billy said. 'We can look them up on Seely's computer and see where they live and—'

'I don't want Seely all up in my business the way you do, Billy D.'

'Fine.' Billy moved to slam the book shut, but I caught his hand.

A face had just jumped out at me. I couldn't put my finger on it exactly, but something was familiar.

'That one.' I pointed to the page. 'I know that guy . . . I think.'

Billy's eyes lit up. 'He looks like you. I marked this page because he looks like you! Dane, it's him. It's him!'

I couldn't figure out how Billy managed to bounce up and down even when he was sitting.

'No, it's not,' I said, but there was no conviction in my voice. The face *was* familiar, but I couldn't lock on to a solid memory – just flashes like you get when you wake up from a dream, and it starts flying away from you, so you can only hold on to a few trails.

'We can find him, Dane. We can use Seely's – I mean, we can use the library computer. I'll say we're doing homework. I'm good at lying, so—'

'We don't have to do that,' I said quietly.

'Yes, we do. You have to find him, Dane. You have to—'

'Stop!' I held up a hand. A memory teetered on the edge of my mind, and I couldn't reel it in with Billy making so much noise.

Billy stopped talking, but he continued to hop around in his seat on the edge of the sandbox.

Finally I said, 'I think I already know where to find him.'

Billy went still. 'You do?'

I ran a finger along the name next to the photo. 'I know this name.'

Vince Martinelli.

As in Martinelli's Pizza and Pasta.

I closed my eyes. Spaghetti and meatballs. A white shirt with a marinara stain Mom never could get out. The man again – adding extra meatballs just for me.

I hadn't been to Martinelli's since I was a kid, but we went so often back then I could remember everything about it. It had the old checked tablecloths and the broken tiles on the floor. It always smelled that amazing way that could make you hungry again, even if you'd just stuffed yourself full.

More flashes now – that face on the other end of a seesaw, in this very playground . . . the inside of a car with no air-conditioning, a melting ice-cream cone dripping on to the seat, and the man laughing and telling me not to worry. But none of them were as clear as the restaurant memory.

Why did Mom stop taking me to Martinelli's?

I looked at Billy. 'You feel like getting a pizza?'

17

A part of me had hoped Martinelli's would be closed. I'd dragged Billy on to the bus without stopping to think about what I was doing. On the ride over, I had time to process it. So what if the guy's face was familiar? That could just be because we used to eat at his place a lot. So what if I maybe looked a little Italian? I could also pass for Greek or even Hispanic from some angles.

By the time we got to the stop, it was Billy dragging *me* off the bus. He'd gotten all pumped up when I'd explained to him where we were going.

'Like a stakeout?'

'Sure, like a stakeout.'

I thought again about what kind of lame crime shows Billy must watch on TV. Then I thought about how lame this whole trip was and tried to turn around, but Billy had taken the reins. He even offered to buy the pizza with the credit card his mom had given him for emergencies. The rumble in my stomach agreed with Billy, so it was two against one, and now here we were, sitting at one of those ugly checked tablecloths, trying to be discreet.

Well, *I* was trying to be discreet. Billy was craning his neck around like some spineless bird, trying to see over the back of the booth into the open kitchen.

'Sit down,' I barked.

Billy sat. And bounced.

'Dude, relax. You're making me nervous.'

Billy leaned across the table. 'Do you see him?'

I pulled my water glass out of the way before he could knock it over. 'No, I don't see him. Sit back. Don't make a scene.'

'Stop telling me what to do.' Billy pouted. But he sat back and buried his face in an oversize menu. 'Can we get pepperoni?'

'Whatever. I don't care.'

I hadn't touched my own menu. I was too busy scanning the kitchen myself. I just didn't have to wiggle around like a jellyfish to do it.

Finally, I saw him. He wasn't dressed in the ugly red-and-white uniform everyone else was wearing. He had on jeans and a T-shirt and work boots – just like the ones I wore. I swallowed hard.

He walked from table to table, asking the guests if they liked their food, whether they'd had a good weekend, and what else he could do for them. When he approached our booth, my hand twitched right into the glass I'd moved away from Billy. Water and ice skated across the slick plastic tablecloth. I watched the flow speed to the end of the table, where it spilled right off the edge and on to the man's boots.

'Whoops!' The man – Vince Martinelli – laughed and shook a cube of ice off his toe.

'I'm sorry – shit – I mean, shoot – damn, I'm sorry. Sorry.' I scrabbled for a napkin and sort of wadded it up and threw it down at his boot.

Billy just stared at me, open-mouthed. His expression proved I looked as crazy as I felt.

'No problem, no problem.' The man pulled a rag from the back pocket of his jeans and pressed it on to the table to stop the waterfall. 'We've got more H_2O where that came from.' He motioned to a waitress to bring a fresh glass of water. Then he turned back to us – to me – and squinted. 'Do I know you?'

I don't know if he asked because he recognised me or because of the psychotic way I was staring at him. I coughed to cover up my speechlessness.

'He's Dane Washington,' Billy said.

I turned my stare to the traitor across the table.

'Don't think I know . . . oh my God.' The change in his voice forced me to look up. 'Are you Jenny Washington's kid?'

Whatever anger and fear had been controlling my face

and making me mute melted away to something almost like excitement. My heart was pounding. I might have started bouncing like Billy.

'Yeah, yeah, that's my mom! Jennifer Washington.'

Ugh. What an eager little puppy dog I was. When I spoke again, I tried to sound only half interested. 'You know her?'

'*Oh* yeah, I know her.'

My leg jumped like a jackhammer – the puppy wagging its tail.

The man pulled a chair up to the end of our booth and sat, leaning forward with an elbow on the wet table and a smile on his face. 'Know you, too.'

Pet me! Pet me!

'You do?' I faked a yawn.

'Sure. Your mom and I dated for a long time after I got back from college – almost a year. You were pretty little – just started kindergarten, I think – so you probably don't remember, but we had some fun, you and me.'

I knew I should return his smile, to make some encouraging expression, but I could feel all the hope sliding off my face. The flashes of memories joined the hope, snaking down to my stomach, where anxiety unravelled and melted along with everything else. All of it slid down my body and settled in my shoes – into my boots, which looked just like this guy's . . . apparently the only thing we had in common.

The man said we could call him Vinnie and told some long story about how he was young when he dated my mom and didn't want to settle down. His eyes were sad and far away, so I didn't have to worry about my face showing any appropriate reactions. I barely even listened. Mom had had lots of boyfriends over the years, and none of them ever felt significant – to either one of us. So this guy was just one of those – nobody special.

'Well, anyway.' Vinnie cleared his throat. 'It sure is good to see you, Dane. You tell your mom I said hi.' He started to stand up.

'I remember you, too,' I blurted.

Vinnie sat down slowly. 'You sure? You were pretty little.'

'Um – just like – this place,' I fumbled. 'And ice cream and little stuff like that.'

Vinnie smiled, sharing my memories, but then he raised an eyebrow at me. 'That why you're here? Something I should know?'

I was about to say no and let Vinnie get back to work when Billy opened his trap.

'Dane is looking for his dad.'

I kicked him under the table.

Vinnie let out a long whistle. 'Wow. And you thought . . .'

'No, I didn't. And I'm not looking for anybody. I just thought . . . I mean . . . It's not like that. Look, don't tell my mom—'

'Whoa whoa whoa.' Vinnie held up a hand to silence me, then lowered it to my shoulder. 'I'm not telling anybody's mom anything, okay? I haven't talked to Jenny Washington in a long time, and I won't be tracking her down to tattle on you. But can I give you some advice?'

No, you're not my dad.

'Maybe you *should* talk to her about this.'

I shook off Vinnie's hand. 'Okay. Thanks.'

He stood up, folding his dishrag. 'Well, you boys want a couple slices? On the house, anything you want.'

'We're not hungry,' I said.

I stood up from the table and glanced down for a second at Vinnie's boots next to my own matching pair. *Same size.*

I spun and headed for the exit without another word. A bell jangled loudly over the door as I pushed it open. Faintly, over the racket of the bell, I heard Billy's voice behind me.

'Can I have pepperoni?'

*

I waited until we were back on the bus to lay into Billy.

His face was a mess of tomato sauce as he crammed two

slices of pizza, stacked on top of each other, into his mouth.

'This is your fault,' I said.

Directly across the aisle from me, Billy lowered the pizza sandwich, but his mouth stayed open. I could see half a slice of mashed-up pepperoni on his tongue and a string of cheese stuck to his lower lip.

I sneered at the disgusting sight, letting it fuel my words.

'Making me look at that stupid yearbook – making me go to that restaurant—'

'I didn't make you—'

'Making me get caught up for a second – making me think I might want to look for ... for ...' My voice cracked, and I balled my hands into fists. I was almost *willing* my palms to itch. Then, at least, I would know I was angry. But my hands were calm. Not even a tingle. The emotions clutching my chest and stomach were something much more frightening, more powerful, than rage. I didn't trust myself to say anything else, so I stayed silent and kept my fists clenched, hoping they would make Billy think I was mad and nothing more.

'I'm sorry Vinnie's not your dad,' Billy said.

I turned away from him, towards the bus window, and squeezed my eyes shut, wishing I could close them as tight as I could close my fists.

'I don't care,' I said.

We swayed back and forth a little with the motion of the bus.

'We can find some of the other—' Billy started, but I held up a hand.

'I don't want to see that yearbook ever again.' I looked hard at Billy so he would know I was serious. 'I mean it. If you put that thing in my face again, I *will* kick your ass.'

'Okay.'

'This is why I didn't want to go looking for anything in the first place. Every road is a dead end or a disappointment or a waste of time!'

'*Okay.*'

'You can't find someone who doesn't want to be found!'

Billy fell silent at that.

Shit.

'I didn't mean *your* dad,' I said. 'That's different. I'm sure *he* wants to be found.'

Billy nodded and dropped his uneaten pizza crusts into the brown paper bag they'd come in. He fished a used napkin from the bottom of the bag and cleaned off his face, avoiding my eyes.

I pointed at Billy's backpack, where I knew the yearbook was hiding. 'Just get rid of it.'

18

I made Billy open his backpack Tuesday morning to verify the yearbook was inside, on its way back to the library.

'I told you,' he said, zipping the bag and hefting it off the garden's brick pathway. 'I'm taking it back. Even though Miss Tanner said I could keep it as long as I want.'

'Who's Miss Tanner?'

'The librarian.'

I thought for a minute. 'The tall, skinny one?'

'Yeah.'

'She's kind of hot. Nice ass.'

'Ew.'

'What? You don't think she has a hot ass?' I gave him a little push down the path. 'C'mon, Billy D. Admit it. You only go to the library to check out Miss Tanner's ass. Or are you a boob guy?'

Billy shushed me, his eyes darting around as if the flowers could hear us. He looked almost as freaked out as when I'd explained why Beaverlick was such a funny name.

'Oh yeah.' I laughed. 'Billy D.'s a breast man. You like 'em real big and squishy, huh? Like water balloons – firm on the outside but all—'

'Gross!'

I turned to walk backward in front of Billy as we left the garden. 'What's the deal? You never kissed a girl?'

Normally I'd ask a guy if he'd done a hell of a lot more than that, but I figured Billy might be behind this particular curve.

'I kissed a girl!' Billy said, but the red that filled his cheeks gave him away.

'I thought you said you were a good liar.' I winked.

Billy harrumphed and crossed his arms.

'Hey, it's no big deal,' I said. 'We just gotta hang out with some girls.'

'Seely's a girl,' Billy said, a little too hopefully.

'Not Seely,' I said, a little too forcefully.

We locked eyes for a minute, both stopping in midstride down a grassy slope.

'You like her,' Billy said.

'I don't like anybody.'

'She likes you.'

My stomach did a strange flip-flop, and I coughed to cover it up, as if Billy could hear it. 'Would it bother you?' I asked.

'What?'

'Would it bother you if Seely and I liked each other?'

Billy adjusted the straps of his backpack. 'I know she doesn't like me,' he whispered.

That wasn't an answer. I waited.

Finally, Billy let out a dramatic sigh and started walking again. 'Okay, it wouldn't bother me.'

'Good.' I smiled, falling into step beside him. 'Because I know some other girls you might like.'

Billy looked up, listening.

'I have to think about it a bit,' I said. 'Sara's usually down to hang, but she's kind of an airhead.' I flipped through my mental black book. 'Annie is nice – to everyone – *real* nice. But she's always with Marjorie. And Marjorie Benson can't close her legs.'

Talking about girls carried us all the way to school.

Billy asked me a thousand questions. *How do you know if a girl likes you? Where do you go on dates? When do you hold her hand?* I told him: if she laughs a lot, bowling, and hand-holding is for pussies.

He asked me how I knew girls who didn't go to Mark Twain High, and I sugarcoated the details about most of the girls I knew getting kicked out of Twain. He asked me if I'd had sex with any girls, and I answered honestly that I hadn't – but I'd been pretty close. He asked me if *he* should have sex with girls, and I pretended I didn't hear him.

At the edge of the baseball fields, before we went our separate ways, I punched Billy lightly on the arm. 'You taking notes on all this? There's a pop quiz on the way home.'

Billy slapped my punch away. 'I don't need a quiz.'

I dodged the slap and gave Billy a shove that knocked him sideways a few steps. 'We'll see about that.'

'Stop that!' a voice called out.

A teacher I didn't recognise was marching across the car park. She had daggers in her eyes, and they were aimed at me.

'Stop what?'

'I saw that.' She reached us and put a hand on Billy's arm. 'Did he hurt you?'

Billy pulled away from her touch. 'He can't hurt me.'

'We were just messing around,' I said.

The teacher glared at me for a split second, then looked back at Billy. 'It's okay. He can't do anything to you. You can tell—'

'Dane Washington doesn't hit retards.' Billy crossed his arms, proud that he had settled it.

I closed my eyes. 'Billy, that's probably not the best—'

'Oh honey, you are *not* a . . . people shouldn't even use

that word.' She looked at me with venom but kept talking to Billy. 'And people who do are not your friends.'

'He *is* my friend,' Billy insisted. 'We were just messing around, like he said. He walks me to school and tells me about girls and teaches me to fi—'

I cleared my throat to shut him up.

'We're going to be late for class,' I said.

The teacher checked her watch and studied us both for another second. 'Messing around. Fine. But not so rough,' she said to me before clacking away in her high heels.

I stared at her back as she retreated. I wanted to believe it was me she was judging – that she looked at me and saw a hoodlum. But I knew it was more likely she looked at Billy and saw a victim.

That realisation put me in a mood that lasted all morning.

*

I was still on edge when Billy plopped a tray down next to mine at lunchtime.

'Mrs Pruitt has the flu,' he announced.

'So?'

'So she doesn't need my help today, and Mr Bell said I should eat lunch in the cafeteria.'

'Then go eat in the cafeteria,' I said through forkfuls of mac 'n' cheese. I wanted to be alone, and if Billy would disappear, I would practically get my wish. I hadn't seen Jake or Marjorie since the abandoned fight with Mark, and the only other person on the patio today was minding his own business at the other end of our table, scribbling in a notebook.

Billy ignored me and dragged the atlas out of his backpack.

I pointed at it. 'What are you doing?'

'I'm trying to solve this clue,' he said. 'What's need – what's needed—'

'Put it away. It's not cool to be geeking out over a bunch of maps at lunch.'

Billy huffed at the interruption and started again, reading even more slowly. *'What's needed for a doo – a doo – for a duel.'*

'If you don't put that thing away, all we're going to need for a duel are my fists and your face.'

I didn't know if it was leftover rage from the teacher that morning or the shame of Billy catching me eating alone that had me so irritated, but I was not in the mood for chatting. I was in the mood for hitting. . . .

Which is probably why I ended up in the disciplinary office not fifteen minutes later, sitting next to a kid with a bloody nose.

The guy had it coming, of course, but that wouldn't matter to the warden.

Billy had started babbling about the clue, and I'd let my eyes drift away – towards the kid with the sketch pad. I could tell the ugly cartoon face he was drawing was Billy D., even before he added the gapped teeth and tiny protruding tongue.

My elbow had connected with his nose faster than he could glance up. Nobody even saw me swing, except Billy. They just saw the aftermath with the blood and all the cry-babying from the cartoonist.

Within seconds, some cafeteria cop had the three of us marching down the hall to let the warden sort it out.

Now we were parked in his office, waiting while he fussed with some paperwork and checked voice mails. I could see Mrs Pruitt's absence did not improve the warden's mood. Not that my timing mattered. Good mood or bad, the warden would know just what to do with me. This was strike seven. Seven and you're out. The only card I had to play – the ace up my sleeve – was Billy. He was there, and he would back me up – assuming he caught on fast enough.

'It was an accident,' I blurted.

The warden slammed down his stack of papers and finally fixed his full attention on us.

'An accident?' he asked, but his question was drowned out by the nasally shout of the guy with the bloody nose.

'Bullshit!'

Except he had so much tissue stuffed up his nose it sounded more like 'Billshid.'

He pointed a finger at me. 'Thad kid hid me in the doze.'

The warden fixed a glare on the boy. 'Watch your language in my office, please.' His eyes flicked back to me. 'How do you accidentally break a nose?'

I had to fight to keep from rolling my eyes. I seriously doubted the kid's nose was broken. 'I was telling my friend Billy D. here a story,' I said. 'And I was gesturing with my arms.' I demonstrated an exaggerated sweep of one arm, and the bloodied boy flinched as my hand came close to his face again. 'And whaddaya know, but I *accidentally* hit this guy in the face.'

I gave the warden a smug smile. Really, I was helping us both out. Keeping me in school kept the warden in the principal's good graces. All he had to do was confirm it with Billy, and we'd all be on our way back to class. Well, maybe not the kid with the crushed nose. He'd probably have to go to the nurse's office – or the hospital. After the picture he'd drawn of Billy, I really didn't care.

As expected, the warden swivelled his chair slightly to face Billy. 'It was an accident?'

Billy squirmed in his seat.

The warden sensed Billy's hesitation and made his voice sharp. 'Because you know I have every reason to suspect that is not how it happened—'

'No, id's nod,' the sketch artist protested.

'It *is*,' I insisted. 'Right, Billy D.?'

My eyes bored a hole in the side of Billy's head, willing him to look at me, but he only stared at his hands.

'Billy D.?' the warden prompted.

Billy rocked back and forth in his chair.

'*Tell* him,' I said in a low, fierce voice.

Billy looked up finally, and his voice was small and miserable when he said, 'I don't feel good.'

'Do you need to see the nurse?' the warden asked.

'Uh, *I* deed to see the durse,' the other boy snuffled.

The warden and I smacked the boy with equally vicious stares, then turned our attention back to Billy, who cowered.

'I just don't feel good,' he repeated.

'Okay, Billy, why don't you wait outside?'

I started to protest, but Billy was already scrambling for the door and the warden was already moving on.

'Dane, given your track record and the severity of the damage inflicted, I'm inclined to disbelieve this was an accident.'

What was with the formal talk?

'Therefore, I have no other choice but to—'

'Wait!' I gasped the word, trying to think as fast as my mouth could move. 'I had a reason . . . I can explain . . .'

The warden pressed his fingertips together, and his voice was almost hopeful. 'I'm listening.'

Okay, so lies were out. I had to come up with another angle quick. Desperately, I latched on to something I'd heard in history or English or, hell, chemistry, for all I remember – *the truth shall set you free*.

I pointed at the boy with the bloody nose. 'He was drawing a nasty cartoon of Billy D. Real nasty, making fun of his face and stuff.' I knew the warden didn't stand for violent reactions to any non-violent offence, but I silently prayed he would make an exception, just this once.

'Yeah, I drew dat kid.' The boy next to me dropped his hand from his nose for the first time. A thin red bubble of snot ballooned under one of his nostrils, then disappeared as he took a breath. When he spoke again, I could hear him clearly for the first time. 'I draw everybody.'

He pulled his sketch pad from his backpack, smudging a little blood from his thumb on the edge. He flipped fast through the notebook – page after page of faces I half recognised from the patio, the cafeteria, the hallways. Each one was as cartoonish as the next.

'I do caricatures.' He sounded almost apologetic. 'I wasn't making fun of your friend.'

'He's not my friend,' I spat, my anger pulling away from the boy with the bloody nose and latching on to the backstabber waiting outside the warden's door.

But the itch in my palms faded. I'd hit the kid for no reason – or maybe just the wrong reason. *It really was an accident, in a way*.

I looked up from the sketch pad to the boy's face. 'I'm sorry.'

The words felt sort of bulky and foreign coming out of my mouth, but I meant them.

The boy mumbled something like 'It's okay' and put his notebook away. His anger had disappeared, too. He looked as guilty as I felt.

The warden finally sent the poor guy to the nurse's office, and a silence fell between the two of us. I broke it first.

'So it *was* kind of an accident,' I said.

The warden just stared at me.

'And you heard the guy. He said it was okay. And Billy—'

'Billy,' the warden interrupted, 'seemed very shaken by what he saw.'

'Nah, he just—'

'You promised to look out for him, and instead you exposed him to violence.'

'No, I—'

'If you ask me,' the warden pressed on, 'you hurt two boys here today.'

I clenched my jaw. Anyone could see it was *Billy* who'd betrayed *me*. All he had to do was agree it was an accident, and this whole mess would have gone away. Sure, that guy's nose would still be jacked up, but what was done was done, right?

The warden spoke quickly, tugging open filing cabinets and pulling out papers as he talked. 'Dane, you are suspended, effective immediately and for the duration of the week.'

I sank back in my chair, speechless.

'This is a final offence before expulsion.' He slid one of the papers across the desk towards me. 'This form states you cannot be on school property and outlines other rules of suspension.'

He dropped another sheet on top of that one. 'This one is for you to take home and have a parent sign, stating they understand you will be expelled for any further . . .'

The warden's voice turned into a low buzz as he kept pushing papers at me – one form explaining how Mom could pick up my homework, one detailing how a suspension would be reported on my permanent school record. The pages blurred together just like the warden's words. This was exactly the moment I'd been trying to avoid when I'd made a deal with Billy. So why did it feel like his fault that I was here?

That's what you get for sticking up for people who don't return the favour.

Billy was sitting patiently in one of the outer office chairs when I opened the warden's door. He hopped up at the sight of me.

'Can we go back to class now?' he asked.

I waited for the door to click shut behind me and gripped the forms in my fist so tight they crumpled. I looked Billy dead in the eye and seethed. 'You go back to class. I'm going home.'

'But—'

I raised my fist full of papers, silencing Billy. Then I shoved as much anger into my voice as would cover up the hurt.

'Deal's off.'

19

Suspension was a little like being on holiday – if that holiday involved the silent treatment from Mom and extra chores for me. After the initial screaming match, Mom had settled into using a new shorthand type of speech. 'Homework assignments' – accompanied by the smack of papers and books on the kitchen table each afternoon. 'Dishes' – as she passed me a rag and pointed at the sink. 'TV off' – whenever she headed out the door to work.

Of course, that TV went on the moment she left, but when she was home, I was off the couch and on my feet constantly – cleaning my room or dusting her damn lottery tickets. Even after my suspension was technically over, by the weekend, she had me outside mowing the sorry patch of grass we called a front lawn.

That's where I was, pushing and sweating in the April humidity, when Seely rolled up in her dad's car Saturday morning. She threw it in park right in the middle of the street between my house and Billy's, then got out and leaned against the bonnet, facing me with her arms crossed.

I slowed the mower to a squeaky stop and stared back.

'What?'

'You avoiding me?' she asked.

I wiped a slick of sweat from my forehead with the back of my hand. 'Been busy.'

'Busy being suspended,' Seely said, climbing the slight slope of the front yard to stand in front of me.

'So?'

'So, you embarrassed or something?'

I tried to press my eyebrows together – tried to look pissed – but it was hard to lie to Seely in any form, so I dropped the scowl and shrugged.

She put a hand on my arm, and it was like the sweat there conducted an electrical current from her fingertips all the way into my chest. 'Don't be,' she said. 'Billy told me what happened. It's not your fault—'

'No, it's *his* fault,' I snapped, pulling away from her.

Seely's eyes swung from me to Billy's house and back again. 'You guys still aren't talking.'

'We aren't *anything*,' I said.

'Well, that's just not true and you know it.'

When I didn't respond, she gave an exaggerated sigh and strolled back towards the street. 'Guess you don't want to come, then.'

'Come where?'

161

'Oh, nowhere. Just a little road trip.' She reached her car and stroked the bonnet dreamily. 'Just thought you might like to drive.'

Damn it.

I could smell a pretty girl setting a trap from a mile away, but she'd found my bait. Hell yes, I wanted to drive that car – any car – if it would get me out of town and away from Mom.

I sucked my teeth for a second. 'Who else is going on this road trip?' I asked, already knowing the answer.

Seely didn't have to respond, though, because just then Billy's front door burst open, and he came slapping down the steps in a rush. He looked up when he hit the street and stopped in his tracks. One corner of his mouth crooked up, like he wasn't sure whether to smile or run away.

Seely caught my eye. 'I'm taking Billy to Mexico, Missouri.'

I felt a twinge of jealousy. Sure, I'd told Billy the deal was off, but I didn't think he and Seely would keep up the search *without me*. And even though I was pissed at him and shouldn't care who he dragged to Mexico, I couldn't help but wish it was me giving him the ride instead of her.

'What do you think you're going to find there?' I asked.

'Oh, we already found something,' Seely said in that

tantalising voice. 'And we'll tell you all about it on the way to Mexico.'

Damn, she was good. And Billy was smart to be keeping his mouth shut, standing there still as a statue with that stupid half-grin on his face. I held my hand out for the keys, but Seely snatched them back at the last second.

'Tell you what. You play nice on our little outing, and I'll let you drive home.'

Snake. I was on the hook, and she knew it.

I thought fast, my eyes flipping from Seely to the lawnmower to the house, where Mom would be waiting inside with more chores for me. Finally, my gaze landed on Billy. I heaved a sigh and growled at him.

'I call shotgun.'

*

Mexico, Missouri, was an even bigger shithole than Columbia. Well, a smaller shithole, technically, since it was barely big enough to be called a town.

I'd spent the whole ride there staring at Seely's legs flowing out from short shorts and trying not to catch Billy's eyes in the rear-view mirror. The tense silence in the car had broken only once, when I'd called Mom to tell her where I was. She'd actually sounded relieved. I think she was running out of shit for me to do.

Now we were crawling along the dusty grey streets of Mexico, and I had to know what we were looking for or lose my mind from boredom.

'Fine,' I said, as if responding to something in the silence. 'What did you figure out?'

'Billy found something,' Seely said. She craned her neck to look at Billy in the backseat. 'Tell him, Billy D.,' she prompted.

I set my jaw to keep myself from making a smart-ass remark. I didn't want to hear a word from Billy, but Seely was obviously hatching a plot to get us talking. Billy knew better, though. Instead of opening his mouth, he took something from his backpack and slid it up to me in the front seat.

It was a stack of envelopes and postcards bound by rubber bands. I snapped off the bands and flipped through the pile. The messages were bland, but they all had two things in common – a return address in Mexico, Missouri, and the same weird signature: *June Bug*.

'These are old,' I said, scanning the dates on the letters. 'How do you know this "June Bug" still lives here?'

'We looked up the address,' Seely said. 'It matches a listing for a June Budger in Mexico. No phone number, though – just the address.'

'Where?' I asked, strapping the cards back into the rubber bands.

'Here.'

Seely pressed the brakes, and I looked up to see we were parked outside a little blue house on a great big plot of land.

Billy pressed his face against the back window glass.

'You want us to come with you?' Seely asked.

'No.' Billy opened the car door, never taking his eyes off the house. 'I can go by myself.'

'He's really sorry, you know,' Seely said the second the door had shut.

'Whatever.'

'He didn't realise—'

'New subject,' I snapped, my eyes following Billy up the pavement.

Seely let out a breath. 'Okay, we figured out the rest of the clues.'

I whipped my head around so fast my neck cracked. 'What?'

'Well, most of them.' Seely reached into the back seat and yanked the atlas from Billy's bag. Little blue sticky notes sliced through the smooth edges of the pages – just as they had in the yearbook – except each of the notes in the atlas was marked with two letters, representing a different state. The handwriting was Billy's, but I was sure Seely had helped him with the abbreviations. Seely opened the atlas to New York. 'You were right. The clues are an unbroken line. Every one leads to another state with a clue, which leads to another and another.' I read the note from Billy's dad at the bottom of the page.

What's needed for a duel.

It was the clue that cost me a week of school. Apparently Seely had been more helpful. The sticky note at the top of the page was marked AZ.

I looked up towards the house, where Billy was pounding on the front door. Maybe if I'd just worked with him on the clue, I wouldn't have ended up in the warden's office at all.

'Two Guns, Arizona,' Seely said. 'What's needed for a duel.' She talked as she turned the pages, showing me how Arizona's clue then led to Indiana, Indiana's to Colorado, Colorado's to Texas. 'It's a lot easier to solve the riddles if you only look for the answers on other maps with clues. So we marked off states where Billy had already found answers, and it narrowed the field.'

'And you figured them all out?'

'All but two,' Seely admitted.

My eyes flicked back to Billy, who had stopped knocking on the door and started peeking into windows. 'Let me guess. You can't solve the clue after Mexico, Missouri.'

'Right.' Seely sighed. 'Billy thinks that means it's the end of the trail.'

'He thinks the clue leads to his dad.'

She nodded. 'And we won't be able to talk him out of it until we solve it.'

I took the atlas from Seely and opened it to the map of Missouri.

This is what happens when you don't give up.

Outside, Billy was now knocking on a side door. I shook my head. 'Is there a town called Bloody Knuckles?'

20

Seely shifted in her seat. 'Should we go get him?'

'Give him a few minutes.'

'Okay.' She tucked the atlas back into Billy's bag and fiddled with the radio, turning up the volume to fill the awkward silence. After a moment, she spun the dial down again. 'So you want to drive home?'

'You sure it's okay?'

'Yeah, my dad won't mind.'

'Which dad?'

Seely tensed and gripped the steering wheel. 'Very funny.'

'Or not,' I said, watching her knuckles turn white on the wheel. 'Sorry. I didn't mean—'

'It's just hard to know when you're joking or being mean.'

It was hard for me to tell sometimes, too.

'Well, I won't do either if you don't like it,' I said.

Seely smiled tentatively. 'Okay.' She stared past me out at Billy, who had stopped knocking and was now just staring at the front door as if willing it to open. 'My dads think you're my boyfriend.' She laughed, but I noticed her cheeks were flushed, and she looked away. Something in my chest fluttered down into my stomach, and I smiled for the first time all week.

'Then I'm in double trouble, because dads usually don't like me, and I've got two to worry about.' I caught Seely's eye to make sure she was still smiling. 'Or is it three? Wasn't there a third guy?'

'You mean bio-dad?'

'Yeah.'

'He's just a sperm donor.'

'But your dads *had* that part.'

Seely nodded. 'Yeah, a lot of people ask about that. Basically, they didn't want either one to be more of a "real" dad or for me to grow up looking like one of them and not the other, so they borrowed someone else's junk.'

'Borrowed?' I snickered. 'Did they return it when they were done?'

Seely laughed, too, and swatted at my leg. I liked the way her hand felt there, but she pulled it away too quickly.

I was thinking about reaching for that hand with my own when the car door flew open and Billy slammed himself into the back. I flipped down the sun visor above

169

my seat and watched him in the little mirror attached to it. He had his arms crossed and his mouth turned down. Pouting. I was still pissed, but now I also felt something like pity. I knew how badly the kid wanted to find his dad, and it occurred to me just then that I wanted to find the guy, too – not because I owed Billy anything, not any more – but maybe because I wanted to see if this too-good-to-be-true dad he always bragged about was the real deal. Or maybe I was just a masochist.

I sighed. 'It's cool, Billy D. We'll just wait. The lady's got to come home sometime, right?'

His eyes met mine in the mirror, and I saw something hopeful there.

'Actually,' Seely said, a note of apology in her voice, 'I have to have the car back before dark.'

I groaned. Having a car with a curfew was like not having a car at all. You needed wheels of your own to truly feel free.

'Well, we'll wait as long as we can,' I said.

Billy started to say something, coughed, and tried again. 'You're not mad at me?'

'Yes, I am. But unlike some people, I keep my promises. So we'll find your stupid dad.'

Seely gave me a warning look, but I ignored it. She wanted us talking; this was what she got.

'I keep promises,' Billy said behind me. 'But you don't.'

'What the hell does that mean?' I snapped, finally turning around to face Billy square.

'You said you only hit people who deserve it.' His forehead was pinched, and he gave me an accusing look. 'Only people who deserve it. That's what you said, Dane. So you broke your promise, too.'

'That's not a promise,' I said, flustered. 'That's a . . . that's a—'

'A lie,' Billy said. 'Because that boy didn't deserve—'

'I thought he *did* deserve it!' I punched the car ceiling, and both Billy and Seely flinched. 'How many times do I have to say it?!'

'That's probably enough right there,' Seely said. She put a hand on my arm, but this time I shook it off.

'I didn't see the picture,' Billy said. 'I just saw you hit him. I didn't . . . I didn't—'

'You didn't know what to do,' Seely finished the sentence in a voice meant to soothe Billy, but she was looking hard at me when she said it.

'So what?' I said. 'You still should have had my back. That's what friends do, deal or no deal.'

I flopped back in my seat, looking anywhere but at Seely and Billy.

'You're still my friend?' Billy sniffled behind me.

When I said nothing, he went on. 'Dane, I'm sorry. I'm really really really sor—'

'I know,' I said quietly.

'Billy will make it up to you, right, Billy D.?' Seely piped up.

'Yeah.' Billy pushed his head between the front seats. 'If you still help me find my dad, I'll help you find yours.'

I sighed. 'Dude, I don't want—'

'We won't look in the yearbook,' he rushed to add. Then, to Seely, 'Dane doesn't want to look for his dad in a yearbook.'

'I don't want to look for him *at all*,' I corrected.

'But—'

'Look, my dad's not in that yearbook, okay? And even if he is – and even if I wanted to find him – I know I wouldn't find him in there.' I looked hard at Billy, so he would see I was serious. 'You know that feeling? When you just *know* something? Even if you can't prove it?'

Billy nodded. 'I know my hamster, Larry, didn't go to a farm. Mom said he went to live with pigs and chickens and lots of other hamsters. She says she calls the farm and checks on him, and I can't prove she's not really calling, because I'm not supposed to listen to her phone calls. But Mark told me hamsters don't live on farms, and

I looked it up, and they don't. So I think Larry is dead, but I can't prove it.' He paused. 'Like that?'

I grinned, despite my mood. 'Yeah. Like that.'

'I think my mom lies a lot,' Billy said quietly.

'A lot of parents lie about pets,' Seely said. 'It's no big deal.'

'Not about pets. I think she lies about my dad.' Billy pulled back into the rear seat and tucked his knees under his chin. 'She says maybe he doesn't want to be found. But he wouldn't have told me about all the cool places unless he was going there and wanted me to find him.'

It sounded to me like Billy's mom was the one who didn't want to be found.

'And she says he doesn't know how to love us, but that's dumb, because how do you know how to love someone? You just love them, right?' Billy looked at me in the mirror for confirmation.

'I don't know, Billy D.'

And I really didn't know. It sounded simple and true enough, but if you 'just loved someone,' then it would have to be true that sometimes you 'just didn't,' and that meant my own dad had probably walked away sixteen years ago because he fell into the 'just didn't' category.

'Billy D.' Seely hesitated. 'Are you *sure* your dad wants to be found?'

Billy's face morphed into a stormy combination of doubt and sadness.

She held up her hands. 'I'm only asking because—'

'I'm sure,' he said.

'But *how* can you be sure—'

Billy leaned back into the front seat and raised his voice. 'Because he said so. I was in the car with all the stuff, and Mom was outside with the keys, and Dad said, "Don't you take him away from me!"' Billy flailed his arms, talking louder. 'He said it just like that. He said it a whole bunch of times. "Don't you take him away from me! Don't you take him away from me!"'

I gripped Billy's shoulder. 'Okay, okay. We believe you. Calm down.'

After a moment, he did calm down, settling back into his seat and staring at the little blue house as though the mysterious June Bug would walk out the front door any minute.

He held still now, but inside, I was shaking *for* him. My guts rattled with rage at Billy's mom. She sounded like some pissed-off housewife whose husband probably cheated or did some other dirtbag thing, and she hit back – but way below the belt – and hurt him in the worst way she could – by snatching his kid.

I thought about how lucky Billy was to have a dad

somewhere who loved him – who wanted him and fought to keep him. I hated Billy's mom for taking that away from him.

'I have to go,' Billy said.

Seely shook her head. 'It's okay. We can wait a little longer—'

'No,' Billy stressed. 'I have to *go*.'

Five minutes later we were parked outside a petrol station while Billy took his time in the bathroom. I got out of the car to stretch my legs, and Seely followed.

'My turn to drive?' I asked, holding a hand out for the keys.

She stuffed the keys in the pocket of her shorts and crossed her arms. 'After you almost punched a hole in the roof of the car? How can I trust you to drive it?'

I flinched. 'Sorry about that. My temper . . .'

'You scared me,' she said. 'I thought you were going to – I mean, Billy—'

'I would never— You thought I was going to hit *Billy*?'

She shuffled her feet a bit and looked down.

'I don't beat up on guys like him,' I said.

'Guys like him?'

'No hitting girls. No hitting retar—' I swallowed. 'No hitting kids who are challenged or disabled or whatever.'

Seely stared up at me. 'So you have rules about who

175

you *don't* beat up but no rhyme or reason to who you *do*?'

'Sure,' I answered. 'Anybody who has it coming.'

'Like Ben Demopolous?'

I lifted my eyebrows. 'How do you know about that?'

'You don't fly under the radar as much as you think you do.'

Ben had been my first detention after Mom got my slate wiped clean. He'd been bragging to his buddy in the bathroom about how he'd felt up some chick at a party after she passed out. Too bad he didn't know I was listening from inside one of the stalls. I'd shoved his face so low in the urinal, he was practically eating the deodorising block.

I explained what he'd said to Seely, but she dismissed my reasoning with a wave of her hand. 'What about Jimmy Miller?'

'Geez, are you stalking me?' I laughed, but Seely was serious.

'I saw it happen. You knocked him off his bike for no reason at all.'

'There was a reason.'

There's always a reason.

'He wasn't even talking to you. You just walked right by, picked up a stick, and threw it in his spokes.'

'Dude, that was months ago. How do you even rememb—'

'I told you. I saw it. I was there.'

'Well, you weren't there when that little puke stole my paper, made the A look like an F, and put it up on my locker for everyone to see.'

Seely's eyes widened. 'Jimmy didn't do that.'

I blinked. 'Uh . . . I think I know.'

'Uh,' Seely mimicked. 'I think you *don't* know. Jimmy didn't do that to your paper. Marcus Fletcher did.'

'What? No . . .' I stumbled. 'He . . . but how could you—'

'Because actually I was there. I saw Marcus messing with someone's paper in art class. He used our special markers to make the red F bigger and darker than the A. I saw the paper up on a locker later, but I figured it was one of his friends' – like a prank.'

'And you didn't tell anyone?'

I don't know why I sounded so shocked. I wouldn't have told anyone, either. I wouldn't have given two shits if I'd seen the paper up on someone else's locker. And I didn't like tattletales.

'No, I didn't tell anyone. Who cares? I'm just telling you now because I happen to know who did it – and it wasn't Jimmy Miller.'

The weight of that sank in. Until that day, Jimmy had never done a thing to me. But I knew I'd left that paper in biology, and Jimmy was the only one still in the classroom when I'd left. I just assumed . . .

Shit.

Every asshole thing Jimmy had said to me, every dirty look he'd shot in my direction since that day was totally justified, because apparently, when he got knocked off his bike, he'd never done anything to deserve it. Unprovoked. That's what the warden would have called it – and for once, he would have been right.

'So Jimmy didn't do anything to me,' I said.

'Nope.' Seely rocked back on her heels. 'He's just an innocent victim.'

'A victim,' I repeated. A queasy feeling seeped into my gut. 'Then what am I?'

Seely shook her head as if it was obvious and half smiled. 'You're the bully.'

21

Seely bought us all sodas from a vending machine before pulling out of the petrol station and apologetically steering the car towards home. She was driving a little too fast for the bumpy back roads, so I don't know how I spotted the sign. Mexico was barely behind us, and the buildings had only just given way to leafy green trees and apple stands racing past our windows. But in the blur, I somehow read the words on one of those stands.

'June Bug's: Fresh from the Farm.'

Actually, all I got out was 'June Bug's' before Seely skidded to a stop so fast I heard gravel pinging against the side of the car. She reversed into the apple-stand parking area, and I felt my stomach growl at the sweet smells that seeped into our open windows.

Billy was out of the car before it was even parked.

I opened my door and looked back at Seely. 'You coming?'

'I'll keep the air conditioner running,' she said. She reached behind her seat and grabbed Billy's backpack off the floor. 'And I want to check something. You go ahead.'

I followed Billy into the open-air produce market, inhaling deeply. I was so dizzy with the smell of fresh vegetables and fruit, I almost didn't notice the woman with the long, wild, grey hair and the crooked smile.

'Hello, there! You boys looking for a snack or you shoppin' for your mommas?'

I opened my mouth to say we were just browsing, to play it cool, but Billy rushed his words out first.

'My mom is Molly Drum. Do you know her?'

The woman peered at Billy for a moment, then she threw her head back and laughed in a deep, raspy roar.

'Oh, heavens, yes, I know her.' She weaved through the stands of carrots and blueberries towards Billy. For a second, I thought she was going to hug him, but she only gripped his shoulders in both of her hands. 'Let me look at you. Part Molly May, part Paul Drum. You are a sight, for certain.'

Billy's eyes widened. 'You know my dad, too?'

I shrank back into the tables piled high with food, so I could watch without staring. I would have been more subtle, but Billy's put-it-out-there approach was apparently getting results. I picked up a purple-and-yellow squash, pretending to study its freshness.

''Course I know them,' the woman said, stepping back

from Billy and leaning against a stack of heavy crates. 'They worked right here in my store.'

I glanced around at the dirt floor and rickety wooden tables. The whole thing looked more like a tent than a store, but I kept my nose buried in the squash and said nothing.

'Name's June.' She stuck a hand out to Billy. 'But you can call me June Bug. Everybody does.'

Billy took her hand, and she shook so hard, his arm looked like it would wobble right off his body. 'I'm Billy D.'

The woman tossed her crazy head of hair. 'Can't believe your momma and daddy would be back in town and not come in to say hello. Lost touch with 'em a few years back, but we did correspond for quite a long time. Doesn't seem right they don't come in.'

'We live in Columbia.' Billy finally found his voice. 'Just me and Mom.'

June Bug's voice softened. 'Ah. I see. That's too bad. Well, good to have her home. Big deal when Molly May and Paul Drum up and married and moved.'

Billy climbed on to a long, large pallet of wood and leaned his elbows on his knees, drinking in June Bug's words.

'Always thought your momma belonged in a small town,' June Bug said. She twisted her face as though deciding what to say next. It made her mouth look even more crooked. 'But a tiny place like this just couldn't contain your daddy's big personality. Not the type to stay still anywhere, in fact. Not surprised he's up and run off on y'all. Sorry to hear it, but not surprised.'

Billy didn't bother to correct who ran off on whom. He was too lit up at the mention of his dad. He leaned so far forward, I thought he might fall off the wood pallet, but he only teetered on the edge. 'Do you know where he is?'

'Your daddy?' June Bug waved a hand. 'Sorry, honey, but I sure don't. I was always a little bit closer to your momma, to tell you the truth. Your daddy could be charming sometimes with all that – what do you call it? – *charisma*. But other times he just got right down to brooding. Like your friend there.'

She whipped her head suddenly in my direction, and I flinched, surprised she remembered I was there. She flashed that one-sided smile at me, then turned back to Billy.

'I guess that's just teenagers for you. No offence meant.' She tossed the last comment back at me.

'None taken,' I said. Then I went back to inspecting my squash, hoping to disappear from the conversation again.

'So you don't know how to find him?' Billy pressed June Bug.

'Oh, honey. If you and your momma don't know, I surely don't. Your daddy always wanted to live in far-off places – places people had never even heard of. And he wanted to live in them all. He used to fret all the time about getting stuck in Missouri. He got real down about his prospects sometimes, but I always told him, "don't give up". The surest way to get stuck is to give up. I told 'em both that, your momma and daddy. If you never give up, you never fail.'

I looked up from the squash I was sniffing. 'What was that?'

She twisted her head to look at me and repeated, 'Never give up. Never fail.'

'Neverfail,' Billy echoed. 'That's the name of a town. My dad told me about it.'

I dropped the squash.

'Billy D.,' I said slowly, 'it's the name of a *town*?'

'Yeah, it's in . . . I can't remember. It's on one of my maps.'

I moved to stand in front of Billy, to catch his eye, and stressed again, 'It's a *town* . . . on your *map*.'

Billy tipped his head to one side. 'You're being weird.'

'And you're being dense,' I said. 'Neverfail is a town. And it's *what happens when you don't give up*.'

Finally, I saw understanding flood Billy's face. 'We have

to go,' he announced. He hopped off the pallet and waved at June Bug. 'Thanks. Bye.'

'Uh, sorry—' I stammered. 'He, um, just remembered he has to be somewhere.'

June Bug's eyes narrowed in a shrewd expression. 'Uh-huh. Well, let me pack you boys a snack for the road. Billy D., what kind of fruit do you like?'

Billy was clearly anxious to get back on the hunt, but his stomach must have been growling, because he let June Bug show him around the stand. He pointed out his favourites, and she stuffed them all into a brown paper bag. She wrote her number on the bag, and Billy tore off a piece and put his own number down on the brown paper. In his hurry, his handwriting was messier than usual, and I doubted she'd be able to make out the numbers.

'Call me if you see my dad,' he said as he pressed the paper into her hand.

June Bug agreed with a sad smile, and she made Billy promise in turn to tell his mom she said hello – a promise I knew Billy couldn't keep if he wanted his search to stay secret. Then June Bug cupped her hands around Billy's face – around the wide cheeks, heavy eyelids, and protruding tongue that told the world Billy was different.

'It made my day, getting to meet you. You look just like your daddy.'

Billy opened his eyes wide. 'Nobody ever told me that before.'

'Well,' June Bug said, standing up straight, 'that's because nobody ever looks close enough at other people these days.'

✱

Billy couldn't contain himself. The car doors weren't even closed when he blurted to Seely, 'We figured out the clue.'

She looked up, surprised. 'What is it?'

'Neverfail!' Billy said. 'It's in – it's in . . .'

'Tennessee?' Seely offered.

'Yeah! That's it!'

I raised my eyebrows. 'How'd you know?'

Seely held up the atlas, a guilty look on her face. 'All the maps with clues lead to somewhere, and something leads to *them*. A puzzle and a solution on every page.'

'Yeah?' I said.

'New York and Tennessee are the only maps left that don't have solutions. But we already know New York leads to Arizona, so I figured the answer had to be in Tennessee. We've been following the clues forwards when we should have been working backwards.' She dropped the atlas into my lap and put the car in gear. 'Check it out.'

I flipped to Tennessee, and saw where Billy had already marked it. *Neverfail*.

'See, Billy D.? You already had the answer. You just didn't know it.' Seely steered the car out of the gravel lot and on to the road.

Billy leaned forward to peer over my shoulder. He was quiet for a long while, staring at the bottom of the Tennessee map. 'Where does that one go?' he asked.

Seely bit her lip. 'Well . . .'

'If all the clues go to another map, where does that one go?'

There was a tremble of excitement in Billy's voice.

'I don't know,' Seely admitted. 'Maybe it points back to New York, to the beginning, like a loop—'

'It's the clue to the town.' Billy smiled. 'The town where my dad is.'

'Well, we don't know—'

Billy snatched the atlas out of my lap and pulled it in close. It was a riddle we'd seen before – we'd seen them all a hundred times – but it wasn't one Billy had memorised, so his reading was slow.

'*In the place with no sh – with no sh—*' He let out a frustrated grumble and shoved the atlas back at me.

I read it out loud.

In the place with no shoes, it's neither city nor town. Your favourite and mine, plus what's paired with a frown.

'It has to be a town in New York,' Seely insisted. 'That would make the clues a circle.'

'Or it's a dead end,' I said.

But Billy was staring at the heavy book in my hands, oblivious to us, and I could see it all over his face. To Billy, it wasn't a dead end at all. It was just the beginning.

22

'In the place with no shoes . . .'

'Socks?'

'You ever heard of a town called Socks?' I raised an eyebrow.

'Nah,' Billy admitted.

We were breaking down the final clue piece by piece on the way home from Seely's. We'd spent all of Saturday evening and most of Sunday in her garage, tossing around ideas. Well, Seely and Billy tossed the ideas. I mostly soaked up the smells of petrol and sawdust. The garage was fast becoming my favourite place – a place for a 'guy's guy' with Seely as scenery.

'What kind of place has no shoes?' I kicked a beer can off the pavement into the street.

It was by far the hardest riddle yet.

Billy lifted his shoulders. 'Don't know.'

'It's neither city nor town,' I recited from memory. 'That's pretty obvious. It's gotta be one of your invisible places not named on the map.'

Billy nodded in agreement.

'Your favourite and mine, plus what's paired with a frown.' I looked at Billy. 'What favourites do you and your dad have in common?'

Billy ticked off items on his fingers. 'Chocolate ice cream, cowboy movies—' His list cut off abruptly as something stopped him in his tracks – literally.

'What's up?' I asked.

Billy didn't answer, but he raised one shaky finger to point ahead of us and to the right, across the street. I followed the line and saw the bus we sometimes rode home. It was parked at our stop, a good block away.

'That's all right. We'll just walk,' I said.

Billy shook his head.

What was with the mute act?

Then I saw it, as the bus pulled away – what he was really pointing at.

A group of guys – three of them – moving towards the bus stop from the opposite direction. One of them hopped right in front of the bus, forcing the driver to slam on the brakes, then hopped back up on to the kerb, laughing hysterically.

What a jackass.

'So?' I said, turning back to Billy.

But Billy was gone. I spun in a full circle. 'Billy?'

'Shh.' The whisper came from the other side of a low stone wall on my left.

I peered over the top and saw him crouched on the ground, pressed tight against the wall.

'Dude, what the hell are you doing?'

'Shh!' Billy commanded again, more fiercely this time. He motioned for me to join him.

I felt stupid climbing over the wall, but not as stupid as I did standing on the pavement looking like I was talking to myself.

'Billy, what is this?' I asked once I was hunched down beside him.

He put one finger on his lips and pointed another over the wall, indicating the troop of guys down the street.

'Yeah, what about them?'

I recognised the guys – seniors, all of them, but not too tough. I'd seen them in detention a few times and behind the Dairy Queen smoking pot after school. I couldn't figure out why Billy seemed so scared of . . .

Oh.

'That's them, huh?' I whispered.

Billy nodded, his finger still glued to his lips.

I peeked over the wall and sized the guys up. They were bigger than Billy but not that rough. I doubted they'd ever been in a real fight. 'Those potheads wouldn't hurt you,' I told Billy. 'They're probably too high to even swing a good punch. I bet you could take 'em.'

Billy's eyes widened. He saw the idea coming before I said it out loud.

'Hey, Billy D.! This is it – it's like your final fight. In *Karate Kid*, there's always a big scene at the end when Daniel-san – that's what Mr Miyagi calls him – has to fight the jerks who have been picking on him—'

'Shh!'

I lowered my voice. 'Sorry. But seriously, what are you afraid of? I'll be with you – oh no, wait – even better. I'll stay down here and you—'

Billy's head shook violently from side to side.

'Come on, it'll be fine. All you have to do is take out one guy. Do your head-butt. Then I'll jump out and help take care of the rest, I swear. But they have to see you knock down at least one guy – just one, so they'll know you can do it. And I'll be right here like – like a secret weapon.'

Billy's head stopped shaking, and he lowered his silencing finger.

'A secret weapon?' he whispered, intrigued.

'Yeah, just like in the movies. You want to be one of the heroes, right?'

'Yeah.'

'Well, let's see it, Billy-san.'

Billy looked up tentatively and loosened his tight huddle. 'You'll be right here?'

'Right here.'

He started to stand.

Just before his head cleared the wall, I grabbed his wrist. 'Remember. Just one guy.'

Billy nodded and climbed over the wall.

I crept to the edge of the wall and into the next yard, where a thick bunch of thorny bushes kept me hidden but got me closer to the action. I watched the scene through a gap between shrubs.

Billy crossed the street with some confidence, but when he hit the pavement, he faltered. The guys had seen him. They stopped joking with one another and stood still on the pavement, watching Billy. When he was within earshot, the biggest of the three called out.

'What's up, Window Licker?'

Billy stumbled a step, and I winced from my hiding place, but I relaxed when he regained his footing and kept walking towards the boys.

Just one Billy, just one. I balanced on my toes, ready to bolt across the street when he needed me.

'Where you going?' the big boy asked.

'The bus stop,' Billy said. I could hear a tremor in his voice.

Don't talk to them. Just get close enough to knock one down.

'Oh, this bus?' The boy jerked a thumb at the bus stop. His voice was dangerously friendly – sweet on the surface but with something menacing bubbling underneath. 'Nah, you don't want this bus. You want the short one.'

The other boys laughed, but even from across the street, I could see the flicker of confusion on Billy's face.

'No, I want the regular bus.'

The boys laughed harder.

Billy was close enough to get a head-butt in now, if he gave it a good running start, but instead, he stopped on the pavement. Their laughter frightened him.

Come on, Billy, just one, then run for it.

'He wants "the regular bus",' one of the other boys mimicked Billy's speech, exaggerating the high tone and affecting a lisp.

My palms began to itch. Billy garbled his words sometimes, but he never sounded like his mouth was full of marbles. I fought the urge to leap over the bushes and take them all out myself. Instead, I focused my anger towards Billy, hoping somehow he might absorb some of it and just go berserk already!

'I don't think the short bus stops here, Window Licker,' the big boy said.

What the hell is a Window Licker?

'What's a short bus?' Billy asked.

I slapped a hand to my forehead. He walked right into that one.

'The short bus,' the big boy said, 'you know, for retards – like you.'

'I'm not a retard.' Billy's hands balled into fists at his side.

Here we go. I leaned into the gap, eager to see Billy do some damage – to see the looks on their faces when he let loose.

The big boy noticed the fists. 'Whatcha doin' there? You gettin' mad? You wanna hit me?'

Billy flinched, and I saw his fingers relax a little.

The boy took a few slow steps forward, and his pals fell into step just behind him. He crossed his arms as he reached Billy, and leaned into his space. I watched in frustration as Billy backed up a step.

'Come on, Flat Face, take a shot.'

Billy hesitated, his whole body arched backward, ready to take another step away.

Now, Billy. Head to the gut. Right now.

But Billy waited a beat too long. As he teetered in that awkward backward lean, the boy unfolded his arms and threw them to either side of Billy's head. *'Boo!'*

The guy didn't touch Billy, but the surprise of it

tipped him off his heels and on to his ass.

I was over the bushes and on to the pavement before Billy's fall was even over, but something grabbed my jacket, holding me back. A thorn from the bush had hooked itself into the zip's lining and was threading its way through the fabric. I played tug-of-war with the bush for only a second before I gave up and struggled to get the jacket off instead.

'Dane?' Billy whimpered.

'I'm coming!' I said, fighting with the second sleeve.

'Dane!' Billy's voice was louder this time.

I finally spun out of the sleeve and jumped into the street, already running, but all I saw on the pavement ahead of me was Billy – still on his ass and beet red.

'Where'd they go?'

'They saw you,' Billy said as I reached him. 'They saw you and said "oh shit". Then they ran away.'

I looked up the pavement and down an alley. 'Which way?'

Billy gestured vaguely at the yards across the street, at the wooded area behind the bus stop. 'All ways.'

I held out a hand to help Billy up, but as soon as he was on his feet, I pushed him hard in the chest – harder than I'd meant to, but it felt good, because my palms were still itching.

'What the hell was that?' I shouted at him.

Billy's jaw dropped, and I suddenly hated the way his tongue stuck out, the way his teeth were spaced too far apart, the way his heavy eyelids always made him seem a little sad. I hated that he looked like such a fucking victim, and I hated that he acted like it even more.

'You had an opening. You had *two*, actually. Why didn't you go for it?'

Billy closed his mouth, and I noticed his lower lip was trembling. I guess it should have made me feel sorry for him, but it only pissed me off.

'Did you even really want to learn to fight?' I asked, putting a finger in his face. 'Or were you just wasting my time?'

He didn't answer. Instead, his eyes went all glassy, and I could see we were about to have a waterfall. I glanced up and down the deserted street. Well, at least if he had a fit now, there was no one to see it and blame me. Although, with Billy standing there on the verge of tears, a little voice in my head told me maybe I *was* to blame.

I clasped my hands, willing the itch to go away, and took a deep, steadying breath.

'Okay, shit, I'm sorry. I just meant—'

'You *should* be sorry!' Billy yelled.

'Wha—?'

'You didn't tell me what to say. You didn't tell me when to . . . or where to . . . or how – how – how—'

Billy's whole body was shaking in a way that frightened me. His hands were in fists again, and they were vibrating worse than the day I'd scared him on the way to school.

I reached for his shoulders the same way I had then.

'*No!*' he screamed, backing up. 'No! No! No!'

He took off at a run, shouting it over and over again. His heavy backpack flopped behind him as he pounded down the street. I was too stunned to follow, so I just stood and watched him run until he finally turned a corner. I could still hear him shouting 'No!' long after he'd disappeared from my sight.

When I finally couldn't hear him any more, I sat down to wait for the bus with my head in my hands. I had been right the first time. I was no Mr Miyagi, and Billy D. was no Karate Kid.

23

Billy didn't show up on the walk to school on Monday. Or the day after that. He wasn't there on the way home, either. At first I was pissed. Wasn't this what he wanted? What had we been doing in the park all those days, if Billy wasn't going to stand up for himself? At the very least, he could have been there for my first day back from suspension – to let the warden know he was still on my side. By the time Tuesday afternoon rolled around, I realised how much that mattered, having Billy on my side.

I wasn't sure how he'd done it, but that little foot-stomping blabbermouth had made me give a shit about him. It kind of ticked me off, like he'd pulled one over on me. I channelled that anger into my fist as I pounded on his door after school. No answer. And Billy's mom's car was gone. I pounded again, harder this time.

'Bang all you want, but no one's home,' a voice called up from the street behind me.

Seely was leaning on her skateboard with one hand stuffed in the pocket of her hooded sweatshirt.

'How do you know?' I asked.

'His mom took him to see a therapist. Four, actually – before and after school. He said she's taking him to a different one every day this week, testing them out.'

'So apparently he's still talking to *you*.' I crossed my arms.

'Relax, you big baby.' Seely propped her board against the kerb and met me on the pavement. 'He's still talking to you, too.'

'You don't know,' I said. 'There was a fight . . . or an almost fight—'

'Yeah, I heard about that.' Seely scowled at me. 'What were you thinking, Dane?'

'Me?' I waved a hand at Billy's front door. 'He asked for it! That's why I've been teaching him to fight.'

'To fight three guys at once?'

I stuffed my hands in my back pockets. 'Maybe that was too much. But he doesn't have to ice me out.'

'He's not,' Seely said. 'He just doesn't want you to know he's seeing a shrink.'

'A shrink?'

'Yeah.'

'Why doesn't he want me to know?'

Seely smirked. 'You really don't know the effect you have on him.'

I shifted my weight from foot to foot, not sure what Seely meant. 'What are you doing here, then? If you know he's not home?' I asked.

She rolled her eyes. 'I happen to know someone else who lives on this street.'

'Oh.' My cheeks felt warm. 'You . . . you want to hang out or something?'

'I actually came over to tell you Billy and I figured out the first part of the clue.'

A flash of anger sent the heat from my cheeks to my palms. 'You guys worked on the atlas without me again?'

'Not really,' Seely said. 'I just guessed at one bit. "The place with no shoes".'

'And?'

'Well, I thought – bare feet. I called Billy last night, and he said there's a town called Barefoot in Kentucky. So we have the state!' She smiled, looking proud of herself.

The twitch in my palms subsided as my brain started whirring. 'Nice. But there's no clue in Kentucky.'

'Right.'

'So if we figure out the town – I mean, that could really be it.'

Seely bit her lip.

'What?' I asked.

'Something just seems . . . *off*. When Billy talks about his dad, do you ever feel – I don't know – like you're not getting the whole story? What if the guy really doesn't want to be found?'

'But what if he *does*?' I asked.

I invited Seely into the house, and we continued the conversation sitting side by side on my bed, with a bag of crisps wedged between us.

I reminded her what Billy had told us about his dad screaming outside the car the day his mom took him away, but Seely wasn't convinced.

'Dane, he's obsessed with his dad. Maybe he has some rose-coloured goggles on, or whatever they say. He's looking at that moment in a rear-view mirror, and maybe it's distorted, y'know?'

I let that sink in. It felt true; Billy might be exaggerating how badly his dad wanted to find him.

'But why won't Billy's mom even let them talk on the phone?' I asked. I mined the last crumbs from the bag, then crumpled it up into a ball and tossed it on the floor. Seely inched over slightly to fill the space it left between our hips. 'It's like the guy just disappeared.'

Seely gasped and grabbed my arm.

'What?' I jumped. 'What's wrong?'

'Dane.' She tightened her grip on my arm, which would

have hurt if it didn't feel so good, and looked straight into my eyes. 'What if he's in jail?'

'Nah. They still let you make phone calls in jail.'

Seely leaned back again and let go of my arm, but I could still feel the pressure where her hand had been. 'You're right,' she said. 'I just thought . . . maybe she's protecting him from the truth – from something bad about his dad that he doesn't know.'

'Yeah, like he's a cheater.'

'What?'

I told Seely my theory about Paul Drum being a shitty husband and Billy's mom punishing him for it.

'But if Billy's mom wanted to keep him from his dad, why wouldn't she just get divorced and fight for custody?' Seely asked. 'Don't moms always win those things?'

'I don't know.'

'Did your mom?'

Our backs were flat against the wall and our legs stretched forward. Her foot kept tipping to the side, so her right pinkie toe touched my left one. I watched our toes gravitate towards each other and away again, like magnets.

'There was no fight,' I said.

Seely was quiet for a moment. 'I wonder why she's taking him to a therapist.'

'Uh.' I almost laughed. 'He's got some issues, in case you haven't noticed.'

'Therapists are expensive,' Seely pressed on. 'It has to be pretty serious if she's spending that kind of money. And how is she paying for it? It's not like they live in a nice neighbourhood.'

She swallowed hard. 'I mean—'

'It's okay,' I said. 'You're right. In fact –' I sat up straighter – 'I tried to ask her where she worked, and she got all weird with me, like it was a big secret. What if she does something – I don't know – *illegal*?'

Seely laughed like I was kidding, but I wondered what other secrets Billy's mom was keeping. My eyes drifted towards the window and through it to Billy's house across the street. Their car was in the driveway now – the car she had used to drag him all over the country – parked in front of the house filled with boxes never unpacked. I thought about Billy calling his mom a liar and about the scene he said his dad made when she drove away.

Was it still kidnapping when someone stole their own kid?

Seely slid even closer to me on the bed. Now our pinkie toes were definitely touching. And our knees. And our elbows. Thoughts of Billy and his mom grew fuzzy and slipped away. Seely's hand slipped into mine. It made my palms tingle in a way that was better than the itch. I reached my other hand to Seely's cheek and turned her face up towards mine. I was wondering how I could feel so at ease and so jumpy at the same time, when she kissed me.

I probably should have been the one to go in for the kiss. Most girls let me lead, but Seely was different. I almost pulled away and started over, but then her hands touched my face, and her lips moved down to my jaw, and I forgot all about how the kiss began. I just didn't want it to end.

I reached instinctively for the hem of her shirt, making the usual attempt to steal second base, but my hand froze when it touched her skin. Her stomach was so soft, my fingers lingered, not caring if they grabbed on to anything more substantial. Seely's skin was enough. And I wanted to touch more of it. My lips found her neck – even softer than her stomach – and every time I kissed it, another girl's name was erased from my memory. I imagined all of the Saras and Annies and Marjories disappearing from my speed dial.

When my lips were back on Seely's, I opened my eyes for just a second, to see what I wanted to kiss next, and my eyes fell on the window and Billy's house across the street.

Billy. He'd had a crush on her first. Maybe he wouldn't like this. I didn't even realise I'd stopped kissing Seely until she pulled away.

'Um . . . Dane?' Her lips were pinker than before and a little swollen.

'I'm sorry.'

'What's wrong?'

'Nothing. Shit. I'm sorry.' I reached a hand up to flatten my cowlick out of habit.

'You always do that when you're nervous,' Seely said.

I half laughed. 'Billy says I do it when I like a girl.'

'You like me.' Seely cocked her head. 'You just don't want to kiss me.'

'No, I do. . . . I just . . . you surprised me, and I'm distracted and—'

Seely touched my arm. 'I understand.'

'No, I'm sorry. I'm glad you . . . I'm glad we . . . I'm glad it happened. I'm just—'

'I know,' Seely said. 'I'm worried about him, too.'

✱

By Saturday, I was done worrying and ready for answers. I watched at the window until Billy's mom drove off at her usual time, headed for work, then I bolted across the street and walked straight through his front door.

'Billy D.!' I thundered, and my voice echoed around the bare house. 'I know you're in here.' I poked my head into the kitchen and moved down the hallway towards Billy's room, shouting as I went. 'I'm over this silent treatment. If you don't—'

'Hi.' Billy's big head popped through his cracked bedroom door.

I scowled. 'Hi? You ignore me for a week, and all you can say is "Hi"?'

'I'm not ignoring you.' Billy opened his door all the way, inviting me in. 'I had . . . appointments.'

'I know you're seeing a shrink,' I said. I flopped down on Billy's mattress.

Billy's face flushed, and he looked away.

'It's no big deal,' I said. 'But why so many? Why every day?'

Billy shoved a pile of dirty clothes off his bed and sat next to me. 'Mom says we're testing them. We met one with glasses and one with a big couch and one with a small couch and one with lots of stuff on the walls, like your mom. He doesn't put pictures in his frames, either, just pieces of paper with lots of words. And one who called me "buddy". And then I had to tell Mom which one I liked talking to the best.'

'And what'd you say?'

'I said I like talking to *you* the best.'

I had to pretend to cough to cover up my smile. It was

one thing to want the kid around. It was another thing to go all soft.

I pointed to Billy's atlas on the floor, open on the map of Kentucky. 'You figure out that clue yet?'

Billy perked up as he showed me Barefoot, Kentucky, and explained how he and Seely had figured out the first part of the clue. I didn't tell him Seely had already shared the story, and I tried to act surprised and impressed all over again. He showed me a list of Kentucky towns with funny names, but he slumped a little as he admitted none of them matched the second part of the clue: *Your favourite and mine, plus what's paired with a frown.*

'Too bad we can't ask your mom for help with the clues,' I said. I cast a sideways glance at Billy to see if I was dipping a toe in dangerous waters. He seemed unfazed.

'Yeah, too bad. She's good at this stuff.'

'She is?'

'My dad used to hide her Christmas present. He gave her a clue, and she had to figure it out to find her present.'

'That sounds kind of fun.'

'Yeah, my dad is fun.'

I slid off the mattress on to the floor, so I could face Billy square. 'So if he's so fun, why did your mom split?' I held my breath, waiting to see if Billy would dodge or get worked up the way he did when Seely quizzed him.

But he only shrugged. 'She says some things are unforgivable.'

'Like what things?'

Billy flipped through the atlas pages, not meeting my eye. 'I don't know. But it's not true. I forgave you for beating up that boy.'

'You mean *I* forgave *you* for not sticking up for me.'

'Yeah.'

'So you don't really know what happened with your mom and dad,' I said.

Billy looked up from his maps and smiled. 'When we find him, you can ask him!'

Oh, yeah right. Hey, Mr Drum, so who were you banging on the side and how did you get caught?

I snatched the atlas out of Billy's lap.

'Hey!' He clawed for it, but I held it out of his reach.

'What I'd like to ask your dad is how to solve this stupid clue.' I read the last riddle aloud, and Billy settled next to me on the floor as we went backwards through the maps.

I stopped on Missouri and tapped the riddle at the bottom that had stumped us for so long. 'It's weird that we actually had to go to Mexico, Missouri, to get the answer to this one,' I said. 'I wonder if you went to all the towns if someone there would always have the answer.'

Obviously Billy's dad didn't expect him to go to all these

208

places, but I wondered if he'd been to all of them himself – if he'd travelled and met people who inspired the clues. I wanted to meet a guy who put that much thought into a gift for his kid. The more I thought about Billy's dad, the more I agreed with Billy – nothing was unforgivable. And the more I thought about his mom keeping him away from a guy like that, the more she seemed like nothing but a kidnapper.

24

Seely wasn't on board with my kidnapping theory. She told me as much with a giant eye-roll Monday morning as she shoved her skateboard into her locker. I'd shooed Billy off to class, hoping for a minute alone with Seely, but I'd spoiled that minute.

'Dane, she's not a kidnapper. She's his mom.'

'I know. But if she's hiding Billy from his dad—'

'Hiding him?' Seely slammed her locker shut and looked at me like I was some kind of moron. 'Hiding him less than an hour away from the town where his parents grew up? I found better hiding spots when I was five years old, and for the record, I suck at hide-and-seek.'

I opened my mouth to disagree but closed it again when I realised there wasn't much to disagree with. It did seem strange that she would move so close to Mexico. It almost seemed like someone who wanted to be found or . . . A new thought tangled with the old ones: Maybe she was looking for Billy's dad, too? Maybe she'd changed her mind about leaving him and tried to go back, but he was already gone.

But that would mean he wasn't looking for Billy after all, and that was an idea I couldn't stomach. I had to believe there was a dad – *any* dad – out there as great as the one Billy had described. A dad worth finding. So I pushed the new nagging thought aside.

A bell sounded in the hallway, signalling we had thirty seconds to get to first period.

'You can't be late!' Seely said, pushing me towards my first class. I laughed at the concern on her face and caught the arm she was using to shove me away. My hand circled her wrist, and I pulled her so close our breath mixed together in a little cloud of heat between our lips.

'You're going to get a detention,' she whispered, but she was smiling as I kissed her. It was a kiss worth getting kicked out of school for, but Seely eventually pressed her hands against my chest and waved me down the hall. 'Go!'

I slid into my seat just as the warning bell went silent.

*

I looked for Seely in the car park after school, hoping to finish what we'd started, but instead I spotted Billy. He was waiting in the usual spot at the edge of the car park next to the baseball field, and he wasn't alone. He was chatting up some girl sitting on the bonnet of a car. No, not just some girl – Marjorie. Not the kind of girl I would have picked for Billy, but hey, great to see the kid giving it a shot anyway.

Just as I opened my mouth to call out to them, I saw Marjorie fly off the car. A second later, her hand connected with Billy's face.

I could hear the smack of contact from thirty feet away.

'What the hell?' I screamed, tearing across the car park. I covered the distance in seconds and lunged at Marjorie, my fist raised. It was all I could do to pull up short and keep from hitting her. She flinched and slumped backwards against the car. I didn't care that she looked like a frightened animal, didn't care that I had no idea what was going on. All I knew was that she had no business laying a hand on Billy D.

I'd always said I didn't hit girls or challenged kids, and when it came to a fight between the two, I didn't know which side I'd pick – I'd probably just stay out of it. But when it came to *anybody* versus Billy, there was no question whose side I was on.

I uncurled the fist and wrapped my hand around Billy's shoulder instead. My other hand pointed a finger in Marjorie's face.

'What the hell do you think you're doing?'

'Your little friend is a pervert!'

'What?'

'I didn't do anything, Dane. I didn't do anything!' Billy's hands flapped. He sounded like he was on the verge of tears.

I tightened my grip on his shoulder. 'Billy D., what did you say?'

'Nothing! She sat on the car, and she crossed her legs, and I told her that's great 'cause I thought they wouldn't stay closed, but she's fixed!'

Oh shit.

My eyes bored into Billy's, and I willed him to read my thoughts.

'Because remember you said—'

'No. Billy.' *Please, shut up.*

'You said Marjorie Benson can't keep her legs closed.'

'Billy D.!'

'You said!'

'Oh, *really*?' Marjorie glared at me.

I turned a diamond-hard gaze on her. No way was I apologising. If she didn't want people to say things like that about her, maybe she *should* have kept her legs closed.

Marjorie straightened up to her full height. 'You're an asshole, Dane.'

'Yeah, and you're a real princess, right?'

I started walking across the ball field, pulling Billy with me.

'Don't call me any more!' she shouted after us.

'Like I ever called you before!' I hollered back.

The last thing I saw before turning away was Marjorie's middle finger up in the air. I waited until we were across the field and fully out of her sight before I pushed Billy up against a truck parked on the street and fixed him with my fiercest look.

'What?' he protested.

'Billy D., saying a girl can't keep her legs closed is . . . is just . . . it's an expression, y'know? It's like saying she's loose.'

Billy's face was blank.

'She's easy. Get it?' I said.

He shook his head.

I sighed and stepped back. 'She likes to have *sex*, Billy.'

His eyes bulged. 'Oh.'

'You basically just called her a slut.'

Billy's eyes opened even wider. 'Then you called her that, too.'

'Yeah, but not to her face.' I laughed. 'I guess it's not your fault, the stuff you don't know.'

Whose fault is it? I wondered. *His dad's? For not telling him about girls? Or his mom's? For taking him away from his dad before he had the chance to tell Billy about girls?*

214

'You want to work on the clue to night?' I asked when we started walking again.

'Can't. Mom says no more friends over when she has to work.' His eyes slipped sideways towards me, but he didn't have to be sly. It was clear when Mrs Drum said 'friends,' she meant me.

'So she works nights *and* weekends?' I was suspicious all over again. Sure, my mom worked nights, too, but her uniform was spandex and sweats, so it was no secret what she did. Mrs Drum's grey scrubs made her look like a depressing nurse. But what kind of nurse came home in the middle of her shift to get a bottle of bleach? 'Do you know what she does?' I asked. 'For work?'

Billy shook his head. 'When she took me to school the first time, Mrs Pruitt said, "What kind of work do you do?" And Mom said, "The backbreaking kind." And then they just laughed. And one time, at the grocery store, the man who wraps up the meat said stuff was expensive, and Mom said, "At least we have jobs" and . . .'

Billy didn't stop talking about his mom until he actually *saw* his mom. We reached the end of our street just in time to see her wrapping her arms around someone in the front yard. We were too far away to make out any details, but the someone was definitely a dude, and the hug definitely lasted longer than your average 'hello' hug.

And anyway, it looked more like goodbye, because when they finally pulled themselves apart, the guy got into a car and drove off while Mrs Drum stood staring after him.

Billy took a giant step forward like he meant business, but I yanked him back by the collar and dragged him behind a car before his mom could see us.

'Who was that guy?' I asked, ducking low.

'I don't know.' Billy scowled and struggled against the grip I still had on his shirt.

'Does your mom have a boyfriend?'

'No!' he practically shouted.

'Shh! Well, if she has a . . . *friend* here, maybe it's someone like June Bug, who knew your dad.'

Billy stopped struggling and finally looked interested.

'Think, Billy D. Has your mom introduced you to anyone or told you about any—'

'I don't know anyone here,' he said. 'Except you. And your mom. And Seely and Mrs Pruitt and Mr—'

I held up a hand to stop him. 'Got it.'

'You think that guy knows my dad?' Billy asked.

'I don't know. But even if he does – the way he was groping your mom, I doubt he'd want to find your dad, you know what I mean?'

I looked at Billy and saw in his face that he did know, and he was not too happy about the idea. He spun away and stormed down the street before I could stop him. I followed him back on to the pavement and spread my arms wide. 'Billy D.! I was just kidding!'

But either he couldn't hear me or didn't want to, because he didn't look back once. He marched all the way down the street and up the steps past his mom without saying hello before slamming the door shut behind him.

The slam echoed across the street for just a second, then a startled Mrs Drum turned her eyes from the door to me and frowned.

Yeah, like this is all my *fault.*

25

Billy's bad attitude lasted all the way into the next morning. The only expression uglier than his was the one on his mom's face as she watched us leave for school.

'Dude,' I said to Billy once we'd turned off our street. 'What's with your mom giving me the evil eye?'

Billy hoisted his backpack higher on his shoulders, and I could tell by the heavy way it flopped back down that the atlas was inside.

'She saw us spying on her yesterday.'

'We weren't spying—'

'And I told her you wanted to know who that guy was.'

'I didn't – you *told* her?'

'She says you shouldn't be so nosy.'

'But I was just trying to—'

Billy silenced me with a glare. 'I don't want to talk about my mom any more.'

'Okay.'

'We have to solve the clue.'

'Fine.'

Billy veered off the pavement towards the gardens, and I followed, slipping on the dewy grass while Billy's heavy stomps kept him steady.

'You figure out the favourite?' I asked.

His silence answered my question.

'All right, let's try a game.' I looked over at Billy, expecting his face to light up at the suggestion, but he kept his features pulled tight and focused on the ground. I pushed ahead anyway. 'What's your favourite song?'

'Don't have a favourite.'

'Well, what's your dad's favourite song?'

'Don't know.'

The garden came into view.

'What's your favourite flower?' I asked.

'Flowers are for girls.'

I clenched my teeth and tried to ignore the tiny tickle in my palms.

'What's your favourite colour?'

'Green.'

'What's your dad's?'

'Not green.'

Anybody but Billy would have been flat on the ground with a swollen jaw. For the first time in weeks, I had to remind myself that helping Billy wasn't just something I wanted to do; it was something I had to do – to keep my record clean. I forced myself to keep a steady voice as we dropped down the slope from the garden to the next pavement.

'Okay, forget that for a second. What about the next part? *What's paired with a frown.* A smile?'

Billy rolled his eyes. 'That's the *opposite* of a frown.'

'Oh yeah, genius?' I spat. 'You learn that in your life skills class?'

'Everybody knows that.'

'Well, then? Let's hear it. What's paired with a frown, huh, Billy D.?' I threw my hands up. 'Seriously. *What's paired with a frown?* What does that even mean? You'd think your dad would leave you easier clues, considering . . .'

I took a deep breath, trying to suck back those last words.

Billy's face was so fierce he could have been growling. 'Considering what?'

'Never mind.'

'Considering I'm *retarded?*'

'I didn't say that.'

'Because I'm not!'

I held up my hands. 'I know you're not.'

'I'm smart enough to figure out the clues.'

'I know—'

'I'm smarter than *you.* At least I know who my dad is!'

He pushed past my outstretched hands and raced down the street before I could say another word.

*

I was sitting in first period, feeling half pissed at Billy and half guilty about losing my temper with him, when they showed up in the doorway.

The warden came in first, whispered something to Mr Johnson, and motioned to the door. They stood there, shoulder-to-shoulder, right outside the doorjamb – my mom and Billy's. Something in their expressions made the hairs on my arms stand up.

The warden raised a hand, beckoning me to follow him. I think it was supposed to be subtle, but because he was standing in front of the class he'd just brought to a standstill, every single set of eyes followed the gesture to me and watched as I grabbed my books and got up. I might have been embarrassed if I hadn't been so focused on those frightened faces. I felt something tight and cold inside my chest.

'What's up?' I asked outside the classroom.

The warden ushered us a short way down the hall, where we couldn't be heard through the classroom door. 'We have a situation, Dane.'

'I haven't done anything!' I said. 'I've been on time for

every class; I haven't started any trouble; I'm all caught up on my missed assignments—'

'Dane, you're not in trouble.' Mom put a hand on my arm.

But I guess I knew that already. I was just too afraid to admit that if I wasn't the one in trouble . . .

'Have you seen Billy D. today?' the warden asked.

'Yes,' I said, but I didn't elaborate. I was picturing those punks from the bus stop. Had they just been waiting for a chance to get Billy alone?

'He walked Billy to school,' Mrs Drum said. There was an edge of accusation in her voice.

'No, I didn't.' I shifted my weight and looked at the floor. 'At least, not all the way.'

'What do you mean?' Mom asked.

'We . . . we got in a fight.'

The warden and the moms all gasped in unison.

'Geez. Relax. Not a fight-fight, just . . . y'know, an argument. Someone got him in a bad mood, I guess.' I looked pointedly at Mrs Drum, who pursed her lips.

'Dane,' Mom said in her warning voice.

'If he was upset, it was probably because the last person he was with upset him.' Mrs Drum's angry words and face dissolved with the tremble in her voice, and I felt a chill. This wasn't just overreacting to a kid skipping school. There was genuine fear oozing off of her.

'Look, I'm not the kid's babysitter.' I locked eyes with Billy's mom. 'I guess it's scary for a parent not to know where their son is, huh?'

Mrs Drum and I stared at each other for a second, seething. The warden twitched next to us and cleared his throat. 'Dane, I'm sure you've gathered – Billy is not in class. He hasn't shown up for first period.'

'He's probably in the bathroom or something.' I wanted there to be a simple explanation.

'We checked the bathrooms,' the warden said. 'We checked everywhere. Normally, we would just mark a student absent, but in Billy's case, there are . . . special circumstances.'

'What kind of circumstances?'

Mrs Drum spoke to my mom in a whimper. 'Jennifer, there's something—'

'What circumstances?' I repeated.

'Please,' Mom said to Mrs Drum. 'Call me Jenny.'

I raised my voice. 'What circumstan—'

'Okay, Dane, you may go back to class,' the warden said. He took my arm to lead me away.

'No!' Mrs Drum's shout echoed down the empty hallway. She lowered her voice back to a whisper. 'He can help us.'

'I don't think—' Mom started, but Mrs Drum cut her off and spoke straight to me.

'You know him bet—' She choked on the word. 'You know places to look that I don't know.'

'Are you guys serious?' Their fear was contagious, and it was growing inside me, making my stomach roll over.

'Please.' The angry edge in Mrs Drum's voice collapsed, and the tears took over. 'Please, can you help us look?'

Of course I was going to help them look – even if it meant cutting out of school and getting expelled right then and there. But that wasn't going to be necessary.

The warden nodded at Mom. 'With your approval, we can excuse Dane from—'

'Yes, that's fine,' Mom said.

Mrs Drum kept her eyes on me. 'You'll help?'

Like they could stop me.

'Fine, I'll help,' I said. 'But only to prove to you guys that you're overreacting. He's probably home watching TV or hugging his stupid atlas or something.'

I don't know if I said it that way to convince them or myself.

*

I told Mom and Mrs Drum to follow the pavement route home while I checked the gardens. I was sure they wouldn't find Billy, but I didn't want them on my heels. I

224

could move a lot faster without two old ladies trying to keep up.

'Call us if you find him!' Mom shouted after me as I trotted away from the car park and across the baseball fields.

I gave her a backward wave in response and started jogging. Our moms were making me so damn nervous I wanted to just hurry up and find Billy to calm everyone down.

I ran all the way to the gardens, even though I knew I'd find them empty.

I tumbled out on to the street on the opposite side. On instinct, I turned right, instead of left towards home. My feet carried me all the way to the Dairy Queen, where those potheads sometimes hung out after school. I was running so fast by the time I reached DQ, I actually skidded to a stop when I rounded the back of the building. There was nothing there but a beat-up metal rubbish bin and one lonely cockroach creeping under the restaurant's back door, trying to find a crack big enough to slip inside. I bent with my hands on my knees, breathing hard. Blood pounded in my brain, making it hard to think clearly.

Why am I looking for those guys, anyway? I should be looking for Billy.

The pounding subsided after a minute, and I started

walking again, without giving the DQ a second glance. Billy hadn't been jumped by a bunch of thugs. He'd run away. I'd watched him do it – right after he'd told me off.

There was only one direction I'd ever seen Billy run in – whichever way led him closer to his dad. And there was only one place I could think of where he'd ever made any progress on that journey.

I called Mom from my cell phone as I veered towards Seely's. I gave her directions and told her and Mrs Drum to meet me on the way.

Halfway there, a short *whoop* like a birdcall caused me to spin in place. When I saw the squad car, I held up my hands, ready to explain why I wasn't in school. But Mom's face came into focus in the back window before I could speak. The window rolled down with a whine, and I leaned into it.

'You called the police?'

Mom started to answer, but Mrs Drum leaned across her lap, cutting her off. 'Did you find him?'

'Just one more place to check,' I said. I tilted my head at the officer in the driver's seat. 'You want to . . . uh, follow me?' I was used to avoiding cops. It felt wrong asking one to tail me. 'It's just down here.' I pointed ahead, past the bus stop where Billy had nearly had the shit beaten out of him – the almost-fight I'd literally pushed him into, when I shoved him out from behind the garden wall. A knot of guilt tied itself up in my stomach.

'You want to hop in?' the officer asked.

No. I want to run.

'I'll walk,' I said.

Mrs Drum fell back into her seat, and I was struck by the image of her in the back of a cop car. It seemed like a fitting place for a possible kidnapper, but what kind of kidnapper called the police for help?

She waved her hands around in a panicked way that reminded me of Billy D. when he was upset. 'We need to do a – a – what do you call them? An Amber Alert!'

I stepped away from the window and back on to the pavement, not wanting her fear to infect me. Maybe it was a mom thing – even a kidnapping mom – to overreact and call the cops, but I was surprised they came along. Didn't kids have to be missing for twenty-four hours or something before police gave a shit? If this was Billy D. getting special treatment because of his Down's syndrome, then I guess for once I didn't mind.

I started jogging along the pavement. Seely's house was only one block down. She'd shown us where they hid the key to the garage, so we could go in whenever we wanted. I would find Billy there and get into the squad car when I could throw him in with me. I was starting to feel pissed at him for putting me in this spot – for worrying his mom and everyone else. After he got an earful from his mom, he was going to get one from me.

Behind me, the wheels of the cruiser turned slowly, following me down the road.

'Dane, what are you doing?' Mom called from the passenger window.

I kept moving.

'Get in the car,' Mom said, but it sounded more like a question than an order.

Still, I ignored her. I wasn't going to say another word until I found Billy in Seely's garage and hauled him outside.

I had one foot in her driveway when movement in the park – *our* park – across the street caught my eye. Past the grassy expanse of lawn and a little to the left of the faded, graffiti-tagged playground, where the trees started to grow thick together and become woods, I saw the motion that had distracted me.

A scream caught in my throat as I ran towards the scene. It was all playing out in front of me in slow motion, but not slow enough that I could get there in time to stop it.

I watched, helpless, as two arms lifted a heavy object

and lowered it in a long slow arc down to the body already broken and bleeding on the ground. Up, down, up, down. Again and again. I ran as fast as I could, but it was like I was deep underwater, pushing against a current. I was nearly there when my chest finally opened up, and the scream soared out.

'BILLY D.!'

26

It was all wrong. I mean, I could see it with my own eyes and knew it was reality, but I couldn't wrap my brain around it. It was just . . . *wrong*.

One boy was curled up on the ground, a bloody mess but breathing. Another boy propped himself up against a tree, clutching his gut and puking. And standing above them both, with one hand wrapped around what looked like a thick tree branch and the other hand curled in the tightest fist I'd seen him make yet, was Billy D.

He was breathing hard, his face red and streaked with dried tears, and he had his feet planted in the stance I'd taught him. He'd stopped pounding the kid at his feet when he heard my scream, but his whole body was still tense, frozen at the sight of me.

Questions fell off my lips too fast to make sense. 'What? How did you . . . ? Why? How . . . ?' I took a breath. 'Dude, what the hell happened?'

Billy's muscles slacked a little, and he started to shake, but he didn't answer.

Behind me, I heard the squawk of a radio and the officer saying something into it. An instant later, he was at my side. He put a hand on my chest. 'Son, I'm going to need you to back up.'

I pulled away from his hand and took only the smallest step backwards.

'Are you Billy?' the officer asked. He knelt next to the bloodied boy on the ground but kept his eyes on Billy the whole time.

Billy said nothing, but I saw him tense up again.

The officer was working on the boy on the ground one-handed, checking his wrist for a heart rate and his arms for broken bones. The boy rolled over on his own and propped himself up on one elbow. He was either still catching his breath or too scared to speak. I didn't recognise him. He wasn't one of the potheads who'd scared Billy, and neither was his buddy.

The officer stood to address Billy again. 'Are you Billy?' he repeated more firmly.

'Billy!' Mrs Drum's scream came from behind us.

Guess that answered that question. I turned my head just enough to see that she and Mom were a short distance away, probably where the officer had told them to wait, but Mrs Drum had broken free of my mom's grasp and was moving closer.

'It's him,' I said.

'Billy, do whatever the officer says.' Mrs Drum was almost next to me now.

The officer put out an arm, silently warning us both to stay back. To Billy he said, 'Drop your weapon.'

'That's not a *weapon*,' I said.

'I told you to back up!' the officer barked without turning around.

I didn't take my eyes off Billy, but a familiar *whoop* told me a second squad car had pulled up behind us. Just what we needed – another cop, so they could circle Billy like some caged animal.

The officer tried a softer approach with Billy. 'It's all right. You're all right. But I'm gonna need you to drop your weapon, son.'

Poor choice of words, I thought. *Poor, poor choice.*

'I'm not your son!' Billy screamed.

Told you. I put my hands in my pockets and leaned back on my heels. *Should have just let me handle it.*

The bloody boy on the ground scooted away at the sound of Billy's shriek. He was bruised and scraped, for sure, but he was moving just fine. Billy hadn't done any serious damage from what I could see.

The boy sitting against the tree had caught his breath and joined the ruckus now.

'Shoot him!' he shouted at the officer. 'Shoot him! He's crazy!'

'You shut your mouth!' I said.

The officer looked back at me. '*You* shut *your* mouth. That's the last time I'm going to warn you.'

Every voice that added to the chorus got louder, until it was all just a collage of screams. The second officer was at the scene now, moving towards Billy's back. The whole thing was about to get ugly. Fear and frustration were an explosive combination inside of me, and I couldn't stop myself from crying out.

'Billy D.! Drop the fucking thing, already!'

Billy obeyed my command in an instant, letting the chunk of wood drop with a thud. On the ground, I could see it was not part of a tree but a broken piece of the wooden railway sleepers that surrounded the sandbox.

The officer noticed Billy's response and used a hand to gesture me forward. 'Keep talking,' he said.

'Oh, *now* I'm allowed to talk?'

He gave me a glare that put the one Mom always used to shame.

'Fine.' I stepped towards Billy. 'Billy D., it's cool, man. You're not in trouble or anything.'

'Oh yeah, he is!' the kid against the tree spat. 'That little retard is going to jail!'

I snapped my head to the side. 'If I hear one more word out of your mouth, I swear to God, I'll—'

'Be quiet!' the officer's voice cut me off.

I whipped my head around and saw it wasn't me he was barking at. His eyes were on the kid at the tree.

'And don't go anywhere,' the officer warned as the kid struggled to stand up. 'We want to talk to all of you.'

'See, Billy?' I said. 'They just want to talk to you. That's all. Just talk.'

'Just talk?' Billy asked in a small voice. He dropped his fighting stance and took on his usual hunch. It was a good move, I thought. It made him look more like a little kid and less like a psychotic, sleeper-toting attempted murderer.

'Yeah. Let's just go with the officers.' I moved closer to Billy until he was within arm's length. 'You tell them what happened, and—'

'I'll tell you what happened!' the kid at the tree said, lumbering towards us. He stretched his arm out to point a finger at Billy and looked at the cops. 'That freak jumped us!'

'Don't you call my son a freak!'

Billy's mom had been so quiet, I'd almost forgotten she was there. Now she stood with her fists clenched at her side, looking like she wanted to do more damage to this kid than Billy had.

'That's what happened!' Mrs Drum powered on, pleading with the officers. 'They called him names. They attacked him. He had to defend himself!' She covered the distance to Billy in two strides and wrapped him in a hug. Billy kept his arms to his sides, not returning the embrace. He looked like he was in shock.

'*Us*? Attack *him*?' the kid said. 'No way! He came after us first!'

Mrs Drum scoffed. 'Oh, I seriously doubt that.'

'He did!' the kid with the blood and the bruises spoke up, stepping into the circle. 'He hit us first.'

'Yeah, right,' I said.

'No, that's true,' Billy said quietly. 'I hit them first.'

I gaped at Billy. 'Seriously?'

'Seriously.'

'Well, dude, in that case – stop talking.'

27

We sat on the pavement with our backs up against one of the cop cars – me, Billy D. and the big mouth. The officers had called an ambulance for the bloodied kid, which I thought was unnecessary and definitely not a good sign for the deep shit Billy was probably in. They let me sit with Billy, since I was the only one he seemed to be listening to, but they made his mom stand back. When she kept insisting on a lawyer and spouting her own versions of what *must* have happened, they finally suggested she go get that lawyer and get him down to the police station as soon as possible, because that's where Billy was going.

She nearly lost it then, but Mom had a soothing way with her and managed to get her in the car with promises that Billy would be okay and that the best thing they could do was get him some help and meet him at the station. It was almost comical how convincing Mom was because I knew there was no way in hell *she* would have let *me* out of her sight if I were in this much trouble.

Leaning against the squad car, Billy focused on his hands, picking little bits of dried blood off his fingers – none of it his own. He'd gone mute since the cops set him down on the pavement. In contrast, the other kid couldn't shut up.

He went on and on about how he and the other boy were just messing around at the playground, skipping school, when Billy came up acting all weird and just staring at them and not talking.

'Then this retard just ducks down and rams his head into my gut,' the kid said.

'If you call him a retard again—' I growled.

'Oh yeah, what are you gonna do?' The boy leaned across Billy to me, but an officer pushed him firmly back against the car.

I wished they'd put him in cuffs, but that might mean they'd have to cuff Billy, too.

'Looks like I don't have to do anything,' I said. 'My boy Billy D. here already kicked your ass.'

'I could take this 'tard! He just surprised me.'

'What did I tell you about that word?'

'Knock it off,' the officer said. He was down on one knee in front of us.

'Well, then he just went crazy,' Big Mouth continued. 'Joe went to help me up, and this kid hit him in the back with that stick or whatever and just kept hitting him.

Jacked him up good, too.' He sneered at Billy. 'You're going to jail for sure . . . *retard*.'

I held my breath, trying to control the itch in my palms. My only comfort was the fact that the officer looked just as disgusted by Big Mouth as I was. And when he looked at Billy, his expression was much kinder. 'Is that how it happened?' he asked.

Billy methodically picked at his bloody fingers and refused to meet the officer's eye.

'His mom told him not to talk without a lawyer,' I said.

The officer nodded. 'Then he'll have to tell us his side of the story at the station.'

Billy looked up at that, fear all over his face. 'They're taking me to jail?' he whispered to me.

'Not jail,' I said. I looked at the officer for confirmation. 'Right? Just the police station.'

'That's right.'

'That's okay, then,' I told Billy. 'And I'll go with you, so it's going to be fine.'

'You can't come with him.' The officer shook his head at me. 'You can meet him down there with his mom, if you like, but he's gotta come with us. You'll have to take your own car.'

'I don't *have* a car,' I said bitterly.

'Sorry.' The officer stood. 'Then you'll have to go on

home. We don't give free rides to the station.'

'Oh yeah?' I said. Then, fast as lightning, I swung my arm all the way around Billy D. and landed a fist smack into Big Mouth's face. His head made a satisfying *thunk* as it hit the metal car door behind him.

I looked up at the cop. 'How 'bout now?'

✳

The police station was brighter and cheerier than I'd imagined. There were lots of windows and clean carpet and shiny desks. Billy and I were seated at one of those desks, across from the officer who had helped us with the search. The cop who'd been called in for backup was questioning Big Mouth at another desk.

Our officer made small talk with us, blabbering on about the station's recent remodel and how it almost made him want to get off the streets and become a desk jockey. He let me call my mom to explain why I, too, would be needing a lawyer, then we all just sat there and waited for moms and solicitors to show up before anyone agreed to start talking.

But Billy couldn't help himself. After a few minutes of silently watching the officer type up his report, Billy burst out, 'Dane, I didn't mean to!'

I was too startled by his explosion to tell him to be quiet. 'What do you mean, you didn't mean to?'

'I didn't mean to make that one kid go to the hospital.'

'That kid's just being a pussy. He's fine.'

The officer across the desk cleared his throat. 'Lucky your friend here's not a little stronger. He could have done some real damage,' he said to me.

He's stronger than you know.

I glared at the officer, willing him to look away, which he did. I lowered my voice when I spoke to Billy again.

'What happened?'

I knew I shouldn't ask him in front of the cop. I knew we should wait for all the legal know-it-alls, but I was going crazy not knowing, and by the way Billy was fidgeting around in his chair, I could tell he was going crazy not telling me.

'I didn't go to school today,' Billy said.

'Yeah, that part I got.'

'You made me mad.'

Maybe Billy's mom was right. Maybe this was somehow my fault.

'I went to Seely's,' Billy continued. 'But she wasn't home. And I couldn't remember where she put the key.'

Billy looked embarrassed at that last bit, so I just nodded, encouraging him to keep talking.

'But I didn't want to go to school, and I was really, really mad at you.'

'Uh-huh. You mentioned that.'

'And I remembered the other time I was mad at you was 'cause you tried to make me beat up those boys.'

I winced and glanced over at the cop. Sure enough, he was listening. But there was no stopping Billy now that he'd started to spill.

'And I was at Seely's house by the park and thinking about how I could fight, and I could show you, and then maybe we wouldn't get mad at each other any more.'

I wished the seat of my chair would open up and swallow me. The more Billy talked, the more his crime sounded like *my* idea. I almost believed it myself.

'And I thought how you said you don't hit retards or girls, but hitting everyone else is okay—'

'Not *everyone* else—'

'Because that was different, and I didn't know why it was different and those guys were right there, over in the park and—'

'Billy D., slow down.'

'And I just wanted to know what it felt like.'

'What *what* felt like?'

'Hitting.'

So, the big-mouth kid had told the truth. I was acutely

241

aware of the officer falling still across the desk. He'd heard what Billy had said. It was basically a confession *and* a motive, all in one. Billy went looking for the fight. There would be no way to pin this on the other guys – to claim they started it.

'So?' I asked. 'How did it feel?'

'It hurt.'

I stretched out in my chair, trying to sound casual. 'Yeah, I told you to keep those shoulders hunched when you go in for a head-butt. Sometimes I bruise my knuckles a little—'

'No.' Billy clutched at his chest. 'It *hurt*.'

Oh.

I thought then about Jimmy Miller – about the way he'd always had a smile on his face, a sort of funny carefree look, until the day I'd knocked him off his bike. Ever since then, the only face I'd seen him wear was one full of contempt. And thanks to what Seely had told me, I now knew I deserved that. I thought, too, about the way other kids skirted me at school or looked down if I caught their eye. Some days that made me angry. Other days it made me proud.

I looked at Billy, still holding his hand to his heart. And if I was totally honest, some days it made me hurt.

'Maybe you're just not a hitter,' I said.

Billy dropped his hand into his lap and stared at it. 'Maybe nobody should be a hitter.'

I smiled. 'That's just what Mr Miyagi would have said.'

'From that movie?'

'Yeah.' I sat up straight and made my most serious face. '"Fighting is not the answer, Daniel-san."'

Billy laughed at my acting. 'He says that?'

'Something like that. He says it in the first movie, I think. Actually –' I waved a hand – 'he says it in, like, all the movies.'

Billy screwed up his face. 'But I thought you said you were the Miyagi, and I was the Karate Kid.'

'I did.' I sighed and leaned my head against the back of the chair, still facing Billy. 'But maybe I was wrong.'

The solicitor showed up and announced he was representing us both. I wondered if our moms were getting a two-for-one deal. The guy looked cheap enough, with his shabby shoes and no jacket or tie or anything else lawyer-ish about him. The police made our moms wait in some outer lobby, which I was thankful for. It was a lot easier to tell the truth to cops and lawyers than to your own mom. And that's what Billy and I did – told the truth. Not that I had much choice. I'd thrown my punch right in front of the police. But Billy's story was more elaborate, and every word of it matched what Big Mouth had said.

We both sighed out loud with relief when the cop and the lawyer agreed we wouldn't be put behind bars or anything. They yammered on about our charges: assault for me and possibly something worse than assault for Billy D. – or possibly something less, depending on how they decided to factor in his disability. They spoke a language I didn't understand with all sorts of legal terms like 'probable plea deal something' and 'knocked down to lesser whatever'.

I rolled my eyes at one point and whispered to Billy, 'I think they're just making those words up to scare us. It's like speaking pig latin.'

It made Billy laugh.

The lawyer went to tell our moms what was going on while the officer filled out little sheets for us that basically said we got arrested, even though it didn't seem like we did. The officer passed me mine, and I thought it looked a lot like the slips I had to take home to Mom when I got detention. Except this time, Billy sure as hell wasn't going to be the one to get me out of it.

28

Billy's mom kept him out of school for the rest of the week. I thought she was taking grounding to the extreme, but Mom kept insisting 'Molly is just being cautious.'

I tried to ask her what that meant and if she and Mrs Drum were friends now, but she brushed me off with sweeping comments about how single moms needed to stick together and teenagers think they know everything. I had to think I knew a little more than Mom, though, because I couldn't imagine she'd be friends with someone who'd steal a kid from his dad. I would have told her so, but every time I brought up Billy, Mom steered the conversation back to my own legal troubles.

The lawyer had convinced us that my charge would probably get knocked down to a misdemeanour if not wiped out altogether, and he was pretty sure he could use Billy's Down's syndrome and crystal-clean record as leverage for lesser charges there, too. It didn't hurt that the kids Billy had attacked had records of their own, including big stuff like car theft. They'd both been in and out of juvenile detention and were barely even welcome at the alternative school.

Maybe it was those little rays of hope, or maybe it was just that Mom was too busy being worried to get mad, but whatever the reason, she decided to go easy on me. Actually, I was starting to realise that, volcanic temper aside, Mom pretty much always went easy on me. My worst punishment seemed to come from Billy's mom, as her keeping Billy at home meant I had to walk to school alone.

By Sunday, almost a week after Billy's bloody battle in the park, his mom finally released him for an afternoon at Seely's. She made us promise to stay out of the park and out of trouble.

Seely sat cross-legged on a rug, while Billy and I stretched out on opposite ends of a sofa. None of us said a word about Billy's fight in the park. I'd already filled Seely in, and Billy was entirely focused on another topic – solving the last clue. He'd spent his week at home coming up with a list of all his favourite things, but we hadn't found any towns with matching names in Kentucky. The whole exercise seemed like a big waste of time, considering Billy and I had bigger problems now than absent dads, but he was obsessed.

'Let's take a break,' Seely said, sounding weary. She

tossed Billy's list of favourites on to the coffee table and reached towards the ceiling in a stretch.

Billy tucked the list into his atlas and collapsed backwards into the couch cushions with his arms wrapped around the heavy book. His face was unreadable, even to me.

Seely tilted her head and gave him a sympathetic look. 'We'll figure it out, Billy D.,' she promised. 'Maybe dads are just harder to find than we thought.'

'Not all dads,' Billy mumbled. He shot me a look.

'What?' I sat up straighter on my end of the couch.

'We could find *your* dad,' Billy said, a note of hostility in his voice. 'But you won't look at the yearbook.'

I rolled my eyes. 'This. Again.'

Seely picked at a thread in the rug, trying to look invisible. She knew enough by now to realise I didn't have a dad, didn't want a dad, and *definitely* didn't like talking about my dad. But she must have been burning with curiosity, because she didn't stick up for me.

'I told you to take that thing back to the library,' I said.

'I did. But I bet your mom has a yearbook. We could see who signed it and—'

'Stop it,' I said. I wouldn't allow Billy to tempt me into another disappointing stakeout. It was hard enough trying to find the dad who *wanted* to be found. Why would I waste time trying to find one who didn't?

Sure, if I ever found him, I could ask him some questions and maybe plant a punch in his eye socket, but I didn't need him. I had taught myself to shave, hadn't I? I did all right with girls, didn't I? And Seely's dad had even offered to teach me a little about cars last time I was here. Anything else a dad could have done for me – show me how to build a snow fort or ride a bike or stay out of trouble – well, it was just a little too late for all that.

When I spoke again, my voice came out louder than I'd intended. 'The guys in those pictures – they're nobody. Signatures – they're nothing.'

'But—'

'Nothing! We're not finding my dad in a yearbook, just like we're not finding *your* dad on a map.'

I wished I could take it back as soon as I said it.

Seely's jaw dropped a little. 'Dane.'

'Shit, I didn't mean it like that.'

Billy fingered the edge of the atlas, silent.

'Billy D., really, I didn't mean—'

'You're just scared,' he snapped.

'Scared of what?'

'Scared of finding your dad.'

'I'm not scared of anything!'

Billy met my eye, and his stare was cold. 'At least I'm not afraid to *look* for *my* dad.'

Seely moved to sit between the two of us on the couch.

I craned my neck around her bony frame to sneer at Billy. 'Too bad you're looking in the wrong places!'

'Too bad I'm not!' Billy held up the atlas and shook it at me. 'My dad is in one of these places. He's just not listed. He's just waiting for me. He's just . . . he's just . . .'

Billy was waving the atlas around like crazy, and Seely grabbed it from his hand before he could knock her out with it.

'Billy D., it's okay—'

'It's *not* okay,' I said. 'He needs to wake up.' I took the atlas from Seely and waved it around myself. 'This is like a baby blanket or Santa Claus. You're supposed to outgrow it. You're too old to believe in fairy tales, and that's all this is.'

'Dane,' Seely hissed through her teeth. 'You are being. A. *Dick*.'

'Yeah, *that dick*, just like Mark said,' Billy spat.

'Screw you, Billy.'

'Screw your*self*.'

'Stop it!' Seely shouted finally, putting a hand in each of our faces. 'If you guys act like this, I'm not having you over any more.'

That shut us both up.

Seely's garage was my sanctuary, and I wasn't going to

throw away my invitation – not even to prove a point to Billy.

Billy and I leaned back in our opposite corners of the couch, both silent.

'That's better,' Seely said. She shook her head. '*Boys.*'

I had more to say – a *lot* more – but I kept my mouth shut and flipped through the atlas instead. Hellhole Palms, California . . . Climax, Colorado . . . Looneyville, Texas. *That's where Billy should be.*

I looked as long as I could at the maps, trying to ignore the growing silence in the garage. Finally I settled for just picking at the loose lining on the inside of the book's hard back cover. I ran my thumb back and forth along a spot where the lining peeled away from the shiny blue edge and revealed the ugly cardboard colour underneath. The more I thumbed the gap, the larger it grew, until I could actually fit the end of my thumb inside the space. And that's where I felt it – another paper edge. It wasn't as thick as the book lining, and it wasn't glued down.

I peeked inside the gap, but I couldn't see anything. Bored and curious . . . and still a little pissed at Billy . . . I tore the lining right open. It made a satisfying ripping sound as the bottom edge shredded away.

'What are you doing?!' Billy tried to climb across Seely to get to me, but she held him back.

'Dane, what the hell?'

'Wait,' I said, holding up a hand.

My vandalism had exposed a sliver of the hidden paper. It was a simple, college-ruled page torn from a notebook. I tried to lift it out, but it was still tucked too far under the lining. I ran a finger along the lining's edge, starting at the gap, and noted how easily it pulled up – almost like it had come loose before and been glued back down.

When the last of the lining gave way, the notebook page underneath fluttered right into my hand.

I held my breath as I read the handwritten words scrawled across it and the signature at the end.

When I'd read it twice, and when Billy and Seely both looked about to burst with curiosity, I finally croaked out, 'No way.'

'No way what?' Seely asked. She sounded as desperate as Billy looked.

I focused on Billy and swallowed hard.

'Billy D.,' I whispered, 'you were right.'

29

Hey Buddy,

Sorry I had to hide this letter, but you know how nosy your mom can be, and some things are just between us boys.

I know I tell you this all the time, but sometimes daddies say things they don't mean, and sometimes they do things they wish they could take back. Your mom thinks you don't understand this, but I think you understand it better than she does.

Well, Bud, here's another secret about daddies: we cannot tell a lie. That's how you know, when I tell you I love you, that it's always the truth. Just like I told you the answers are usually in the back of the book, and look! I wasn't lying.

Listen:

Everyone knows you need Two Guns for a duel, but only a lucky few know Santa Claus lives in Indiana.

There's a Dinosaur in Colorado and a talking frog in Texas.

'Kermit!' Seely burst out.

I'd been reading the letter out loud, but I stopped when Seely snatched the atlas out of my lap and started flipping through the pages tagged with sticky notes. As I watched Seely, Billy watched me.

'What else does it say?' he asked. He leaned across Seely, reaching for his letter.

Seely gripped his outstretched arm, excited. 'It says the answers to the clues, Billy D.'

He twisted his head ever so slightly to her, distracted, but not enough to lower his greedy hand, still open and grasping for the paper I was holding.

'Look.' Seely turned the atlas to face Billy and moved quickly from one map to the next. 'See, I was wrong. It's not a circle. The clue in New York is just the start – *What's needed for a duel.* That leads to Two Guns and Santa Claus and Dinosaur and—'

'And *It ain't easy bein' green*,' Billy recited from a glance at the bottom of the Colorado map. His hand finally dropped, and he moved it instead to the atlas, fingering the clue written by his dad.

'Exactly,' Seely said. 'The clue for Kermit, Texas.' She nodded at me and the letter in my hands. 'It's an answer key.'

A quick scan of the letter proved she was right. Billy's dad revealed all the solutions in exactly the order Seely had plotted. Texas led to Washington, then to Florida, Alabama, Montana, Ohio, and so on. Finally, in two quick sentences, he solved the clue that had taken us weeks to figure out – and the one we never did.

If you never give up, you'll Neverfail.

And if you're ever Barefoot in Kentucky, I'll meet you in Monkey's Eyebrow.

'That's it.' I turned the paper over to confirm the backside was blank before passing it to Billy.

He pressed it flat on the coffee table and leaned low over it, as if getting closer to the ink itself would somehow get him closer to an explanation. The silence that fell in the garage made the pounding of rain on the roof even louder.

'Monkey's Eyebrow,' Seely said after a moment. 'That can't be right.'

'Yeah, it is,' Billy said. He grabbed the atlas and opened it to Tennessee, where the final clue anchored the page. 'Read it,' he ordered Seely.

She sighed. '*In the place with no shoes, it's neither city nor town—*'

'Barefoot, Kentucky – just like you said.' Billy beamed at Seely. 'Keep going,' he insisted.

Seely went on. '*Your favourite and mine—*'

'Dane, remember I told you? Dad and I spent the whole day at the monkey cage at the zoo.'

'Yeah, I remember but—'

'Monkeys are my *favourite*. And—' He looked at the map for the end of the clue. *Plus what's paired with a frown.* 'Eyebrow?'

'Sure,' Seely said. 'You know, when you frown, you kind of scrunch up your eyebrows.' She made an exaggerated sour face, which cracked Billy up. 'But I thought the last clue would lead back to New York to make a circle.' She flipped the atlas to the New York map. 'Nope. Nothing here.'

Billy looked first at me, then at Seely, and whispered in a conspiratorial voice. 'I know where it is.'

I knew, too. It was one of the towns already marked on Billy's maps – or not a town really, but one of the places Billy had written in. I reached down to turn the atlas to Kentucky.

'Here, right?' I pointed out the spot at the very top edge of Kentucky's bumpy western border, where the state slipped under Illinois and winked at southern Missouri.

'Yeah,' Billy said.

'But there's no clue on this page,' Seely said. 'So now what?'

'So it's either a dead end, or—' I sucked in a breath. It was possible. Anything was possible. Maybe Billy's dad had known what was coming. Maybe he'd guessed that Billy's mom might take him away. I don't know how he ever expected Billy to find him with such a complicated trail, but it had to be complicated, to keep Billy's mom from figuring it out.

'He's there,' Billy said, his eyes all light and hope.

'He *could* be there,' I agreed. I was excited by the possibility, but I wasn't completely convinced Billy's dad was actually in this not-really-a-town in Kentucky, and I didn't want Billy to be let down if we were wrong.

We both looked at Seely for confirmation.

'I suppose we could do an Internet search.' She sounded hesitant.

'Yeah, what are we waiting for? Fire up the computer,' I said. 'See if there's a Paul Drum in Monkey's Eyebrow.'

Seely chewed a fingernail.

'What's the big deal?' I asked. 'If he's not there—'

'He *is* there,' Billy stressed.

'Oh, yeah. Yeah, sure he is. We just have to figure out how to get in touch with him,' I said.

Seely took the letter gently from Billy and sat back to read, still munching on her nails.

Billy shoved the atlas inside his backpack and forced the pack's zip closed. 'We don't have to check. We have to go home.'

'Right now?' Seely looked up from the letter.

Billy held his hand out for it. She started to give it to him but pulled back at the last second, clutching it in both hands.

'What are you doing?' I asked her. 'Give him his letter.'

'I just don't understand,' Seely said. 'Some of this doesn't make sense.'

'Oh,' Billy said. 'Sometimes he calls me Buddy. It's like a nickname. That's when you call someone something that's not really their name, but they still know you mean them when you say it.'

'No, not the greeting,' Seely said, frustrated. She moved her head back and forth as she read the words on the paper. '*Daddies say things they don't mean* and *do things they wish they could take back?* What is that?'

Billy suddenly became very distracted, tightening the straps on his backpack and making sure his shoes were tied.

'Billy D.?' Seely said.

'I don't know.' Billy threw up his hands and rolled his eyes. 'It doesn't mean anything.'

Billy took the letter from Seely, folded it carefully, and tucked it into the front pocket of his jeans. Then he marched out the garage door without so much as saying goodbye.

I started to follow him, but Seely caught my arm and pulled me back.

'Dane, it *does* mean something. You know it does.'

'It could mean anything,' I said. I took her hand from my arm and held it. 'I think his dad *was* a cheater – or at least some kind of jerk to Billy's mom. And I think maybe Billy knew about it and just doesn't want to say so.'

'It's more than that.' Seely stared down at our hands wrapped around each other. 'The atlas was a really special gift to make, and the letter in the back is like the secret surprise at the end.'

'So?'

Seely chewed a fingernail on her free hand. 'So why would his dad start that letter with an apology?'

'Who knows? Maybe things got really ugly before his parents split up. Maybe he saw something or heard something—'

Seely shook her head. 'But even then, I'm sure he wouldn't use the atlas to say sorry to Billy about cheating on his mom – not in a present like that.'

'Yeah, that does seem weird.' I was feeling kind of stupid, but I didn't have any other ideas, and I wasn't sure it was the big deal Seely was making it out to be.

'It doesn't make sense, unless—'

'Unless what?'

Seely dropped my hand and paced away a few steps. 'And the fact that he's not here in Missouri looking for Billy . . . ' she muttered almost to herself.

'Seely, what?' I stopped her pacing by hooking an arm around her waist and pulling her body to mine. 'What's wrong?'

Seely let out a deep breath. 'I think it's a goodbye letter. Dane, maybe Billy's dad was leaving *them*.'

I shook my head fast, but Seely caught my face between her hands and forced me to look into her eyes. In her expression, I could see the parts of the letter she was talking about – the odd apology and the love-you-always message. If you picked apart the pieces, Seely was right. It sounded an awful lot like a man about to walk away from his son.

I had to physically shake my head to knock that thought loose. *No way. No way is Billy's dad like mine. Isn't that the whole point of looking for him? To find the dad worth knowing?*

I countered the idea with the memory Billy had of his dad screaming outside the car. *'Don't you take him away from me.'* It was enough to convince me. I didn't know what that letter was all about, and I didn't think the guy was hiding out in Kentucky, but I did believe – wherever he was – he wanted to be found.

And I was going to help Billy find him.

'I'll call you later,' I said.

'But, Dane—'

I tried to silence her with a kiss, but she kept talking

through our smashed lips until finally we broke away, laughing a little.

'You're impossible.' She was smiling, but there was still something sad in her eyes.

I gave her one more kiss – so hard on the lips she couldn't breathe, let alone talk – then I followed Billy out of the garage and into the storm.

*

Billy had got tired of waiting for me, and I had to jog to catch up with him. The rain fell harder with every step towards home, and by the time we reached the bus stop, we were soaked through. Our teeth were chattering too much to talk, and the thunder was too loud and frequent to have a conversation anyway. We rode the bus in silence, concentrating on getting warm, then got drenched and freezing again walking the final leg of the trip home. When we reached the spot in the street between our houses, I stuck an elbow in Billy's ribs.

'Walk to school tomorrow?'

I couldn't see his face well under the big hood of his jacket, but I saw his shoulders lift and fall. 'I guess.'

Either the rain had washed away his enthusiasm, or the reality of the situation had finally sunk in. Maybe I wasn't the only one who didn't know what the hell I'd say to my dad if I ever found him.

'You all right?' I asked. But a big clap of thunder drowned out my words, and Billy was already walking away before I could say anything else.

*

I found Mom in the kitchen warming up a cup of coffee in the microwave.

'Hey, sorry I'm late,' I said.

She flattened my cowlick, then ruffled my hair, making it stand up again.

'You're not late,' she said.

'I'm not?'

The digital clock on the microwave flickered 5:16. The dark brought on by the storm had made it feel a lot later.

'You're soaked,' Mom said. 'Why didn't you call me to pick you up?'

'Why can't I have a car to pick *myself* up?'

'Dane.'

I shrugged. 'I thought you had a class.'

'I do.' She checked her watch. 'And I'm late. Gotta run.' She half hugged me with one arm and lifted her coffee to her lips for one last sip with the other. Then she slammed the mug on the kitchen table and rushed out the door.

I sat alone at the kitchen table, smelling Mom's coffee and staring at the hated lottery tickets. I wondered if getting pregnant so young drove Mom nuts, or whether she was always a little off – with her strange theories about luck and life and with that cheery personality that could turn into a temper on a dime. Maybe all the crazy is what drove my dad away. Maybe it wasn't *me* he didn't want.

I couldn't figure out if that thought made me feel better or worse.

A massive wave of thunder shook the front door. I jumped up from the table, startled, as lightning pierced the windows and lit up the kitchen. The thunder rumbled away, but the sound at the door was constant. I waited a moment, not trusting my own hearing, but the pounding became more insistent. It definitely wasn't thunder.

I peered out the peephole, half expecting to see some crazy meth-head trying to get inside. It wouldn't be the first time. But the only thing I saw was Billy D., soaked to the bone without his jacket and shivering.

I flung the door open.

'You scared the shit out of me,' I said. 'What are you doing?'

'I'm f-f-freezing.' Billy was shaking.

I pulled him inside.

'Stay right there,' I commanded. 'Don't drip on anything. I'll get you a coat—'

'We have t-t- to g-go,' Billy chattered.

'What? Go where?'

'To find my dad.'

'We are. We're working on it. We're getting closer, right?' I looked at Billy sideways. Had the soggy trip home made him sick? Maybe he had a fever.

'No.' Billy wrapped his arms around himself, and the chattering slowly stopped. 'We have to go *now*.'

And then I understood.

'Now? To Monkey's Elbow?'

'Monkey's *Eyebrow*,' he corrected. 'We have to go now.'

'Billy D., that's crazy.'

'Why?'

'Well –' I dragged a hand through my hair – 'for one thing, Kentucky's gotta be at least a six-hour drive from here. You saw it on the map. We wouldn't get there until the middle of the night.'

'So?'

'So – so—' I spluttered. 'So we don't have a way to get there. We don't have a plan. We don't even know if he's there.'

'He *is* there.' Billy raised his voice. 'I have to go. You have to drive me. You promised you would help!'

Billy glared at me, not breaking the stare even as raindrops rolled off his forehead on to his heavy eyelids. 'You *promised.*'

'We wouldn't find him until morning!' I cried. 'We wouldn't get back in time for school tomorrow! I can't skip school, Billy D. I'm one detention away from getting expelled.'

'Fine, I have to go.' Billy turned and stepped back into the storm.

'Billy! Stop!' I followed him right out into the rain. A huge clap of thunder caused us both to flinch. 'You know what happens if I get kicked out of school?' I yelled at his back as I chased him down the steps. 'That's it! I don't get to come back in a week. It's over. I'm out! Is that what you want?'

We were both in the street now, ankle-deep in water rushing off the road and standing under what felt like Niagara Falls.

Billy spun round to look at me, and even through the long bands of water falling between us, I could see the difference between the raindrops and the tears on his cheeks.

'You promised!' he wailed.

'Stop saying that!'

Billy took two fast steps towards me with his arms out and pushed me – hard.

I staggered backwards, splashing through the street.

'What the—'

'You lied to me!'

'I didn't—'

'You said you would help me, but you lied. You're a liar!' Billy was still crying, but he sounded more angry than hurt.

I lifted my hands to my forehead, to shield my face from the rain. It was pointless.

'Where's the fire, man?'

'What?' Billy D. stopped raging for a second to give me a confused look.

'It means . . . what's the hurry? Let's figure this out – plan it. Maybe we can go next weekend or—'

'No. Tonight.'

'Billy D., what's the difference? If he's really there, he'll be there still in a few days—'

'What if *I* won't be here in a few days?' Billy stomped as he said it, throwing up a huge spray of water.

'What the hell are you talking about?'

'I might not be here,' he repeated.

'Is this about the cops? It's not like you're going to jail tomorrow or something—'

'I could *die*!' Billy exploded.

'You could *what*?'

'I have . . . I have . . .' Billy fidgeted, twisting his hands together and swaying back and forth. 'I have a broken heart.'

I rolled my eyes. That was overdramatic, even for Billy.

'Dude,' I said, 'I get that you're upset, but—'

'No! I have a *broken heart*.' He pointed to his chest. 'I need a new one. Mine is broken, and I might die, Dane. I might *die*.'

I dropped my hands and let the full force of the wind and rain slap me across the face.

'You what?'

'I might die.'

'Die?' I echoed the word but didn't feel its meaning. It was a nonsense word – empty on my lips.

Billy nodded emphatically, little drops of rain flying off his head. He didn't seem upset about this bombshell – only excited that he'd maybe broken through to me.

'Yeah, so see, Dane? See? We have to go now.'

I shook my head, trying to understand what Billy had just said – or maybe trying to erase it.

'I think we should go inside and talk about—'

'No. We have to go.'

'Go where? Go *how*?' I thundered. The storm backed

me up with a thunder roll of its own. 'We don't have a ride! We don't even know how to get there!'

'Fine. Don't come. Liar.' Billy started to turn away, but I grabbed his elbow.

'I didn't say I wouldn't go. I just said let's go inside for a second.'

Billy's eyes grew as wide as possible. He looked up at me, his face all tears and raindrops. 'You'll go with me?'

'Yeah, fine. Fine!' I shouted, dragging him back towards my house. 'I'll go with you, okay?'

I must be out of my damn mind.

30

It always came down to the wheels. Ever since I'd turned sixteen, my whole life had been divided into car or no car, drive to school or walk, get a ride to the party or take the bus. You could either afford a car or you couldn't, and Billy and I definitely fell into the second category.

I convinced him not to call Seely. I knew she wouldn't go for it, and on top of that – she'd probably tell on us.

Hell, I should probably tell on us.

But I knew I couldn't stall Billy long enough for our moms to get home. He'd already stomped off into the night once. If I tried to keep him in the house much longer, he'd have a fit, and then he'd be gone. Who knew what he'd do – where he'd go? The kid could catch a bus; that much I knew. I tried to imagine Billy sharing the bus with the thugs who rode it down to the park at night. We'd seen them show up a few times, when we'd stayed and sparred a little too late. They were bigger and tougher than the boys Billy had run into in the park during the day. He definitely couldn't take them if they messed with him, and on a bus there was nowhere to run.

'We can't take my mom's car,' I said, pacing the kitchen. 'She won't be home with it for hours, and then she'll be here and know something's up. We'll never get out of here.'

Billy sat at the kitchen table, his chubby hands wrapped around a mug of hot chocolate. It was all I could think to give him to calm him down for a second so I could think. Mostly I'd tried to think of ways to get out of this, but short of tying Billy to a chair, I couldn't come up with a way to stop him from going. And I wasn't letting him go anywhere without me.

'I have a car,' Billy said quietly. 'I know where Mom keeps the keys.'

A low roll of thunder rattled the windows, but it was much tamer than before.

I stopped pacing and leaned on the back of a chair. 'Oh yeah, Billy? And how do you think we're going to steal your mom's car without her knowing?'

'She won't know, because she's not home. She's on a *date*.' Billy spit out the last word like it tasted bad.

I sat in the chair across from Billy. 'A date?'

'Yeah. She said she was going to a movie with a friend. But it was that guy – the one we saw before – and he picked her up in his car, just like boys pick up girls in the movies, so I know it's a date.'

I sighed and put my head in my hands. 'Dude, is that what this is about? That your mom is on a date?'

'No!' Billy jerked, causing some hot chocolate to splash out of his mug. 'I told you. It's because of my heart.'

There it was again – the heart thing. I had already asked Billy more about it, but he blew me off with vague statements about kids with Down's syndrome and holes in the heart. A heart with holes in it sounded pretty fucking serious to me, but Billy was too impatient to get on the road to answer my questions. When he stood up and threatened to leave again, I stopped asking.

I didn't know anything about hearts or Down's, but I had seen Billy work himself breathless in our fight sessions and get so fired up about something, his whole head turned red. And yet he lived. So I just couldn't process this new information. I couldn't figure out why the trip couldn't wait a week. Billy didn't look any more likely to die before next Saturday than he did *last* Saturday.

But Billy seemed to believe it – believed it enough to go stomping out into a storm in the middle of the night to find his dad before that broken heart exploded or whatever. I had a feeling if I didn't go with him he'd *walk* to Kentucky if he had to. I thought of what little old ladies said about 'catching your death of cold', and

I shivered. If there was any chance Billy was right about his short life span, the least I could do is make sure he had a ride.

'Fine, we take your mom's car. But what about money?'

It always came down to money, too.

'I have my emergency credit card,' Billy said.

I shook my head. 'Credit cards can be traced. Haven't those lame crime shows you watch taught you anything? We need *cash*.'

'Why?'

I pounded the table. 'We need gas; we need food; shit, we probably need a hotel, because there's no way we're finding your dad before morning.'

Billy pushed his mug aside. 'Can we just go now?'

'And then we'll probably need money to bail my mom out of jail when she tries to kill me. . . .'

'Dane!' Billy snapped me out of it.

I stared hard at Billy, trying to come up with an answer for him. Then my eyes slid above his head and landed on the answer – right in front of me the whole time. I let out a long breath, resolved.

'You get the keys, Billy D. I've got the money.'

*

As soon as Billy was out the door, I stood in front of the wall of lottery tickets, summoning courage. Mom and I were about as close as a mom and a son could get, but her temper was something to be feared. And this thing I was about to do – this betrayal – would blow the lid off that volcano. It might even be unforgivable.

My hand reached for the largest frame – the king of all kitchen lotto tickets – five thousand dollars, but I froze halfway there. How was I going to redeem a ticket that big on a Sunday night? Even if a lottery office was open, I had to be eighteen to cash it in, and I doubted the fake ID stuffed in the bottom of my underwear drawer would be convincing. I needed to redeem the ticket somewhere they'd only glance at the fake licence – or better yet, not even card me.

My eyes crawled over the other tickets on the wall – a hundred here, fifty there. I could cash in those smaller winners at a petrol station, and maybe taking those but leaving the golden ticket would give Mom some room to forgive me.

I hesitated only a minute before pulling five tickets free. I left the empty frames on the table next to a hastily scrawled note.

> DON'T PANIC.
> Weren't robbed.
> Took tickets.
> With Billy D.
> Explain later.
> Dane

It wasn't much, but it was all I had time for.

*

Billy knew how to start the car, and he had it all warmed up when I hopped into the driver's seat.

I fiddled with the headlights and windscreen wipers, which we barely needed now, the rain had let up so much. I adjusted my seat and the mirrors, feeling my way all around the car.

'Atlas?' I asked.

'Got it.' Billy held up the big blue book with the shredded lining. Man, how I wished I had never picked that scab.

'Snacks?'

Billy produced a grocery bag full of goodies.

'Drinks?'

He dropped a bottle of diet green tea in the cup holder next to me.

I raised my eyebrows. 'Really?'

'That's all we had.' Billy gave an apologetic shrug.

'It's okay. We'll restock on the road.'

There, behind the wheel, with the warm car vibrating under my feet, a friend in the passenger seat, a bag of road-trip food, and full control of the radio, I forgot for a moment where we were going or why. I just felt the total freedom of having wheels.

*

The rainstorm had left the night cool, but I was still sweating under my jacket as we pulled up at the first petrol station. What if this didn't work? I'd had the fake ID for years, thanks to a guy from the alternative school who sold them on the cheap, but I'd only ever needed it twice – once to get into a bar where Marjorie knew the bouncer anyway and once to buy a case of beer from a liquor store clerk who was half asleep.

'This might be a bad idea,' I said, more to myself than to Billy.

'Why?'

'Because it looks suspicious, cashing in a lot of tickets at one time. They'll think I stole them, or maybe they'll look closer at my ID or – I don't know. Shit.' I rubbed a hand over my face.

Billy thought for a moment.

'Why can't you cash in one ticket at a lot of places?' It was so innocent the way he said it. He was just anxious to leave – to say anything to keep me from changing my mind – and he didn't even realise he'd hit on something brilliant.

I gripped his shoulder. 'You're a genius!'

Billy's face cracked open in a grin. 'I know.'

My hands were shaking a little as I passed the first ticket to the first clerk, but by the time we hit the third petrol station, I felt like a pro. I even cashed one in at the Buy & Bag customer service counter, just to change things up. I only got carded once, and the ID did its job.

I used the last ticket to fill up the petrol tank and buy us some better drinks; then I counted up our spoils – more than three hundred dollars.

Billy watched me stuff the bills into the glove

compartment, and for the first time, when he spoke, he sounded less than excited.

'Will your mom be mad?' he asked.

'Yep.'

'Because it's stealing?'

I shook my head. 'It's different when you steal from family.'

'Why?'

I laughed, but it was a grumpy, uncertain laugh.

'Because your family probably won't press charges.'

Billy bit his lip.

'Anyway,' I said. 'It's done. No turning back.'

Even as I said it, I somehow knew it was true. It was time to make good on my promise. Even if Billy's dad wasn't waiting for him in Kentucky, I could still say I helped – still took him as far down this path as it could go. So we turned off our cell phones to avoid the inevitable calls and hit the road.

It was after eight o'clock by the time we got on the freeway, but at least the rain had stopped, replaced by the sweet smell of wet grass. We rolled down the windows and flew through the dark, leaving Columbia, Missouri, and all my doubts behind.

Billy hung his head out the window for a while, looking as free as I felt.

When he finally settled back in his seat, he couldn't stop talking about Monkey's Eyebrow and his dad and how sure he was that this was right.

'And after we find my dad,' he said, 'we'll come back and find yours.'

I leaned into the wheel, peering through the windscreen at the long, dark road ahead.

'You know what, Billy D.? I'm not sure if dads are really worth all this trouble.'

31

'Is it an animal?' Billy asked.

'No, it's not an animal.'

'Is it a vegetable?'

'No, not a vegetable.'

'Is it bigger than a bread box?'

'What the fuck is a bread box?'

Billy shrugged. 'I don't know. That's what my mom always asks. She says it's this big.' He made a square with his hands.

'Yeah, it's bigger than that,' I said.

'Is it bigger than an elephant?'

This game was getting old. The pure thrill of rolling down the open road with the radio blasting and the engine roaring had worn off after about an hour. Now Billy was trying to keep me entertained by pulling out every road game his mom had taught him on their trip from Oregon to Missouri. It made me want to fall asleep at the wheel. At least a car crash would be more exciting than playing Twenty Questions.

'Dane?'

'Mm?'

'Is it bigger than an elephant?'

'Dude, it's a bicycle.'

'Hey! You're not supposed to tell.' Billy crossed his arms and huffed.

'This is stupid. I'm bored.'

'*You're* stupid,' Billy muttered under his breath.

A sign loomed up ahead of us. 30 MILES TO ST LOUIS. My stomach clenched. We hadn't seen a single cop car on the drive so far – only wide-open fields on either side of the road with nothing but clusters of cornstalks for police cruisers to hide behind. But I knew cops would be crawling all over the freeways around the city. If Billy's mom had reported her car stolen, this was where they'd catch us. Billy hadn't left his mom a note, like I had. I could only pray my mom had taken her note and marched it across the street to Mrs Drum. They'd still be looking for us, but at least then I'd just be a runaway and not a thief and a kidnapper. If I had to see the inside of a squad car again, I'd rather do it as a delinquent riding home than a criminal riding down to the police station.

'Billy D.,' I began carefully, 'there's still time to turn around. We can take this ride another day and—'

'No.'

Billy knew as well as I did that when we got home, we'd both be locked up in our houses for life. Our moms probably wouldn't let us go to the park, let alone Kentucky. The fear of Mom's wrath made me push the accelerator, to put more distance between me and whatever lecture or punishment was waiting for me back home. But even though it *felt* like I was moving away from trouble, I knew I was actually driving deeper into it with every mile.

'What's our exit?' I asked.

Billy consulted the atlas and guided me to a bypass that took us south of the city. My knuckles were white on the wheel the entire trip around St Louis. I jumped at every car that passed, sure it was a cop.

'It shouldn't be this hard, y'know,' I said to Billy as an actual police car cruised by us.

'What?'

'Finding a person. It shouldn't be this hard.'

'It's because our phones don't have the G . . . the GP . . . because our phones don't have the maps.' Billy swivelled his head towards me. 'You said we couldn't turn our phones on anyway.'

'I don't mean finding a person on a map. I mean just figuring out where someone is. Like, you don't have family back in Oregon, right? We wouldn't be doing this if you had a grandma or someone who had your dad's number.'

Billy stared out the window.

'*Right?*' I pressed. 'Because if there's someone you could have called this whole time—'

'No,' Billy said. 'I had a grandma, but she died.'

'Oh. Sorry.'

'And a grandpa. He lives in a smelly building with metal on the windows. Mom says he doesn't remember us. He calls me Edward.'

'And that's it?'

'And Aunt Jean. I don't know her number. Dad doesn't like her anyway 'cause she said he couldn't come to Christmas this one time, and Mom got really mad and said Aunt Jean doesn't have any company . . . or passion . . . or—'

'Compassion?'

'Yeah, that. So we don't ever see her now.' Billy propped his feet up on the dashboard and studied his shoes.

'At least you've got people,' I said. 'Maybe they don't know you or like you or whatever, but at least they're out there. If I've got any of those people, I don't even think they know my name.'

'Why not?'

'I don't really know the whole story, but I don't think they liked it that my mom got knocked up in high school. All my baby pictures are, like, me and Mom and a bunch of her friends and her friends' families and stuff.'

Billy stayed silent, so I talked to fill the space.

'I think maybe they kicked her out – when she had me. She's always bragging about how she graduated high school even though she had a kid and a job, and how she did it all on her own.'

'You don't know who your dad is *and* you don't know who your grandma is. Or your grandpa. Or *anything*,' Billy said.

I kept my eyes focused on the road ahead. 'Sounds pretty pathetic when you put it all together like that.'

'Maybe they all live on our street, and you don't know.'

I laughed, imagining our neighbours as my long-lost family. 'Nah. No way I'm related to a prick like Mark. Anyway, if you ask my mom where they are, she'll say they're all behind bars or inside a bottle.'

'That doesn't make sense.'

'It just means . . .' I wrapped my fingers tighter around the steering wheel, my laughter slipping away. 'I don't know – that they're not worth finding.'

'Even if it means you'd find your dad?'

'Even then.'

A siren sliced through our conversation, and a flash of red and blue lit up the rear-view mirror.

'Shit!' I hit the brakes on instinct, but a second later, my foot was on the accelerator again.

The cruiser was right on our tail, the wail of the siren filling the car.

'You're supposed to pull over,' Billy said, all calm, like we weren't about to get arrested.

'You're also supposed to not steal cars!' I snapped, but I eased up on the accelerator and flipped the turn signal. Better to just face the crimes I'd already committed than to add a high-speed chase to the list. I veered off to the shoulder, my heart pounding right through my chest.

Billy squirmed in the seat next to me. 'Are we in trouble?'

Not we, I thought. *Most likely just me.*

A hand rapped at the window, and I jumped.

'Licence,' the officer said as I rolled down the window. I fumbled for my wallet.

'We weren't speeding,' Billy said from the passenger seat.

I shot him a silencing look. No, we weren't speeding. Which meant we'd been pulled over for another reason – like driving a stolen car, or—

'Busted taillight,' the officer said, taking the licence I handed him.

I would have breathed a sigh of relief, but I knew we were still on the brink. Even if Billy's mom hadn't reported the theft, the cop would ask for my registration next, and he'd realise I didn't belong in this car.

A radio clipped to the officer's shoulder squawked, and an urgent voice shouted a string of numbers and nonsense words through the speaker. The officer didn't respond, but he tossed my licence back at me.

'See about getting that light fixed.'

An instant later, he was back in his cruiser, and the red-and-blue spinning lights were beside us instead of behind us. Then they were disappearing down the freeway ahead.

I stayed parked on the shoulder, momentarily paralysed, my heart pounding.

'Why did he leave?' Billy asked.

I shook my head, almost laughing as I remembered something from studying Shakespeare last semester in English. 'Because fortune favours fools.'

'What's that mean?'

I pulled back into traffic. 'It means we're going to Monkey's Eyebrow.'

The road got darker as we drove south. The open fields fell into thick shadows that crowded our car. All of Missouri was falling asleep, and we were still tearing through the night. Billy had started snoring in the seat next to me, and I felt my own eyelids slip down once or twice.

I flicked Billy in the ear.

'Ow, Dane!'

'Wake up.'

'I am.' His eyes were still closed and his speech slurred by sleep.

I gave his shoulder a rough shake. 'Seriously, come on.'

Billy stretched, sticking one arm right in front of my face. 'Where are we?' He yawned.

'You tell me. We left St Louis, like, an hour ago.'

'How far is that?'

'I don't know. It's sixty minutes. Just check the map.'

'The map is in *miles*, not minutes,' Billy huffed. He rubbed his eyes and squinted at the atlas. 'We have to take the Seventy-four road thing over the river.'

'Seventy-four road thing? Thanks, that's helpful.'

'It's at Cape Girar . . . Girar . . .'

'Girardeau?'

'Yeah.' Billy smiled.

'Damn it.' I pounded the steering wheel.

Billy shrank. 'What?'

'We just passed it.'

'Did it say Seventy-four?'

'I don't know. I was too busy trying to understand your directions.'

'I bet it said Seventy-four.'

We argued all the way down the freeway, through the turnaround, and all the way back to the missed exit.

I slowed down in Cape Girardeau, looking for hotels

along the highway. The town was all single-storey buildings separated by big stretches of untended grass. Here and there, a stream crossed a lawn, and I could tell we were about to run out of town and into a river.

Billy pouted about my hotel hunt, wanting to push through the night.

'But we're almost there,' he whined. 'I'll stay awake, I promise.'

'No way, man. If we keep driving, I'm going to drive us right off the road.'

'Just one more town.'

'Why? Where's the next town?'

Billy closed the atlas as if I was trying to peek.

'Billy D.?'

He picked at the corner of the book.

'There is no other town, is there?'

'There's a town.'

'Where?'

Billy stared out the window.

'That's what I thought. Dude, I'm not trying to be a dick. I'm just trying not to kill us here.'

But the truth was, I didn't really want to stop in a city like Cape Girardeau. I felt uneasy being anywhere with cops close at hand, so I pushed through, hoping Billy was right about there being hotels across the river.

'It's good Seely didn't come with us,' Billy said.

'Why's that?'

'Because she couldn't stay in our hotel room.'

'Why not?'

'We can't stay in the same room with a *girl*.' Billy looked thoroughly grossed out.

'That's bull.' I laughed. 'I wouldn't mind sharing a room with Seely. She could sleep in my bed – no problem.'

Billy caught my drift.

'Whooo!' he sang. 'You *looove* her.'

'Shut up.' I gave his head a playful push towards the window, but he only bounced back, singing for real this time.

'Dane and Seely, sitting in a tree! K-I-S-S-I-N-G!'

'Billy D.' I shook my head. 'That song dies in fourth grade.'

'Why?'

'Because if anyone hears you singing it after that – well, let's just say that's a good way to get your ass kicked.'

'You'd beat someone up for singing a song?'

'If it got on my nerves, maybe. If they were trying to annoy me on purpose, then definitely, yeah.'

Billy fell quiet, thinking.

'You smell that?' I asked.

Billy D. rolled down his window and sniffed.

287

'That's the river,' I told him. I couldn't see a bridge yet, but the city lights were becoming fewer and further between, and the sweet stink of muddy water told me we were close.

'Not just a river,' Billy said. 'The *Mississippi*.'

He opened his atlas and ran a finger up and down the thick waterway.

'You see one river, you've seen 'em all,' I said.

'How can you see them all if you just see one?'

'It's just a . . . it means . . . never mind. I'm too tired to explain. There better be a hotel on the other side of this damn river.'

32

The moonlight that slammed into the Mississippi and shot back up again, turning everything silver, plunged into utter darkness on the other side. There was barely an outhouse, let alone a building suitable for sleeping. Billy was quiet as we weaved down narrow roads and through trees crowding close over the car.

He could tell I was pissed – pissed about being stranded without a bed in the middle of the night – pissed about not taking time to make a better plan – pissed about coming on this whole damn trip.

'Maybe there will be a hotel in the next town,' he tried once.

I shut him down with a glare.

There was no hotel. There wasn't one in the sleepy river town of East Cape Girardeau and there wasn't one in the even sleepier towns after that. We were travelling a smaller, darker path now, and the sleepiest place of all was inside my head. I had to close my eyes, even if it was just for a minute. Finding a hotel wasn't even an option any more. I just had to stop moving.

Long stretches of forest rose up on either side of the road between towns, the thick trees broken up here and there by a dirt or gravel road. I hit the brakes at the next one I saw and turned into it.

Billy grabbed the dash to brace himself against the sudden motion. 'Where are you going?'

'To sleep.'

He cowered a little at the edge in my voice.

I only went as far down the bumpy road as my heavy eyelids would allow, then pulled the car into a grassy area right off the side. A little more tree cover would have been nice, but anything was better than crashing into a tree, which was the only other option at this point. My eyes were closing before I'd even turned off the car.

'We're sleeping here?' Billy asked.

'Yep.'

'Cool. It's like camping.'

'Sure.'

It wasn't like any camping trip I'd ever been on, but at least he wasn't complaining. I opened my eyes in the dark as a realisation struck me: I'd never been camping at all.

We pushed our seats back and zipped up our jackets against the cold.

'Hey, Billy?' I asked quietly.

'Yeah?' He yawned.

'Did your dad take you camping?'

'Yeah, one time. We saw pine trees and mountains and fish and spiders and—'

'That's cool.'

'Yeah, my dad is cool.'

Billy rolled over in his seat to look at me through the dark. 'Maybe he'll take us both camping after we find him.'

I rolled, too, so Billy and I were face-to-face across the car. 'You think so?'

'Yeah.'

'Cool.'

We didn't need to whisper in this empty stretch of forest out of sight of the main road, but something about the stillness of the car, the thickness of the dark, kept our voices low.

My eyelids had just slipped down again when Billy said, softer than ever, 'Hey, Dane?'

'Yeah?'

'You don't remember your dad at all?'

'Not at all,' I said sleepily, keeping my eyes closed.

'Then who hit you?'

'What are you talking about?' I grumbled. I was ready for more dreams, less chatter. 'Nobody hits me.'

'Maybe you just don't remember getting hit,' Billy said.

I opened my eyes and saw Billy staring at me.

'Hit by who? What the hell?'

Billy's voice was quiet and matter-of-fact. 'Mom says people hit because they got hit first.'

I fought the sleep that kept threatening to pull me under and tried to focus on what Billy was saying. 'You think I hit because I got – why is your mom even—' I gave my head a little jerk, to shake the bedtime fog out of my brain. It cleared, revealing a terrible thought. 'Wait, what?' I opened my eyes wider. 'Billy D., does your mom *hit* you?'

'Not my mom,' he whispered.

The last of the sleep went up in flames – flames sparked by a ball of fire growing in my chest. I sat straight up in my seat.

No. No no no no no. He is not saying what I think he's saying. I tried to keep my voice steady, but it was shaking.

'Your dad?'

Billy nodded, still curled up on his side. 'Mom says Dad hit because his dad hit him, and *his* dad hit *him*.'

'Stop.' I held out a hand to Billy, then ran it through my hair. This wasn't happening.

'Fuck,' I said. It was barely a whisper – more like a breath.

'You didn't get hit?' Billy asked.

'No.'

'Then why do you—'

292

'WHAT THE FUCK ARE WE DOING?' I exploded.

Billy jumped back, pressing his body against the car door. 'Why are you yelling?'

I shifted around in the seat, wishing I had room to pace. I curled my hands over the steering wheel and realised my palms were itching – no, not just itching – they were on *fire*. I was burning up with rage from the inside out.

I tried to point my fury in one direction, but it kept bouncing back and forth between Billy's dad and Billy himself. Five seconds ago we were talking about Billy's dad taking us camping. Now we were talking about him using Billy as a punching bag.

Questions spun around my brain. *How often? How hard? Why?* I tried to picture someone who could hit a face like Billy D.'s – especially if he was your own kid, but all I kept seeing were monsters. The fire was moving past my palms, spreading into my fingers, and up my arms. I was looking around for something to punch when a disturbing thought hit me: *I wonder if Billy's dad got the itch before he hit.*

All the questions in my head were eclipsed by just one, so I asked it again, softer this time.

'Billy D., what are we doing?'

'We're going to find my dad.'

'But he hit you.'

Billy sank down in his seat and curled back into a ball. 'Not all the time.'

'But more than once?'

'Just when he couldn't help it – like when I acted wrong or when he tried to show me how to do something, and I messed it up.'

'But that's not fair. You're . . . you're different, so—'

'Dad says I'm not different. He says I'm like everybody else. I should be able to do stuff and know stuff like everybody else. He doesn't treat me different.'

'No, he treats you worse.'

'It's not his fault.'

'I swear to God, Billy D., if you say it's your fault, I will drive us back to Columbia right fucking now.'

Billy stayed quiet. He knew I meant it. He could already see my brain working – calculating how long it would take us to get home in the morning, whether I was awake enough now to just leave that very minute.

'You promised,' Billy whispered.

I looked down at him rolled up in the seat and thought how much he looked like a little kid – not a teenager and nearly a man, like me.

'I promised to take you to your dad, not take you to get a beating.'

'He doesn't beat me up,' Billy said. 'He just hits

sometimes. He doesn't mean to. He always says sorry, and it makes him really sad.' Billy paused, stifling a yawn. When he spoke again his eyes were closed and his voice low. 'It makes me sad, too.'

'Then why do you want to find him so bad?' I asked.

'Because,' Billy mumbled, his words full of sleep. 'He's my dad.'

A second later he was snoring.

My own chest rose and fell in time with Billy's. I was gasping in deep, ragged breaths, on the verge of some kind of attack. I had risked getting expelled for this? Not a dream dad but a nightmare.

I guessed it was around 1 a.m. If I raced all the way home without stopping, I could get back in four hours. If I wanted to get to my first class on time and avoid expulsion, that meant I'd have to be back on the road by 4 a.m. I pulled my cell phone from my pocket to set an alarm, then remembered we'd shut our phones off. I couldn't risk turning it on and giving Mom a way to reach me. As ready as I was to head home, I wasn't ready to deal with the wrath of Mom yet. I had to pray the cramped sleeping quarters would be enough to wake me up in three hours.

I knew that was wishful thinking, but there was no other choice. Sleep was pulling me back down into the seat. I watched Billy breathing in and out until my eyes wouldn't stay open any longer. When they closed, I could still see his face there painted behind my eyelids – innocent and trusting and forgiving – just like he'd been with me. Billy saw a friend where others just saw a thug. And he saw a father where others would have seen a monster. I fell asleep with the uneasy feeling that, to Billy, I looked a lot like the man who showed him how to build a campfire with one hand and knocked him around with the other – that Billy had gone searching for his dad and found the next closest thing.

33

I woke up to sunlight and sweat. I turned on the car long enough to read the clock on the dashboard. I already knew it was too late to get back in time for school, but a glance at the digital display confirmed – school had already *started*. I sat up with effort, groaning at pains in strange places from the awkward way I'd slept. If this was anything like camping, I was glad I'd missed it.

Billy was already outside the car, kicking a rock around the grassy clearing. I opened the car door and felt a cool rush of air. I stood and stretched, relieved to be out of the sauna. The muddy river smell on the breeze told me we were still close to the water – but on the wrong side of it, as far as I was concerned. We should have been home by now.

Billy saw me get out of the car, but he didn't say anything. I moved into the clearing, staring across at him. We locked eyes. A silent duel of wills.

Billy spoke first, but it didn't make me the winner.

'I know you want to go home.'

I squinted across the grass, not sure how to answer. It

297

wasn't that I wanted to go home so much as I wished I'd never come in the first place. At this point, the way I saw it, there was nothing but trouble at *both* ends of this road, and I just didn't know which way was worse.

'Did he really take you camping?' I asked.

'Yeah.'

I nodded. I figured. Billy wouldn't have lied about that. His dad probably did all the things the good dads did – even the extra-special things, like show Billy all the funny town names and write him secret letters and press them in the back of books. But he did the bad things, too – the things only some dads did – the things you don't think about when you imagine what it would be like to have a dad at all.

I threw my arms out, helpless. 'I don't know what to do, Billy D. You're going to hate me forever if we go back, but I can't drive you to find this guy who . . . I mean, that's crazy! Right?'

'You don't understand.' Billy kicked his rock.

'No, I don't. I don't know why you'd want to see this guy for any reason other than to kick his ass.' *Hey, wait a minute*. I looked up, hopeful. 'Do you want to kick his ass?'

Billy scowled at me. 'No.'

My shoulders slumped. *Damn. That I could have helped with.*

Billy kicked his rock across the grass towards me. 'Don't call him "this guy". He's my dad.'

'He doesn't act like it.'

'Yes, he does.' There was no anger or pout in Billy's voice – only truth.

His last kick rolled the rock into the toe of my boot, and when I looked up he was right in front of me, honesty all over his face. He must have known it was wrong for his dad to hit him – enough to make excuses for him, anyway – but I could see he still believed he had a good dad. Or maybe he just loved the guy despite the hitting – took the bad with the good because the good was worth it. And I couldn't talk him out of it, because I didn't know what it was like to have a father – good or bad or otherwise. All I could guess, seeing Billy's earnest expression, was that *any* dad was better than *no* dad.

And there I was, still jealous of Billy, still wishing I had a dad who wanted me – even if that dad was someone I'd be better off not knowing. It was sick, and I figured it probably made me even more messed-up than Billy.

Billy could see I was teetering on the edge, so he played his trump card.

'I have to see him before I die.' He pointed to his heart.

Shit.

'Don't do that.'

'I have to see him, Dane.'

'For what?'

'To make sure he's okay.'

'To make sure *he's* okay? Like he made sure you were?'

'I didn't say goodbye, when Mom took me away – I didn't say goodbye.'

'Screw "goodbye"! Say you want to cuss him out! Say you want to tell him how . . . how the hitting makes you sad – like you told me last night. Say you want to find him so you can rip his crappy letter up in his face!'

'It's not crappy!'

'It is!' I spun around and pushed off the car in frustration. I didn't have the itch, exactly, but I definitely wanted to punch something. 'All that shit in there about dads doing things they don't mean. It makes so much sense now. Give it to me!' I reached for Billy's front pocket, but he clamped his hands over it and backed up.

'No!'

I balled my hands into fists, but it was pointless. I was losing this fight, and there was no punching my way out of it. I sat on the bonnet of the car, defeated.

'If I promise to rip up the letter in his face, will you take me?' Billy asked.

'Yeah, right.'

'I promise.'

'Please. I know you're not going to rip up your precious letter.' After a moment, Billy sat next to me, and the car made a deep metallic pop under our weight.

'Dane.'

'Yeah?'

'He won't hit me if you're there, right?'

'So?'

'So, if I just say goodbye, then we go home, then he won't ever hit me again.'

'Dude, you've been yapping about your dad since practically the day I met you. And you expect me to believe you just want to see him this one time, then you'll never look for him again?'

'I can't,' Billy said. 'Because of my heart. Because I'm going to die.'

'You are not going to die—'

'How do you know?' Billy asked.

I looked away from Billy. I *didn't* know, and I didn't want to think about it.

'You seem fine to me,' I mumbled.

'I'm not fine. I have holes, and I need a new heart. Mine is brok—'

'Yeah, yeah, your heart is broken!' I jumped off the car and stomped over to the driver's side. 'I got it, okay? It's broken and you need a new one and blah blah blah! Just get in the car!'

Billy scampered over to his own door. 'Where are we going?'

'We're going to fucking Monkey's Elbow.'

I threw myself in the driver's seat, slammed the door shut, and started the engine.

Billy climbed in carefully next to me and waited until we were in motion to whisper, 'Monkey's *Eyebrow*.'

34

The sun inched higher into the sky as we drove south through Illinois. We peeled off our jackets and commented on how much warmer it was just a few hours below Columbia. We talked about Seely and how her spiky white hair wasn't as pretty as Nina's dark waves but much cooler. We talked about anything and everything except where we were going. I couldn't stomach it, and I think Billy was afraid talking about it at all would talk me *out* of it.

His warning about his heart had tripped some wire in my own. I knew I wasn't on this road trip – this entire journey – with Billy just to repay some favour. Not any more. If I let Billy down – if I cut this trip short and he actually died – I'd never forgive myself.

A voice inside my head still screamed that making Billy happy meant driving him towards danger, but I hushed the voice by reminding myself that the odds of Billy's dad actually being at the end of this road were slim to none. If we didn't find his dad, he'd be disappointed, but at least it wouldn't be me who'd disappointed him.

Our trip through Illinois had a lot more turns and slower speeds than the Missouri route. Billy was practically drooling at all the signs telling us how close we were to Kentucky, but our stomachs were growling too loud to be ignored, so he agreed to stop when we spotted a greasy-looking diner alongside the road.

'Greasy' didn't actually begin to cover it. There was no word for how nasty the place was, with its wood-panelled walls stained by smoke and its floor with every single tile chipped or missing entirely. We picked two stools at the counter and prised apart a couple of menus stuck together by grease and some other, unidentifiable, gunk.

A guy in suspenders and a shirt as dirty as the diner was on the opposite side of the counter, at the far end, talking to the only other customer – a man missing two of his front teeth and half of one of his fingers. He had the half-finger wrapped around a mug of coffee and his eyes straight on us. He nodded in our direction and said something to the guy behind the counter, who finally came our way, moving like a slug.

'You boys need some breakfast?'

He addressed us both but looked only at Billy – stared is more like it.

Billy was either oblivious or so used to unnatural staring that he overlooked it. 'I want bacon – lots and lots of it –

like this much.' Billy pantomimed a mound of bacon in front of him. 'And orange juice.'

'OJ and bacon,' Dirty Shirt repeated. He tore his eyes off Billy to glance at me. 'You?'

'The sausage-and-cheese omelette and a coffee.'

I despised coffee. The awesome smell was a big lie about the taste. But something about the way this guy held himself stiff in front of us, the way he stared at Billy, made me feel like I had to do something grown-up, like order coffee.

He looked once more at Billy, then at his friend down the counter, before moving to the kitchen to fry up our food. Apparently he was the cook, the host, and the waiting staff all in one.

The silence that followed would have been comfortable if it had just been between me and Billy, but the freak show at the other end of the counter made it awkward. He must have been uncomfortable, too – or just bored – because he broke the silence first.

'You guys travellin'?' He had a coarse voice, like tyres skidding on gravel.

'Why?' I asked, at the same time Billy said, 'Yeah.'

Old Half Finger slid off his stool and moved towards us. He stopped right next to Billy and leaned deep over the counter, getting a good look at Billy's face.

'Where ya headed?'

'Kentucky,' I said quickly, before Billy could spit out anything more specific.

'You special?' Half Finger asked Billy.

I sat up straighter on my stool and gripped the edge of the counter. I wished there were more people in the diner. Something told me this guy wouldn't be so 'friendly' if there was an audience.

'I guess so,' Billy said, casting his eyes away from the stranger.

'Yeaaah, you're special.' The guy drew it out long and slow. I couldn't tell if he was talking like that because he thought Billy was stupid or because *he* was just stupid.

Dirty Shirt came out of the kitchen with our plates, and I noticed Billy's had less than half the amount of bacon he'd asked for. *Not that he asked for a reasonable amount.* I coached myself not to read too much into anything. We were just strangers in a small town, which would make us interesting anywhere, I figured – but especially since one of us looked a little different.

'This one's special,' Half Finger said to Dirty Shirt, pointing a thumb at Billy.

Dirty Shirt stroked his jaw and leaned on the counter. 'Oh yeah? Why you so special?'

They both laughed like he'd told some great joke.

'I don't know.' Billy munched on his bacon.

My own plate was untouched.

I cleared my throat. 'Uh, my coffee? And he ordered an orange juice.'

Dirty Shirt shot me a look. 'Coffee's brewin'.' He looked back to Billy. 'And you don't mind waitin' on your OJ, right, special? What's your name?'

'Billy Drum. But everyone calls me Billy D.'

'Is that right?'

'That's right.' Billy tried to smile, but it wasn't his usual ear-to-ear grin.

I braced my feet against the bar at the bottom of the stool, poised like a cat ready to pounce.

'You don't like them eggs?' Dirty Shirt nodded at my plate.

'Just want to wait for the coffee,' I said.

'Hey, I know what he is!' Half Finger said in that gravelly voice. He was looking at Billy but talking to Dirty Shirt, as if they were in a museum or a circus staring at something they'd never seen before. 'I heard about these guys. There's always somethin' that freaks them out – like a . . . a . . . whadayacallit? A trigger.'

'A trigger?' Dirty Shirt asked. I didn't like his tone of voice, like he was in on a joke I didn't get.

'Yeah,' Half Finger said. 'A trigger, like . . . like the colour *yellow*!' He shoved his ugly toothless mug right into Billy's

307

face and barked the word. Then he pulled back quick like something was supposed to happen. When nothing did, he tried again. 'How do you feel about *yellow*?'

Billy stared back. 'I like yellow.'

'Knock it off,' I said.

I kept my voice steady and tried to control how much my chest rose and fell as my breathing quickened. I should have started kicking some ass right then and there, but here's the thing about sizing guys up for a fight: it's not just about how big they are. It's about deciding whether they've thrown punches and taken hits before. The more guys fight, the more willing they are to take a beating and keep coming for you. And there was no question these two had been in their share of scrapes. Plus, despite those big, round guts from years of filling their bellies with beer, they looked pretty muscular. I might have been able to take either one individually, but together – and with Billy to look out for – I wasn't so sure. And I wasn't in the business of starting fights I couldn't win.

I dropped one of our hundred-dollar bills on the counter, hoping that would be enough to get us out the door and back in our car without a scene.

Dirty Shirt didn't even glance at it.

'Yeah, what are them guys called?' He looked right at Billy. 'What are you guys called?'

'And they're geniuses, too! Wicked smart,' Half Finger said.

Dirty Shirt snapped his fingers. 'Autistic! That's what it is.'

They were talking to each other like we weren't even there.

'Oh, maybe it's not a colour,' Half Finger said. 'Maybe it's like a sudden movement or something.'

'Like this?' Dirty Shirt dropped below the counter quickly and popped back up even faster. *'Boo!'*

Billy flinched, but so did I. So would anyone.

The guys laughed their asses off.

My palms were really burning now, but I still just wanted to go before things got ugly.

'He's not autistic, all right, man? Leave him alone.'

But I was speaking so low under my breath that maybe they just didn't hear me, because Half Finger was already taking a saltshaker and sprinkling some salt on to the counter. As soon as it touched the Formica, he turned the shaker right side up and set it down flat, covering the grains he'd just tossed out.

'Quick!' he said to Billy. 'How many bits of salt were there?'

Billy said nothing. To the guy, Billy's face must have looked like it first looked to me – blank, uncomprehending.

But I knew that face so well by now, I could see the subtle shifts – the twitch of an eyelash, the faint flush of a cheek, the tongue that usually stuck out pulling back as he sucked his lips.

And I recognised fear.

'Come on,' Half Finger said in what he probably thought was an encouraging tone of voice. 'Just tell me how many bits of salt—'

'He can't,' I said, and it came out louder than I'd intended.

Half Finger cocked his head to me, and I could see in his face all the evil that really simmered under the sickly sweet tone he'd used with Billy. I wanted to use his ugly mug as a scratching post for my palms.

When he spoke to me, his voice was full of grit again.

'Oh yeah? Well, if he's not a genius, he must be a regular old retard.'

'I'm not a retard.'

I could hear the stress in Billy's voice, could hear him breathing in and out.

'Well, then?' Half Finger was now issuing Billy an out-and-out challenge. He inched closer to Billy with every word. 'How. Much. Salt?'

'He's not Rain Man, you fuck!' I punched the saltshaker right off the counter and heard it shatter on the tile floor.

Everything happened really fast after that.

My first move was pushing Billy out of the way so I'd have a clear shot at Half Finger's face. Then, there was my fist connecting with a jaw and a tooth dropping right into a cup of coffee. *Easier to knock 'em out when there're already holes on either side.* I opened my fist to grab the back of a stringy-haired head and slam it into the counter. There was a sick cracking sound as a nose caught the counter's edge. Something sliced open my right earlobe, and I knew it was my cue to turn and punch.

I dodged the return swing from across the counter and grabbed a ketchup bottle on my way back up. I didn't really plan to do anything with it. I just wanted to show that I had a weapon. Unfortunately, Dirty Shirt had a better one. His back was to me, opening a cabinet, and I saw it – all shiny and black with one of those chambers you can spin after you put the bullets in. Instinct kicked in. I flipped the ketchup bottle in my hand so the heavy bottom was aimed out, dived across the counter, and lowered the bottle as hard and fast as I could.

Dirty Shirt went down like a bag of rocks. I winced as his head smacked the tile floor. I spun around, ready to finish off Half Finger, but he was already done. He was flat on his back on the floor, with his head twisted to the side, blood gushing out of his nose. I knew there were ways to hit a guy's nose that could be deadly, and I could only hope I hadn't accidentally figured out how to do it. As it was, I'd caused more damage in two minutes than I'd ever caused before. Two guys sprawled on either side of the counter – two guys who probably had friends. We needed to get out of there.

'Billy, come on!'

I spun – then spun again. *Where did he go?*

A glance around the diner told me he wasn't hiding under any of the tables. And he wasn't stretched out on the floor like the other guys, so I was pretty sure he hadn't been hit. The guy behind the counter groaned. Chances were good they'd both be awake in a minute and on their feet shortly after that. I didn't think I'd knocked anyone out cold – probably just stunned the shit out of them.

'Billy D.! Come on!'

No answer.

I tore out the front door, praying he was already back in the car. No luck. I was too freaked-out to shout, afraid the noise would draw people. Finally, I heard him – first a sniffle, then a long whine and a choked-back sob. I followed the noise around the side of the diner and spotted him crouched between a filthy Dumpster and a paint-peeled wall.

'What are you doing? Let's go!' I called.

Billy only leaned away from me, tucking himself further

back into the narrow space and crying harder.

I crouched at the opening and almost gagged from the smell of garbage.

'It's over, okay? But we gotta get out of here.'

I reached an arm into the space, offering Billy my hand, but he smacked it to the side and let out a cross between a wail and a scream. The noise reverberated off the metal Dumpster and soared out into the car park. I clutched my ears and fell sideways against the wall.

'What the hell, man?'

Billy's scream died down to a hysterical high-pitched cry, and he started to hyperventilate.

'Billy D., it's me. It's Dane. It's okay.' I forced myself to sound calm, but I wanted to wail like Billy. If he kept making that noise, we were dead. It didn't matter how isolated the diner was. That sound could carry all the way across a cornfield. I was desperate to get back in the car.

'Are they dead?' Billy cried.

'No, they're not dead. Shh.'

'They're dead!'

'Dude, stop saying "dead". Someone's gonna hear you!'

'I don't care.'

'I promise they're fine, but we have to leave. If someone comes, we won't be able to leave. We won't be able to go to Kentucky.'

Billy swallowed a sob. 'We won't go to Kentucky?' he said between breaths.

'Not if you stay in there. Not unless you come out right now. Come on.'

But Billy still didn't move. He crouched on the ground, wiping his nose on the sleeve of his jacket.

'Why do you hit?' he asked quietly.

'What?'

'Why do you hit?' He raised his voice this time.

'Shh. What do you mean, why? I hit them because they were messing with you – because they might have hit *you*. I was looking out for you, see?'

'No.' Billy shook his head. 'Why do you hit everyone?'

'I don't hit everyone. I don't hit you.'

'Why do you hit *any*one?'

'Can we talk about this in the car? We really have to—'

'If your dad didn't hit you, why do you hit?' Billy's voice was fierce and desperate.

'I don't know, Billy—'

'Why do you hit?!'

'Shit! We don't have time for—'

'Why does he hit?'

'We have to go—'

'Why does he hit?'

Wait. What?

'Why does he hit, Dane? Why does he hit?'

Billy was sobbing openly again, and this time he collapsed like a jelly on the ground. I reached deep into the crevice between the Dumpster and the wall, holding my breath against the smell, and grabbed Billy by the collar of his jacket. He let me pull him out of his hiding space and stand him up, but once he was on his feet, he pushed away from me.

The question was still there in his eyes, but he didn't ask it again.

'Let's go,' I said quietly.

I was so relieved to see Billy finally get in the damn car, I almost started crying myself.

35

I aimed the car south, continuing our planned route out of sheer momentum. Billy dried his eyes, but he was still breathing heavy, worn out from his fit. I stopped at a petrol station to fill up the tank and get a Band-Aid for my split ear. I also picked up a bottle of aspirin and chased down twice the recommended dose with soda. My shoulders and wrists were killing me. I didn't know if it was from the fight or from the fact that I'd been tense since the moment we walked into that shit-hole diner.

We reached the river that divided Illinois and Kentucky and followed it, looking for a way across. Billy consulted the atlas and swore a bridge was coming up, but no matter how long I drove, the river stayed on our left, trapping us inside Illinois. It was a sign, I thought – a sign that Kentucky didn't want us, and I wasn't sure I wanted Kentucky. It wasn't until we hit a town called Cairo, where I saw cop cars for the first time since Missouri, that it hit me – we'd left the scene of a crime. *Was it a crime? It was self-defence ... sort of.* But we'd still left two guys bloody without calling for help. Even if they hadn't seen our car, we were easy enough to identify. I felt a selfish surge of anger towards Billy. He made it impossible for us to blend in. We wouldn't be able to make any more stops – to risk being recognised – all because of Billy.

Because of Billy? Or because of me?

I closed my hands tight around the steering wheel. It wasn't Billy's face that got us in trouble; it was my fists.

'What's wrong?' Billy asked.

Everything.

'Nothing.' I shook my head. 'You really freaked me out back there, man. I thought I got it. I thought it was complicated – the dad stuff, y'know? I thought you could just see him and say whatever you have to say and that I'd be there so—'

'Yeah,' Billy said. 'I'll say stuff and tell him about my heart and the letter—'

'What? He doesn't know about your heart?'

Billy shifted in his seat. 'Um, no?'

'No? You sound like you don't know.'

'I don't . . . I'm not . . . I don't think he knows. I have to tell him, Dane. I have to tell him about my heart.' Billy fidgeted with the atlas in his lap.

'You just moved from Oregon. You just left your dad, like . . . a few months ago, right? Not even?'

'I told you we lived some other places.'

'But it can't be longer than – what? – a year?'

'I don't know,' Billy said. He picked up the atlas and clutched it to his chest.

'Billy D.' I pressed the accelerator, forcing the car to pick up speed along with my temper. 'You said you were born with holes in your heart.'

Billy refused to meet my eye. 'Yeah.'

'You don't think your dad would know about that?'

'He doesn't know I'm going to die!' Billy hugged the atlas tighter, his eyes wild and scared.

Oh my God.

'Oh my God.'

A sign rose up fast in front of us – a warning to slow down. A second sign right beyond it practically screamed at me – junction ahead. Arrows marked the directions – left for Kentucky, straight ahead for Missouri.

I hit the brakes and skidded into a dirt parking area. Dust curled into the air around the car as I killed the engine. When it settled, I could see only one other vehicle – a burned-out old pickup truck parked a little way from what looked like a barn with rotting wood. The sign outside the building was so faded, I couldn't even tell what the business used to be.

'You passed the bridge,' Billy said. 'I saw it.'

I got out of the car and slammed the door.

Billy followed me out of the car and spread the atlas open on the bonnet. 'See, Dane? We're right here.'

He was so cheerful – like nothing had happened – like we were still on some happy-go-fucking-lucky road trip.

I stepped close to him, my hands curled into fists, my breath stressed. 'You don't even have a heart problem, do you?'

'I bet you can see the bridge still,' Billy mumbled. 'On the other side of that building, I bet you can still see—'

'Do you?' I felt like I was breathing fire.

Billy pulled the atlas up over his face like a shield. 'We should go now. We should go to Monkey's Eyebrow.'

'*Do you?*' I shouted.

Billy stumbled backwards a couple of steps and dropped the atlas.

'No.'

'Oh my God!' My hands flew back and forth between reaching for the sky and trying to rip out my own hair.

'But I *could*!' Billy stepped forward again, eager to get me back on board. 'I *could* have a heart problem!'

I pressed my fists to my temples. 'What? What does that even mean?'

'Lots of kids with Down's syndrome have broken hearts – and holes, just like I said.'

'So you *might* have one?'

Billy stuffed his hands in his pockets. 'Well . . . no.'

'Not even a little bit?' I was leaning into Billy's space now, my voice a hiss.

'Not even a little bit,' he said.

'Not even one tiny hole?' I made a pinch with my thumb and finger and shoved it under Billy's nose.

He looked ready to cry but just shook his head. 'Not even one.'

'Unbelievable!' I raged.

'You're mad,' Billy said.

'Mad. Ha!' I strode up and down the car park, punching the air and kicking up gravel. 'Mad doesn't even begin to . . . I mean – are you kidding me with this?'

'You still promised,' Billy said. 'You said we could go and rip up the letter. And – and – he's *right there*.' Billy pointed towards the bridge. 'It's not that far. He's right over there. Please, can—'

'I don't care!' I screamed. 'I don't care if he's right next door. You tricked me.'

'No, I didn't.'

'You lied to me.'

'You lied, too! You said you'd help me find my dad.'

I tore back to the car, pointing my finger at Billy as I came. 'Fuck your dad. Fuck your lies. And fuck Monkey's Elbow!'

'Monkey's *Eyebrow*!' Billy finally lost it. He picked up the atlas and hurled it in my direction. 'And fuck *you*!'

His words stopped me in my tracks more than the flying atlas. I almost wished he'd fall apart and give me an excuse to drag his cry-baby ass into the car and all the way back to Columbia. But instead, he was in a rage. Even his stance – legs apart and arms curved at his side – said he was ready to put up a fight.

Well, I'd had enough fighting for the day. He'd have to find someone else to go berserk on.

I ripped open the car door and threw myself inside.

'Where are you going?' Billy pounded on my window.

I opened it and pushed him back. 'I'm going home.' I started the ignition and put the car in gear.

'You can't leave!' Billy screeched. 'You can't take my mom's car!'

I squeezed the wheel, wondering whether it was possibly a crime to dump a disabled kid in the middle of nowhere. *He'd probably just trick someone else into giving him a ride.*

'Get in, then,' I growled.

Billy crossed his arms in response, and I pressed the accelerator.

'No!' Billy threw himself on the car's bonnet.

I slammed on the brakes, and he tumbled off to one side.

'Shit! Billy D.! Are you okay?' I jumped out of the car and rolled him on his side.

He pushed me away.

'Are you hurt?'

'I hate you,' he said.

He was fine.

'I *hate* you!'

'Hate me all you want, but decide! Stay here or come with me. I'm . . . I'm . . .' I dreaded how much I was about to sound like my mom. 'I'm going to count to ten.'

And I did.

At three, I was back in the car with my hands on the wheel.

At five, Billy was on his feet. He took a long look at me, then a long look towards the river, like he was thinking about swimming for Kentucky.

At eight, he picked up his atlas and stomped over to the passenger side of the car.

And at ten, we were pulling out of the car park without another word.

36

'Put on your seat belt.'

Damn, I was sick of sounding like my mom.

'No.'

'Come on, sit down. I don't want to get pulled over.' Billy was on his knees, his arms hugging the headrest and his eyes trained out the back window. At first, I thought he was watching the bridge to Kentucky disappear, but now I couldn't imagine what he was looking for behind us.

'Billy D., turn around. I need you to tell me where to go.'

'Go back,' he said, still staring out the rear window.

'No. Seriously, there's a freeway coming up. Do I need to get on this?'

Billy D. finally let go of the headrest and flopped down in his seat. 'I don't know.'

'Check the map.'

'You check it.'

'I'm driving.'

Billy stared out the window.

'Fine,' I said. 'We can drive all the way to Texas, then. But I'm not going back. You can either tell me how to get home, or we can spend the rest of our lives sleeping in this car.'

That's not a half-bad idea, actually. Anything would beat facing Mom.

Billy opened the atlas reluctantly.

'I-Fifty-five,' I said. 'Isn't that the one we took from St Louis?'

'I guess so.'

'So yes? Get on it?'

We were one exit away.

Billy closed the atlas and looked out the window.

I cursed under my breath and took the 55 north. Fortunately, the first sign listed both Cape Girardeau and St Louis ahead. Somehow, we'd come full circle, winding up just south of the Missouri state line, where it stretched east and curled under Illinois. Now I knew I could get home even without the atlas – and even if Billy played mute the whole way. In fact, that would have been preferable, because when he did open his mouth, it wasn't pretty.

It started with begging. When we passed the exit we'd taken to Cape Girardeau, Billy cried and pleaded and called me a liar through his tears. When I veered on to the bypass around St Louis, he began to scream. The insults he was throwing at me melted into nonsense syllables swallowed up by these terrible sounds from somewhere inside his chest. He thrashed in his seat and kicked the dashboard over and over. He even reached for the wheel at one point, and I had to grab his wrist so hard, I left a mark.

The injury stopped Billy's tantrum instantly. He sucked in all the horrible noises he'd been making and settled for shrinking down in his seat and whimpering. I had a sick feeling in my stomach that Billy had been silenced this way before.

When we cleared St Louis and pointed the car towards Columbia, Billy finally exhausted all his tears. In fact, he was just exhausted, period. The sniffles and whimpers faded to faint snores, and for the first time, I could hear my own thoughts.

What kind of sucker was I to have fallen for Billy's broken heart story? Hell, I was a sucker from the very beginning, with my rules about who to hit and who to spare. Really, I should have just knocked the little punk down the first time he followed me to school. Then none of this would have happened. Instead, I was stuck with him – stuck in a car with him, in trouble with him, and stuck giving a shit about him.

I shook Billy out of his sleep.

'Are we home?' he asked, rubbing his eyes.

'Close. Listen, we need to get our story straight.'

'What do you mean?'

'I mean, where did we go? What did we do? Why?'

Billy gave me one of his famous blank stares. 'You don't remember?'

'No, that's not—'

'We went across the river and to the restaurant and back across the river. And we got in a fight because you got mad at me. And we got in another fight because you got mad at those guys. And we got in another fight because you got mad at me again. And—'

'Oh my God, stop talking.'

'But you asked—'

'I don't mean what *really* happened. I mean, what do we tell everyone else?'

'You want to lie?' Billy asked.

I shot him a look. 'Like you don't know how to lie.'

Billy frowned. 'Why do we have to lie about where we went?'

'You want your mom to know you went looking for your dad?'

'No,' Billy admitted.

'You want *my* mom to know we had to steal her lottery tickets because *you* wanted to leave right away?'

Billy twisted his fingers in his lap. 'No.'

'And do you want—'

'Don't tell my mom we slept in the car!' Billy burst out.

I jumped. 'Okay. Why?'

'She says only homeless people sleep in cars. She says no matter what happens, we are not homeless. She says it all the time. "We're hungry, but we're not homeless" – "We're hurting, but we're not homeless" – just like that.'

I thought then about how hard I was on Mom about money – always asking for a car or a computer. We were never hungry, never hurting. And we sure as hell weren't homeless. Okay, our kitchen floor was in bad shape, and my cell phone was a dinosaur, but at least I'd never had to worry about the basics.

'Right,' I said. 'So we won't tell your mom about sleeping in the car. But what do we—'

'It didn't feel like being homeless,' Billy said, more to himself than to me. 'It felt like camping.'

'That's it!' I reached over to high-five Billy, and he met my palm, both of us forgetting for a second that we might not be friends any more. 'We'll say we went camping!'

'Awesome!' Billy got caught up in my enthusiasm. 'And fishing! 'Cause we were at the river!'

'But we don't have any rods,' I pointed out.

'That's why we didn't catch any fish!' Billy exclaimed.

We both laughed out loud.

'Okay, but Billy D.,' I said, 'that doesn't explain why we went "camping" without permission . . . in the middle of the week . . . in a stolen car.'

'Maybe we thought we'd be back in the morning before school,' Billy said.

My laugh caught in my throat at the word 'school', and I swallowed hard, remembering why I was supposed to be pissed at Billy. He'd flat-out conned me into this trip with his heart lies and his threats of taking off alone in the middle of the night. But no one would see it that way when we got back. Even my own mom would take one look at Billy's innocent mug and point the finger at me. Not that I blamed them. If even a guy like me could get suckered by a kid like Billy, then moms didn't have a prayer.

And it wouldn't matter if the warden believed me or not. He'd already suspended me for sticking up for Billy. He would be signing my expulsion letters before I could even tell him that I'd missed school to look after the kid. Hell, the expulsion notice was probably already waiting for me at home.

'What about the lottery tickets?' Billy asked.

I sighed. 'I'll figure out something to tell my mom.'

In fact, I planned to tell Mom the truth – partly because I owed it to her for stealing those tickets, but mostly because she wouldn't buy this bullshit camping story we were cooking up for one second anyway.

'Is she going to be really mad?' Billy asked. 'About the tickets?'

'I think she's going to be really mad about the whole thing.'

'So you're in big trouble like me.'

'Bigger.'

Billy propped his feet up on the dash and inspected his shoelaces for a long time. Finally he looked up and took a deep breath.

'I'm mad at you because you lied.'

I gaped at him. '*You're* mad at *me*? You . . . you're . . . ' I spluttered. '*You're* the liar.'

'You lied about helping me find my dad,' Billy went on, as if he hadn't heard me. 'And I'm mad at you because you promised to take me to Monkey's Eyebrow, and you didn't.'

'And *I'm* mad at *you* for being a con artist.'

'What's a con art—'

'You lied about having holes in your heart. You lied about your dad being awesome.'

'He *is* awes—'

'You lied about why you wanted to learn to fight.' I was raging now, shouting the lies at Billy as fast as I realised them. 'It was never about those punks from the bus stop, was it?'

'You didn't take me to Monkey's Eyebrow,' Billy repeated. 'And you're not going to help me find my dad, are you?'

'Hell no.'

'Then you broke your promise.'

'And you broke yours,' I said. 'I'm going to get kicked out of school because of you – because of your lies.'

Billy didn't have an answer for that, so for a few minutes we both sat and stewed.

Finally, Billy broke the silence, and his voice was much softer than before.

'I'm still mad at you.'

I snorted. *That makes two of us.*

'I'm so mad, I might be mad forever,' Billy said. 'But . . . but . . . I don't hate you.'

I let out a breath I hadn't realised I'd been holding and felt something unclench in my stomach. I wanted to tell him I didn't care if he hated me or not. I wanted to tell him I hated him. But I couldn't even think it, let alone say it, because the only thought that forced its way into my mind – as much as I tried to shove it down – was, *I don't hate you, either.*

'Okay, Dane?' Billy said. 'I don't hate you.' He searched my face for understanding.

I set my jaw, to make sure my expression didn't give away too much, and I gave Billy the smallest nod.

'Okay, then,' I said.

'Okay, then.' Billy sat back, satisfied.

'And hey, Dane?'

'Yeah?'

'Are we supposed to see a big sign that says "Columbia" with, like, an arrow?'

'Probably like that, yeah. Why?'

Billy pointed behind us. 'We just drove past it.'

*

It was a long time before Mom stopped screaming. Sometimes she would pause to cry a little bit or attack me in a bear hug and tell me how much she loved me, but then she'd go right back to screaming. I half hoped she'd cry herself to sleep the way Billy had in the car, but no such luck.

I only caught snatches of Mom's rant – words like 'dangerous' and 'underage' and 'disappointed'. That last one hurt.

Finally, she calmed down enough to let me tell her the story – and not the story Billy and I had concocted about camping. I told her the truth, every bit of it – including what I'd learned about Billy's dad. She didn't seem surprised. Apparently, while Billy and I were missing,

331

Mom and Mrs Drum had had a few pretty intense conversations of their own.

She stopped me at one point to call that lawyer she and Mrs Drum had hired. When he told her that getting into another fight meant I might have to sit in jail until my court date with Billy, Mom burst into tears. The lawyer told her not to panic until he made some calls to the sheriff's department down in southern Illinois, and he promised to get back to us.

Mom hung up the phone, dried her wet cheeks, and sank into a kitchen chair with her head in her hands.

'Oh my God,' she whispered, more to herself than to me. 'My kid is not a criminal.'

I am scum.

'But close enough to criminal that he needs a lawyer.' She looked up, talking to me now. 'You're sixteen years old, and you have a lawyer.'

Mould on top of scum.

Mom's eyes drifted to the wall where her remaining lottery tickets hung.

'Mom,' I began.

She held up a hand to silence me.

'But I just want to say I'm sor—'

'No,' she said.

'What?'

'I don't want to hear "I'm sorry" from your mouth until I know you've taken some time to really think about it – to *really* regret your poor decisions. Then you come back and say you're sorry.'

'Okay.' I moved to stand up, then turned back. 'Um, Mom? How much time should I take? You want me back out here later or . . .'

Her death glare silenced me, and I shrank away to my room, wondering how long I should sit in there and pretend I was thinking about what I'd done.

It turned out I would have plenty of time to sit in my room because the warden called an hour later. As of today, there was one less student enrolled at Twain High.

37

'You should have covered for me – told them I was off sick!'

'Off sick? I thought you were off dead! Disappearing in the middle of the night – your cell phone turned off . . . I thought . . . I thought—'

'I left you a note!'

'Which said nothing!'

Mom and I had been having this same fight for two days.

When the school called to report my absence, Mom had already been up half the night with Mrs Drum looking for me and Billy, and it must have made her delirious because she said she didn't know where I was and let them mark me truant. By the middle of the week, calls to the principal and requests to appeal to the school board had been exhausted and denied, and now we were filling out papers to enrol me in the alternative high school.

Mom shoved the forms across the kitchen table and stared hard at her wall of lottery tickets. She'd made a point of hanging the plundered frames back up empty. I guess it was supposed to make me feel guilty, but the only betrayal I saw when I looked at that wall was in the frames still full of unclaimed winners.

'We always have the option of fighting this in court.' Mom took a deep breath and ran a hand over her face. 'But by the time we get a hearing, the school year will be over. Maybe private school?' She seemed to be talking to herself now.

'Like we can afford private school,' I said.

Mom's eyes flickered back to the wall of tickets, but she didn't say anything for a minute. When she did speak, her voice was thin. 'We'll figure something out.'

And I believed she would. The only times I'd ever seen Mom fight harder than when she fought with me were when she fought *for* me. And I suddenly felt bad for making her have to put up a fight at all.

I couldn't quite bring myself to apologise, but I dragged the papers scattered across the kitchen table into a neat pile in front of me and started filling out my application to the alternative school.

*

Billy got into a little bit of shit himself. Skipping school rubbed the shine off his perfect image, and the warden

335

actually gave him a detention. He seemed pretty proud of it, too, judging by the way he waved the truancy slip around a few nights later. He'd already apologised for getting me kicked out of school, but he seemed to think his detention was truly the final penitence.

He got grounded, too. First for running away and then for lying about it. He'd actually tried to use the camping story, but Mrs Drum had gone straight to my mom for the truth. After all that, I was surprised our moms were letting us hang out, but they made an exception for my birthday.

Once upon a time I would have celebrated my seventeenth with a very different crowd and probably pushed Mom for a car. But under the circumstances, I was just glad to have a little company.

Even if that company's idea of a birthday gift was a detention slip.

When Billy finished showing it off, he tucked it back into his bag, which he had dumped on my bed. I caught a glimpse of the atlas there, still in its place of honour up front and always by Billy's side. A book behind the atlas caught my eye, too – just as familiar and nearly as dangerous.

'It's not the same yearbook,' Billy said, following my gaze. 'It's a different year.'

As if that made it okay.

But if I couldn't hold a grudge against Billy for getting me grounded and expelled and arrested, there was no point getting pissed about a stupid yearbook.

When he sensed I wasn't going to explode, he pulled the yearbook out cautiously. 'You should look at it,' he said. 'Only if you want to. It's . . . *better* than the other one.'

I let him leave the book on my bed, but I made a mental note to hide it under a pile of laundry later.

Seely came over after dinner, and we filled her in on everything I hadn't already told her over the phone. We stuffed ourselves with birthday cake, then we all crowded on the couch in the living room and *finally* watched *The Karate Kid*. Billy smiled through the whole movie, and Seely let me cop a feel under the blanket. I could almost pretend I was on vacation and not expelled from school.

The cherry on top of the whole night was a phone call Mom got from my lawyer. I watched her nod and 'uh-huh' her way through the call, and every few seconds her smile got bigger. Then she thanked him over and over and hung up.

'What was that?' I asked.

Billy and Seely had gone home, and Mom and I were side by side at the sink, doing dishes.

She dropped the phone and went back to drying a plate. 'Well, you'll be happy to know your "friends" from the restaurant are going to be okay.'

'I will?' I raised my eyebrows.

'Well, you *should* be. And better yet – they're not pressing charges.'

'We should press charges against *them*,' I grumbled, 'for being dicks.'

I wasn't surprised they'd wanted to drop the whole thing. After all, they'd been armed, and we were just a couple of teenagers. But I hadn't told Mom about the gun – one detail too many might have put her over the edge.

'You dodged a bullet there,' she said.

You have no idea.

'Anyway, your lawyer talked to the sheriff or someone down there, who says one of the guys – the owner of the restaurant – is on probation for some other crime and doesn't want any trouble. So as far as he and his buddy are concerned, they never saw you or Billy D., and nothing ever happened.'

Mom was practically dancing in celebration, but all I could think was something *did* happen. Somewhere between Mom's lottery tickets and Billy's lies, I'd discovered a part of myself I wasn't proud of. The way Billy's tantrum had ended under my too-firm grip, the way those guys looked all sprawled out on the diner floor – the images were all pointing to a single question.

'Mom?'

'Yes?'

'Do you think I could end up like . . . maybe, like Billy's dad?'

Mom stopped drying the dishes and leaned on the counter, facing me. 'What kind of a question is that?'

I shut off the water and took her towel to dry my hands.

He's a hitter; I'm a hitter. And Billy likes us both, even though most people don't.

'You know what I mean' was all I said to Mom.

She pulled a chair from the kitchen table and flopped down in it. 'You are nothing like that man.'

I took the chair next to hers. 'How do you know? You don't know him.'

'I know you.'

I opened my mouth to argue, but Mom cut me off.

'You've had it harder than most kids. You're angry a lot of the time, and that anger occasionally gets misplaced.'

I thought of Jimmy Miller and the anger I'd misplaced on his face when I'd caused him to nosedive off his bike and on to the road.

Mom took a deep breath. 'Would you want to talk to someone about it?'

'About what?'

'Your anger.' She rushed on. 'Molly has a list of names – doctors – just people you could talk to—'

'No,' I interrupted Mom's nervous ramble. But then I looked down at my hands, the ones I so often balled into fists. 'Maybe. If you think it would keep me from . . . I mean, I don't want to turn out like—'

'You won't.' Mom closed her hand over one of mine. 'You would never do what he did. You'd never hurt someone like Billy D.'

'Don't do that.'

'Do what?'

'Don't say "someone like Billy D.", like he's not like you and me.'

'Dane. He's not like you and me.'

I pulled my hand out from under hers and leaned away.

'It's not a bad thing,' Mom said. 'Recognising that difference and still accepting Billy just the way he is – that is what separates you from his dad.'

'What do you know about him?' I asked.

'Billy's dad? I know he's a cruciverbalist. I think that's what it's called.'

'What's that?'

'It's like a puzzle maker. He designs brainteasers for books and sometimes makes the crossword puzzles for big newspapers.'

I flashed on Billy's atlas. 'That makes sense.'

'Molly says he's an extremely intelligent man, but when

Billy was a baby, his dad was in denial about his condition. He went into debt taking Billy to specialists and trying to find a way to . . . to . . . I don't know, really. Cure him, maybe? Or at least help him advance?'

'That's good, right?'

Mom rubbed her forehead. 'It's good that Billy got the best care and the best education at an early stage, but . . . there's only so far he *could* advance. And Molly says when Billy hit that point, his dad just couldn't accept it. He kept trying to push Billy past his limits, and when Billy couldn't keep up, his dad would become violent.'

'He hit him.'

'Yes, he hit him. Molly said it got to a point where Paul became obsessed with creating riddles for Billy to solve. He thought if Billy could understand riddles and puzzles, he could understand anything. But the more Billy struggled, the more violent his dad became. She thinks he even created some puzzles with no answers on purpose – whether for an excuse to hit Billy or because he'd just lost it, she doesn't know.'

Images from the atlas papered my brain – a town pencilled in on one page, a clue lurking at the bottom of another. It was always just one big test to torture Billy. And the letter in the back held nothing more than meaningless answers to meaningless questions.

What's black and white and read all over? Who gives a shit.
What seems cool and fun but is really evil all over? Billy's dad.

I wondered if that guy knew he'd created the greatest riddle of all: How does a kid still love his dad, even when he turns out to be such a bastard? That one sure had me stumped.

'So she ran for it?' I asked. 'She just packed up Billy D. And took off?'

'And they've been running for a while,' Mom said. 'Molly worked odd jobs where she could, but Billy needs stability – needs to stay in one school. So she brought him here, where she knows people. A friend offered to set her up in a house – got her a cash-in-hand job.'

Cash-in-hand. So that explained why she was so secretive about it.

'What does she do?'

'She's a janitor.' Mom's eyes caught mine, and she continued in a sharp voice before I could reply. 'And there's no shame in that.'

'I know, I didn't—'

'There's no shame in anything a mother does to take care of her son.'

'I know.' I said it more firmly this time, and I held her gaze. 'I know it better than anyone.'

Mom's eyes softened just a little bit, then she stood up and did something so bizarre, I nearly took her temperature to make sure she wasn't crazy with a fever. She marched over to the wall of lottery tickets and pulled down the largest frame. I sat frozen as she prised the clasps off the back and pulled the golden ticket from its trophy case. She scanned the back and muttered to herself. 'Still time.'

I swallowed hard. 'Mom?'

She waved the five-thousand-dollar winner between her fingers and looked at me. 'It's enough for a computer – a nice laptop, maybe.'

'Mom?'

'And a college fund – a start, at least. We'll need to add to it, obviously, but we've got a couple of years. I think maybe you ought to think about getting a job this summer. I know you've been wanting to—'

But she couldn't finish, because my hug choked off her last words. I held her tight around the neck and shoulders. 'Thank you, Mom. Thank you.'

Mom let me hug her for a few seconds longer. Then she used her strong, lean arms to push me back into my chair. I would have thought she was angry if it wasn't for the tear I saw her wipe away.

I pointed to the empty frame on the counter. 'I thought you said you were "saving up your luck".'

Mom took my hand and smiled. 'I cashed in on the luck the day you came home safe.'

'If I get a job, and I promise to put most of the money in a college fund, could I – could we maybe – save up just a little for a car?'

I held my breath until Mom finally winked. 'We'll talk.'

I went to bed in such a good mood, even the sight of that yearbook waiting for me in my room couldn't wipe the smile off my face.

I went to swipe it off the bedspread and on to the floor, but something stopped me. Little bits of pink paper peeped over the top of the yearbook. Billy had gone crazy with the sticky notes again. It was a good bet he'd marked every page with anyone who looked even remotely like me. I had to smile. Maybe it was better Billy was spending time looking for *anybody* but his own dad.

Instead of tossing the book to the floor, I cracked it open and flopped down on my bed. I turned the pages slowly, studying every face. I wondered how many of them grew up to be dads – how many of them maybe hit their kids – how many of them walked *away* from their kids. But I couldn't see answers in any of their faces. They just looked like confused, screwed-up teenagers. In that way, they *all* looked like me.

38

I borrowed the car to run some errands for Mom the next day, which included dropping off my enrolment forms at the alternative high. There were only a few students in the halls, but I saw enough to know there were a lot of itchy palms walking those hallways and that being in class there was going to look a lot like being in detention at Twain.

So my mood was already foul when I turned up the street towards home and saw it. Another damn removals van, its back doors open. Just what we needed – more strangers on our street – probably some low-rent family with a thousand noisy kids and . . .

I blinked. The van was parked exactly where I'd seen it the last time – tight against the kerb in front of Billy's house – and Mrs Drum was pushing a huge box into the back.

I stopped Mom's car right in the middle of the street and got out with the engine still running.

'What is this?'

Mrs Drum turned at my voice and brushed the dust off her hands. When she finally met my eyes, they looked at me with more kindness than they ever had. 'Dane, I'm sorry.'

'Sorry for what? What's going—'

'Dane!' Billy flew down the front steps, tossing a box of toys aside on to the lawn as he ran.

Mrs Drum scooped up the toys and disappeared into the house.

'We're moving,' Billy said, breathless.

'What? Why?'

Billy stared at his toes.

'Billy D., what's going on?'

The front door opened again, and Mrs Drum appeared with an armload of smaller boxes. 'Billy, I told you to take the sheets off your bed. And none of your books are packed.'

'I'm talking to Da—'

'Now.'

Billy obeyed, stomping up the front step without even a backward wave.

'Mrs D., what the hell – uh, what the heck is going—' I started, but she cut me off again.

'Dane, I'm sorry, but your mom can fill you in. We're in a hurry.' She dropped the pile of boxes on the pavement and started back up towards the house.

'No way! What's happening? Where are you going?'

'I'm sorry,' she said. And she looked it. Her hair was wild, and she was moving at a frantic pace, but just for a second I saw that 'I'm sorry' echoed in her eyes. I started to follow her right up to the front door, but two small hands caught my arms from behind. I spun on instinct, my fist raised.

'Whoa.' The hands let go in an instant, and I saw Seely's eyes opened wide – her forehead wrinkled all the way up into her spiky white hair.

'Sorry,' I said. I dropped my fist and used the hand to grab her around the waist instead. She hugged me back.

'Did you know about this?' I asked, my face in her hair.

'I just got here.' She pulled out of my arms. 'I was looking for you. My dad didn't need me at the shop after school, so I came by and—' She swung her arm to indicate the truck and the house where Billy and his mom were now shut up inside. 'I have no idea what's going on.'

'I do,' a voice said beside us.

Mom was standing on the kerb, her arms crossed and her lips set in a thin line. 'Come inside.'

I would have rather gone inside Billy's house and demanded answers there, but Seely took my hand and pulled me up the steps after Mom.

Mom motioned for us to join her at the kitchen table and got right to the point.

'Billy called his dad.'

'What?' Seely and I said in unison.

Mom combed her fingers through her hair. 'He got the number from an old family friend – someone named June Bug or something ridiculous like that.'

I set my jaw, trying to keep my face as still as possible, but inside, my heart was beating a racket against my rib cage.

'Apparently, she talked to someone who had seen Paul recently—'

'Seen him?' I repeated, a chill crawling up my spine. Had Billy's dad been in Missouri looking for him after all?

Mom nodded. 'That's what she said. So this woman got a contact for Paul and called Billy up and gave it to him without talking to Molly.'

'I'm – uh – I'm sure she meant well.' Seely's voice cracked. I gripped her hand under the table to keep her from saying anything more.

'Where is he?' I asked.

'Billy's dad?' Mom blew out a long breath. 'By now, he could be anywhere. But I think Molly said he told Billy he was in Detroit.'

A little piece of me – the tiny chunk that understood why Billy would still want to know the camping, monkey-watching, ice-cream-sharing dad – died. I felt it go black

348

and shrivel up inside me. Of course he wasn't in Monkey's Eyebrow. I'd always known he wasn't. *Hadn't I?*

'Anyway,' Mom said. 'Billy, of course, told his dad where he was.'

'Oh my God,' Seely breathed.

'When?' I asked.

'Just this morning. Molly overheard him, but she was careful not to say anything until he hung up. She thinks if Paul doesn't know she knows, he might not show up right away.'

'Do we really think he'll show up *at all?*' I asked. Couldn't we get a little perspective here? The guy had moved to Detroit, of all places. Maybe he just came home for a visit. Maybe he knew he was messed up and wasn't even looking for Billy.

I said all this, in so many words, but Mom and Seely didn't look convinced. Seely pointed out that it was suspicious he hadn't called the police after Mrs Drum ran away with Billy – almost like a man wanting to do his own detective work. Mom added that Mrs Drum knew him best, and if she was scared, she probably had good reason.

I wasn't buying any of it. Or maybe I was just in denial, but running sounded like the worst possible option to me. I knew the further Billy's mom pulled him from his dad, the more desperate Billy would be to find him. And it wasn't like they were in witness protection. They'd be leaving a trail all over the country, and sooner or later Billy's dad would find them. Right here in Columbia, he'd find Billy's name on record at the school, at the police station – *the police station*!

'Mom!' I said. 'Billy can't leave! We're supposed to go to court. Aren't you, like, automatically guilty if you don't show up or something?'

It felt like grasping at straws, and I expected Mom to come back with an easy answer, but she surprised me by pressing a hand to her forehead and leaning back in the chair, deflated.

'I'm worried about that, too,' she said.

'I didn't even think of that,' Seely whispered.

'I'll try to persuade Molly to at least contact the detective and explain the situation – try to work something out – but honestly, I'm just not sure she cares about that right now. She's on one track, like this runaway train.' Mom shot her arm out, pantomiming that imaginary train going off the rails. 'I do think she knows that she's going to eventually have to deal with all this through the proper channels – divorce, custody, all of that. But she wants to get Billy to a safe place first. Then maybe she'll get her ducks in a row and go back to Oregon to sort it out.'

'But we'll never know, will we?' I asked.

I imagined Billy's mom wiping my number from his phone the way she'd wiped out his dad's.

Mom shook her head. 'I don't know, Dane.'

The defeat in her voice made us all fall quiet, and in the silence we could hear the occasional muted thud of another box being loaded on to the removals van across the street.

39

Mom said Billy and Mrs Drum were leaving first thing in the morning, so we got up at the crack of dawn to meet them outside and say our goodbyes. Seely had stopped over the night before on her way home. I wondered what they had said to each other – what *I* was going to say.

The windstorm had ripped up the street pretty good overnight, and I had to jump over a huge tree branch lying across the road to get to the removals van. The sun was still too low to be seen, and only sharp rays of light poked through the houses, casting spotlights, making one side of the street look like a stage and the other like the dark audience. The removals van was in the shadows, but with our moms' eyes on us, I felt like Billy and I were standing in one of the spotlights.

'Do you know where you're going?' I asked.

'No,' Billy admitted. 'I hope it has a cool name.'

'Yeah, as long as it's not Monkey's Eyebrow.'

Billy lowered his gaze. 'I don't want to go there any more,' he whispered.

'Nah, you probably want to go to Detroit, right?' There was acid in my voice, and I wished I could start over. This wasn't how I wanted to leave it with Billy, but I was so pissed.

I'd been up all night trying to figure out who to blame – Billy's mom for being paranoid, his dad for being a monster, myself for giving a damn. But I kept coming back to Billy D. I wished he'd never called his dad – wished he'd never even *mentioned* his dad.

'I'm sorry,' I said. 'I'm not going to give you any shit, okay? I just . . . I think maybe you should stop looking for your dad.'

'One of those doctors – the ones Mom made me talk to – says I'm not really looking for my dad.'

'Oh no?'

Billy looked up. 'He says I'm looking for *answers*.'

'Sounds like a smart guy.'

'I don't think so.' Billy wrinkled his nose.

'Why not?'

'Because how can I be looking for answers when I don't know the questions?'

Not questions, I thought. *Question. Singular. Just one: Why do people hit?*

Billy had been asking me that in his own way practically since we met. It'd just taken me a long time to figure it out. And apparently, Billy still hadn't.

353

'Then what do you think?' I asked.

Billy shrugged. 'I think the doctor wears funny glasses.'

'Well, um . . .' I coughed and looked at my feet. 'I'm going to miss your ugly mug.'

'I'm not ugly,' Billy said. 'I'm handsome. Everybody says so. They say, "Oh, he's so handsome."'

'Dude, when old ladies say it, it doesn't count.'

'Billy, hurry up,' Mrs Drum called. 'You're going to make Dane late for school.'

I started to let out an empty laugh, but it died on my lips when I saw the expression on her face. She was beaming.

'Dane's back in,' she said, more to Mom than to me.

'What?' Mom and I said at the same time.

Mrs Drum bounced a little on her toes, looking so much like Billy and so unlike herself that I had to blink a few times to make sure I wasn't seeing things.

'I wrote a letter to the school board, and I spoke personally to Principal Davis. I explained the trouble Billy had caused trying to run away.' Her smile faltered for a second as she shot Billy a look he shrank under. Then her face turned to mine, and her expression melted into something apologetic. 'And I explained how you skipped school because you were trying to protect him. Principal Davis says the board was very moved.' She looked now at

354

Mom. 'I meant to tell you yesterday. I wanted to surprise you, but I got . . . distracted. The school is supposed to call you sometime today.'

Mom threw her arms around Mrs Drum, and I didn't have to see her face to know she was crying. When she pulled back, she held Mrs Drum's arms tightly in her hands. 'You won't reconsider?'

'No.' Mrs Drum's smile disappeared, and she looked again like the worried, frazzled woman I'd come to recognise. 'I should have never come here to begin with. So close to home – stupid – I just thought—'

'Shh.' Mom wrapped her in another hug, and now they were both sniffling.

It was obvious to me now that Mom was losing a friend, too. But I wondered if they would have become friends without Billy and me getting into so much trouble – what everything would have been like if we'd never gone looking for Billy's dad. Billy and I could have played video games and watched movies and made fun of Mark and hung out with Seely. Then again, would we have ever hung out with Seely if we hadn't needed her computer for the dad hunt? Would Billy and I have even been friends if he hadn't needed *me* for that search? There was no way of knowing, and I was too selfish to really wish I could go back. Somehow,

I had come out ahead. Now Billy was leaving empty-handed, while I got to stay and hang out with Seely and get a job and watch Mom finally spend those lottery tickets. Billy was losing everything, and all I was losing was Billy.

But at the moment, that *felt* like everything.

'Will you be able to call me?' I asked.

Billy's face lit up. 'I have your number,' he whispered. He reached down to his backpack, which was lying open at his feet, and pulled out the atlas. He moved, putting my big frame between him and the moms so they couldn't see, and cracked open the back cover. I saw he'd resealed the torn paper with tape, save for the corner. He folded that corner back now in a triangle, and two edges of folded paper peeked out from underneath.

Billy inched the two bits of paper out and unfolded one. Inside he had printed 'Dane Washington' with my phone number below it. I smiled.

'I have Seely's, too,' he said.

He tucked my number away carefully, then pressed the second slip of folded paper into my palm. I started to open it, but Billy stopped me.

'Don't look yet!'

'Why not?'

'Because you might not like it, and I don't want to know

if you don't like it, because I really, really, *really* want you to like it.'

'Okay, okay.' I laughed. 'I'll look at it later.' I stuck the paper in my back pocket. 'I have something for you, too.'

From another pocket, I pulled out a slim plastic case with a DVD inside. I handed it to Billy.

'*The Karate Kid*,' I told him. 'Sorry I don't have the original box. It's just the disc, but it still plays and all—'

'It's awesome!'

Billy dropped the atlas back into his pack and grasped the DVD case in both hands. 'Thank you.'

'Yeah, whatever,' I said. My cheeks felt hot. 'Just remember. *You* are Mr Miyagi,' I said.

Billy tore his eyes from the case to meet mine. 'No,' he said seriously. 'You're the Miyagi.'

The first curve of the sun appeared over Billy's roof, signalling it was time to go. I started nodding like an idiot and backing up with my hands in my pockets.

'Well . . . ' I drifted off.

'Yeah,' Billy said.

We locked eyes for one more second.

'Okay, then,' I said.

Billy grinned. 'Okay, then.'

Not five minutes later, the removals van was pulling

away with Mom and me in the middle of the street waving like you see people do in the movies. I dropped my hand and stuffed it back in my pocket, feeling stupid.

*

Walking to school alone sucked more than I thought it would. I mean, I'd been walking to that damn high school by myself for three years. There was no reason it should suddenly bother me now.

But I guess it doesn't matter how long you walk alone; once you get used to someone travelling next to you, you sort of come to count on it. And once it's gone, no matter how hard you try, you can't remember what it felt like to have no one there. Now, instead of just me, it felt like me and the big empty space next to me.

The sun beat down on me as I walked, and for the first time that whole stormy spring, I wished it would rain. I was about to take the turn to cut through the gardens when a horn honked, startling me out of my own thoughts.

Somehow, I expected to see a red Mustang with some asshole behind the wheel and maybe across the street a slightly stooped-over kid with a blank expression who would watch while I taught the asshole a lesson. But what I saw instead was surprising enough to chase the memories away for the moment.

'Get in!' Seely said, leaning over the passenger seat to call out the window.

'What is this?' I smiled, despite my sour mood.

This was no Mustang, and there was no asshole behind the wheel – only a beat-up old Cadillac and the girl who reminded me I hadn't actually lost everything.

'*This*,' Seely said, opening the door from the inside and waving me in, 'is *all mine*.'

I dropped into the passenger seat. 'You finally settled?'

'Well, Dad said if I made any more money, he wasn't going to be able to afford to match me dollar-for-dollar, so it was time. Picked her up this morning.' Seely caressed the dashboard. 'Like her?'

'Love her,' I said.

An awkward moment of silence followed, which I covered up with a cough and stammered, 'Um, so . . . anyway . . . uh, how did you know to pick me up or—'

'Billy said you might need a ride today,' she said softly.

'Oh.'

Seely put the car in motion while I stared out the window at the pavements moving slowly past. I thought of the tread Billy and I had worn in those pavements over the last few months. I hoped wherever he wound up that

359

he wouldn't be lonely. I hoped he would find a doctor who spoke his language and could help him figure out both the answers and the questions. I hoped he'd meet someone with a skateboard and someone else who could walk him to school. I chuckled to myself thinking of who that person might be and how the poor sucker had no idea what he was in for. I almost pitied the guy – and envied him.

I shifted in my seat and felt a crinkle in my pocket. I reached back and pulled out the little folded piece of paper from Billy.

'What's that?' Seely asked.

I opened it without answering and read two short lines followed by a name and an address.

Dane,

This is your dad.

40

I was on the homestretch.

Only one more week of keeping my fists to myself and making it to class on time. The doctor Mom had set me up with helped with the fists, and Seely got me to school by giving me a ride every morning.

On this morning – the last Monday before summer break – we were in her car, idling at a stop sign for longer than necessary. Seely was waiting for me to make a decision. She checked her rear-view mirror to make sure no cars were behind us, then she looked back at the slip of paper in my hands.

Billy had taken a lot of care to make sure the words were as neat as possible. I didn't know how he knew – what research he'd done, who he'd talked to, or how he'd found him – but I knew Billy wouldn't make it his parting gift if he wasn't sure.

I'd carried the paper around for two weeks, but I hadn't opened it again until today. It sat heavy in my back pocket, a physical weight pulling me down, and I wanted to be free of it before summer. Plus, I expected to hear from Billy any day, and he would want to know what I'd found.

'Are you ready?' Seely asked quietly.

I looked out the window, down the road to the place where Billy and I always veered off the pavement to cut across the ball fields – a turn I'd probably never make again, now that I had a girl with wheels and possibly my own car coming in the future. Just past that turnoff was the entrance to the car park, and beyond that – only a few blocks away – the street that Billy had printed on this piece of paper.

Seely tapped the clock on the Caddy's dashboard. 'We still have time before school,' she said. 'But we have to go now.'

I nodded, thinking how much Billy would have wanted to be on this stakeout. 'I'm ready.'

Seely passed the school and picked up speed. It only took a few minutes to find the house, and too soon we were parked in front of it.

'Back up!' I hissed. 'You're being too obvious.'

Seely backed up calmly and killed the engine. And just in time, too, because right then the front door opened up, and a man in a suit stumbled out looking like he was in a hurry. There was a woman, too, leaning out the door and saying something, and a little girl toddling down the steps after her dad, but I didn't notice them much. I was too focused on the man in the suit – the hard line of his jaw, the dark skin and hair, the way he smiled at the little girl.

The way he kept reaching up to flatten the chunk of hair that sat up on the back of his head.

Something stuck in my throat.

'He looks just like you,' Seely said. But it wasn't necessary. Anyone with eyeballs could see this man was like a crystal ball into my future – exactly what I would see when I looked in the mirror in sixteen years or so.

The man ushered the little girl back to her mother, who he kissed in a hurry before rushing to his car.

'You want me to block the driveway?' Seely asked, her hand on the gearshift and a fierce tone in her voice.

Right here the whole time, I thought. *Right here in town, right by school. Right here with a wife and a kid and a decent house and a life.*

'Dane?' Seely moved her hand from the gear stick to my arm.

I looked at the name on the paper, trying to remember if it was one we'd pulled from the pictures in the yearbook. I couldn't recall.

I lifted my eyes back to the scene, to the man getting held up one more time by a last-minute something-or-other shouted by his wife in the doorway. I watched him, waiting to feel something – anger, excitement, maybe . . .

363

Nothing.

Well, not nothing – just nothing about this guy. I was feeling a little bit sorry for Mom, that she could have had this house in a nicer neighbourhood, and a little bit defensive of her, that she was prettier than the woman in the doorway. I was feeling grateful for Seely's hand on my arm and still feeling depressed about watching Billy drive off in the removals van – but feelings about this guy?

Nope. Nada.

The man finally got into his car, and I saw his hand stick up out of the window to wave at his family – his family – not mine.

'He's leaving,' Seely said, stating the obvious.

'Let him leave.'

Seely studied my face. 'You sure? You want to come back later or someth—'

'No.'

Well, not 'no' exactly, but just not later that day – maybe *later* later, like years from then later – or maybe not ever.

The guy looked nice enough with his little family. He definitely didn't look like someone who hit his kids, but then again, who can tell? Still, I felt relieved for some reason. He just looked like a guy who maybe made a mistake in high school that he couldn't deal with, because he was probably too weak. I knew right then who I'd gotten my strength from – who I'd gotten *everything* from – and it wasn't him.

'I don't know that guy,' I told Seely as we watched the car pull out of the driveway and roll away.

'Well, he's obviously your dad,' she said.

'No,' I said. 'He's somebody else's dad.'

'Dane—'

'Whoever he is,' I cut her off, 'he's not worth getting kicked out of school for.'

I pointed at the clock on the dash.

Seely jumped at the time and put the car in gear. As mixed-up as I was feeling about Billy and the man in the suit and everything that had happened over the last few months, I still managed a smile when I rolled down the window and felt the sun on my face, the wind rushing by, and the wheels rolling under the Cadillac.

I could tell my smile was making Seely nervous, like she thought I was about to crack up on her or something, and she was hesitant to leave my side when we got to school.

I promised her I'd meet her back at the Caddy later for a ride home and shooed her off to class. I jogged down the hallway towards my own first period, focused on getting into my seat before the bell, but something pulled me up short.

I stopped and turned to look back at the scene. Two familiar faces were the only ones left in the hall as kids cleared out: one of the potheads who had picked on Billy had Jimmy Miller by the collar – pressed up against a locker in a way that looked painful. Jimmy was on his toes, his face red from the choke hold. I recognised the panic in his eyes. I'd put it there myself once.

'Hey!' I called.

Both boys' heads spun in my direction.

'Is there a problem here?' I sauntered towards them casually, like I wasn't at all in danger of being late for class and getting the detention that would be the final nail in my educational coffin.

'No problem,' the pothead sneered. 'Just settling something.'

He looked at me with this glint in his eye, like we were kindred spirits or something. I wanted to spit in that eye, extinguish the flame there.

I waited for the itch, but it didn't come. I felt more in control somehow – my hands calm at my sides instead of tingly and tense.

'I think you've settled it,' I said.

The pothead made a face. 'I'll say when it's settled.' He tightened his grip on Jimmy's collar, making him actually gasp for breath.

I pulled myself up to my full height and set my jaw in a way I knew was intimidating. Then I got right up inside the pothead's personal space and growled in his ear.

'And *I say* . . . it *is* settled. So you can let go now, or you and me can settle it later.'

The pothead shrivelled, letting go of Jimmy and backing out from under me. 'Hey, I don't got any problems with you, man.'

'You don't if you walk away right now, you mean,' I said.

'Sure.' He held his hands up and kept walking backwards.

'Yeah. No problems.'

A few steps later, he spun on his heel and ran the rest of the way down the hall.

Jimmy slumped against the locker and rubbed his sore neck.

'What'd you do that for?' he asked.

'Just making things square,' I said.

I started to walk away, but Jimmy stopped me.

'Well, uh, thanks. I guess I . . . I guess I owe you one.'

Still moving down the hall, I looked over my shoulder.

'No, I owed you one. But now we're even.'

The bell started to ring – a thirty-second warning to get to class.

'Trust me,' I called back to Jimmy. 'I don't do favours.'

SOUTH DUBLIN MOBILE LIBRARY

Acknowledgements

For a book about two boys who walk alone until they find each other . . . it sure did take a whole crowd of people to get them here!

My first thanks go to my first readers – Michael Lange, whose professional expertise was invaluable to this novel, and Holly Lange, who loves these characters even more than I do. You are the only people to suffer through Every. Single. Draft. And you just happen to be the best parents a girl could ask for.

It took one month to write this book. And then it took one *year* to *rewrite* it, with the help of Gemma Cooper and Kelly Thompson. Endless thanks to you both. I treasure your talent and your friendship. And a special thank-you to Marie Saavedra, who provided the kind of insight that can only come from personal experience.

My books would not exist without the tireless work of Caroline Abbey and Jennifer Laughran. One million thanks to you both. Thank you, too, to my UK publishing family at Faber, especially Alice Swan, Leah Thaxton,

Emma Eldridge and James Rose. You make my books feel at home overseas.

Finally, and above all, thanks to my family and friends. You blow me away with your support and encouragement – especially Matt Helm, who deserves all of the credit but never wants to take any. I love each and every one of you.

Q&A

Get to know Erin Lange . . .

Dane and Billy D are incredibly powerful characters. How did you come up with them?

Their voices came to me first. These two boys just kind of walked into my head and started talking to each other. Instead of getting an idea for a scene, I would get a rush of dialogue in my mind, as if overhearing a conversation. It came on so fast and so frequent, that I started dictating the dialogue into a voice recorder whenever I wasn't near a computer. I had no idea what the story was at first, but eventually, I had so many snippets and scenes, the story just developed around them.

Dead Ends **is set in Columbia, Missouri, near Illinois where you grew up. Did you use any of your childhood memories when creating the book?**

I actually lived in Columbia for years. It's where I went to college! But even though the place is familiar, I was careful not to include anything too personal. I experienced this town as a university student, so my Columbia would be very different from Dane and Billy D's Columbia. However, the first leg of their road trip is the same route I would take home to Illinois for holidays and long weekends. I spent a lot of time driving those roads, so writing the scenes with the boys in the car really took me back there.

Which of your characters do you most identify with?
Probably Seely. I like to think I was pretty mature and well-adjusted as a teenager, like she is. Although, I couldn't fix a car to save my life. I envy her that.

What advice would you give your teenage self, if you could?
It would take all the willpower I could muster, but if I could talk to my teenage self, I would try very hard not to give any advice. I believe all things happen for a reason, even if that reason is just to change us in some way. So I wouldn't want to influence teenage me for fear of changing who I turned out to be.

Have you ever been on a road trip like Dane and Billy D?
One road trip in particular comes to mind! When I was in college, it was quite the fad to follow certain bands around from tour stop to tour stop. A few of my guy friends and I

took a weekend to see some shows by the band Phish. We had no place to sleep for the last night of the trip, and everyone was too exhausted to drive, so we ended up just pulling the car off the road and falling asleep in our seats – just like Dane and Billy D!

Why did you choose to write a book about two characters with missing fathers?
My poor dad! Once again, I've written a book with some sort of paternal problem. People are going to think I'm writing from personal experience. In truth, I have two wonderful parents who are my very best friends, but I recognise that we may not be the norm, and I'm fascinated by all kinds of family dynamics, so I explore them in my writing – and explore how family shapes who we are as individuals as well. In this case, those missing fathers are what gave these two boys their initial connection.

How long did it take you to write *Dead Ends*?
I wrote the first draft of *Dead Ends* in one month, but I had been dictating snippets of dialogue between these boys for months before that, so by the time I sat down to write, it was mostly a matter of putting those snippets together. However, the first draft was a bit of a mess, so it took me almost a year to rewrite the story and turn it into something worth sharing.

When did you know you wanted to be an author?

I think it was the first time I got to 'The End' in a manuscript. I had started and abandoned so many novels over the years that finishing one felt huge. I wanted to share it with everyone! Until that moment, writing was just something I did for fun – for me. Now, I still do it for fun, but it's no longer just for me, and that is amazing.

What's a typical working day like for an author?

I have no idea! That is to say, I'm not sure I'm typical. For one thing, I do not write every day. I am a full time journalist as well as an author, and I simply can't write daily – or even weekly. Instead, I write in bursts. When working on a novel, I will typically wake up around 6 a.m. and write for three hours before work. Then, at night, I'll catch up on emails, do any book-related research and continue writing. During these bursts, dishes pile up and laundry gets neglected. After each draft, I will take time off to catch up on life!

How do you generate ideas for your storylines?

A lot of my ideas come from my work as a journalist. Too often, the facts I write for the news are the kinds of terrible things you can't just brush off. They tend to fester in my subconscious mind until they somehow find their way into my fiction, where I can mould them into something a little more hopeful.

When you have finished writing a book, who is your first reader?

My parents are always my first readers, even before I finish a book. I tend to send them chapters as soon as I write them. It's great motivation when I'm in the trenches of a rough draft, because my parents are cheerleaders. However, once I've completed a draft, it goes off to my critique partners, who are much tougher to impress!

Are you influenced by any other authors?

I am inspired by just about everything I read, but if I had to name just one influence, I would say Judy Blume, because growing up, I always felt her books were so honest. She tells the truth about the childhood and teenage experience, even if it scares the adults.

Which were your favourite books when you were a teenager?

I read a lot of Christopher Pike and R. L. Stine – anything creepy with teenagers getting into trouble. I also read the *Vampire Diaries*, which I think surprises teens today who don't realise how long those books have been around!

What ingredients, in your opinion, does a good book need?
Great characters, high stakes and the element of surprise.

Do you have any tips for new writers?
Write what you want to write. Don't try to follow trends or figure out what's going to sell. The best book you can write is the one that entertains YOU.

What do you like to do besides write?
I love snowboarding, though I'm not very good at it, and I play guitar, though I'm very, very bad at it. I also love scrapbooking, eating and of course – reading!

Are you able to tell us anything about your next book?
My next book is **REBEL BULLY GEEK PARIAH**. And that's all I'm saying about it for now!

Look out for Erin's next book

REBEL
BULLY
GEEK
PARIAH

Coming in spring 2015

Don't miss . . .

'Bold and striking, powerful and courageous.' *Booktrust*

'I love it. It reminds me a bit of John Green's
A Fault in Our Stars and R. J. Palacio's *Wonder.*'
Jo, Victoria Park Bookshop